GW01401252

CHLOE: PRIME VICTIM

CARL SANT MURDER MYSTERIES
BOOK 3

DAN LAUGHEY

1

Her laughter rose in the night sky to greet the screeching gulls. They looked down at her and stretched out their necks approvingly. Wisps of sea fret coated their white wings and her dark hair. The yellow of a Victorian street lamp portrayed her face in profile, the ring on her nose a halo in miniature.

'Why me?' he said.

She laughed again, tied her hair back, dropped both hands to the barrel strapped by her side and caressed its steel touch.

'Allow me to talk.' He shifted his weight along the iron railing, the dog lead wrapped around his bony wrist. Bullseye, moments earlier, had darted into darkness. 'This is no way to solve your grievance.'

She raised the barrel and levelled it. The dog lead flew up in self-defence, almost tipping its holder off balance.

'Please, give an old man a chance.'

She grinned a reply and placed her index finger on the trigger of the Remington. There were many on her hit-list. Not one of them, she imagined, would argue with this beauty – loaded or otherwise.

'Can't you allow me to live out my life in peace?'

She cocked the gun and stood with her legs apart, anticipating recoil. Then she walked slowly towards him, nose ring glittering.

'What are you trying to achieve?'

Rifle trained at a spot between his sagging eyes, she drew alongside him, pressed her shoulder against the rails, rolled her eyes and looked down from the bridge. The tide was out. Careless currents glided in from the north, fizzling out in foam.

'The beach,' she said at last. 'Lovely, isn't it?'

He was too scared to look. She knew it.

'You've quite a track record, pigface.'

'I don't know what you mean.'

'You do.'

'Elaborate, young lady.'

'It would take too long, pigface.'

'You don't know a thing about me.'

'Cover-ups, brutality, abuse of authority, perverting the course of justice. Need I go on?'

'You're mistaken, young lady.'

'I think not. You're a sorry excuse for a retired officer. You and your wife both. But you live on, withdrawing your pension, soaking up this sea air without a care in the world.'

He peered up at the circling gulls and shook his head. 'You've got the wrong man.'

She tapped the barrel against rusty iron, pushed herself off the rail and levelled the weapon again, pressure applied to the trigger. The temptation to pull it was erupting.

'I know everything about you, and her. You can blame your late spouse in the next world for what you're about to receive.'

She widened her stance and began counting: 'After three. One, two–'

'No! Please, I can explain. It was a different world back then.'

'Correct, pigface. A world where you got away with murder.'

'Not true, young lady.'

'Oh, I forgot.'

'Forgot?'

'To count to three. One, two–'

'No!'

'Three!'

He threw a hand over his face and crushed his spectacles against the ridge of his eyebrows, a red pinprick pooling at the top of his nose. But there was no explosion of fire. Just the faint click of the hammer being released. Harmless fun.

It did the trick, though. Overbalancing as his back arched, he caught his right ankle between metal bars and capsized over the edge, the snap of his tibia like tubular music to her ears. She approached her overturned prey and heard his muffled howl as he stared hundreds of feet below him at sandy hell. The dog lead dangled and twisted in his wrist, fishing in vain for a change in gravity. Her laughter rose once more in chorus with the guffaws of the seagulls above, and when she finally forced the splintered ankle free, she couldn't get enough of those sweet endorphins pulsating through her brain.

2

THEY GATHERED IN THEIR HUNDREDS CARRYING PLACARDS with STOP STREET SEX and KEEP OUR KIDS SAFE inked on them. They wore hi vis vests and woolly hats and sturdy boots and steadfast frowns. They came on a gusty afternoon after the school run, and not from far because this was their home, next to what the council called its Managed Approach. It was actually a licensed brothel; a red-light district with everything but the red lights.

Carl Sant hadn't come to protest. Instead of a placard he sported a 2X-Large black duffle coat over his customary black Mackintosh to ward off the wind chill. His superior, Superintendent Harry Hardaker, had told him to gauge the mood ahead of a public consultation meeting with the SAVE OUR EYES pressure group. But Sant was also recruiting witnesses. A violent mugger wielding steel toe-capped boots was doing the rounds.

Several hapless souls had been drugged, indecently assaulted and relieved of their belongings, the latest victim three days ago in the park Sant was walking through. It was hoped that someone might have seen the thug in action. There was a prime suspect, though he was missing, and so was any interest in the appeal for information. The poster fastened to the park gates had barely received a backward glance.

The suspect's wife was a local nurse known to the police. Diplomacy wasn't her middle name, but at least she was talking. Sant and his trusted colleague Detective Sergeant Amanda Holdsworth were due to meet her later that day.

'Just cos I happen to live here,' said a grey-haired woman clutching a NO PROSTITUTES placard, 'I get drivers beeping their horns, asking how much for this and that. It's a disgrace. Whores are meant to stay in one spot and not come out till after dark. Instead, they're here and everywhere, every frigging day.'

'One slut had a customer outside my front door last night,' her friend remarked. 'Left a couple of dirty johnnies on the pavement. They should be forced to tidy up after them.'

The two women nattered on. Sant sympathised with their plight. They'd lived in this city since birth, when the white heat of technology had radiated promises of better times, and now they were faced with a sex shop on their doorstep and sex workers as neighbours.

The future told of newfound prosperity. Grand regeneration hinted at a share of the spoils eventually. This part of the city bordered the shiny new South Bank and was set to benefit from the *digital green economy*: eco parks and eco homes, music and film studios. Who wants to make a movie here? That was the question on every Leodensian's lips.

Despair stretched far and wide from the smashed-up bus shelters to the boarded-up wastelands of cash-and-carry failure. The only thing flourishing was fornication. The Managed Approach had decriminalised soliciting and kerb crawling, bringing a boom in both. A boom no longer manageable; an approach without direction.

Sant scanned the line of protestors and recognised a young man championing their cause. Independent Councillor Rory Dobson had been elected to serve the locals as a reward for his stance on sex. He was all smiles, the darling of the crowd. The other two councillors in the ward represented the Labour Party and so were duty-bound to back the Labour-run council to the hilt. Rory, free of political affiliation, spoke his mind and the people loved him for it. His straight-talking attitude towards the powers that be made him a hero in their eyes.

The vibrating phone in his inside pocket disturbed Sant's ruminations. Brad Capstick and his vintage NHS-style specs popped up on screen.

'What is it, Capstick?' Heavy breaths blew down the line. 'Speak up, man.'

'Sir, I've got a runner.' Sant watched the constable wipe a bead of sweat off his specs. 'I tried to detain him but lost him.'

'Where's he heading?'

'Springwell Road.'

'What's he done?' asked the inspector, waiting for his partner to catch his breath.

Capstick fumbled for a while but caught it eventually. 'I'm with a girl called Jenner.'

'Real name?'

'I've not verified–'

'Never mind. Go on.'

'She's crying hysterically. She says he assaulted her. Tried to grab her bag. Shall I pass her on?'

'Not now for Christ's sake.' Sant began weaving his way through the crowd towards the park exit. 'If your bearings are right, he'll be in my sight any moment. Describe him.'

'Skin fade haircut. Light grey sweatshirt. Black jeans.'

Sant rang off and took off at the same time, doing his best to dodge demonstrators marching in the opposite direction. He craned his neck and spotted the boy fifty yards ahead. Skin Fade was sprinting, his top-heavy head of hair ruffled by the wind. The boy looked both ways before leaping over a wall by an industrial estate and hitting tarmac hard.

Sant followed suit, puffing out air as he vaulted over the wall, forcing oxygen into his lungs every four strides. He was approaching fifty and chasing criminals didn't feature on the wish-list any longer. Still, a job was a job and Capstick had handed it to him – with compliments. And besides, the time to call for reinforcements was long gone.

Skin Fade scampered down a narrow ginnel and joined a disused road lined with derelict mills. Sant took a short cut through an abandoned yard and decided to flank the boy from the other side of the road rather than come from behind. Quarry wasn't aware of pursuer, which suited Sant just fine. He didn't fancy his chances in a straight race. The kid was thirty years his junior.

Ignoring the stitch in his side, he picked up speed to keep apace, took the outside of a bend and was on the inside of the next. Dashing past a posse of schoolchildren, he found a gap between parked vans, charged across the road and threw himself at his target, executing a rugby tackle Jonah Lomu would have been proud of. Skin Fade went with him as they hurtled through a hedge bordering vacant office blocks. Struggling on top, Sant dug a knee into the boy's chest, pulled his arms down, then worked at pinning his wrists. I'm too old for this, he thought. Why not draw that pension now?

'Before I read your rights,' he panted, 'tell me about the girl.'

Skin Fade spat out twigs. 'I dun nowt,' he choked.

Chest beating like a mallet, Sant searched pockets and

unearthed a bag of pills in three colours. MDMA. The boy dealt in ecstasy, but the last laugh wasn't his.

'This'll do as evidence.' Sant took a moment to recover his lungs before calling Capstick. 'Put her on,' he told him.

A distant sobbing faded to a hesitant sniffling. A cagey feminine voice finally garbled something unintelligible.

'How much did he charge you?' Sant asked.

'Uh?'

'For the molly.'

'Uh?'

'He says you didn't pay.'

'The twat! I paid all reet but he pulled wool over me eyes. And afta he tried blackmailin' me.'

'Jenner?'

'Who? I mean, uh?'

'Hand the phone back to the nice officer.'

More sniffles were interrupted by an apologetic cough. 'Sir?'

'Let her go and get here sharpish to take this low-life peddler off my hands. And before you ask, he's not our mugger.'

'Any idea who he is?'

Sant followed the trail of bleached track marks punctuating the entire length of the dealer's frail arms. 'One gets born every minute, Capstick.'

'I'll be right there, sir.'

That overzealous constable will learn eventually, Sant mused, hauling Skin Fade to his feet and displaying him for the passing mob of whore haters to shake their wind-swept heads at.

* * *

The Romanian passed by and chuckled under his breath. He'd bought some gear off the crackhead the week before. Charges were reasonable. Sadly, he was another supplier who'd bitten the dust; the usual *Engleza* operator. Plain stupid. He should've known he might be tracked. Even if the pig was plainclothes, that didn't excuse the crackhead's error of judgement. Pigs of one sort or another were bound to be roaming around a protest.

The Romanian tossed a coin. Tails up. Avoid this area like the plague, he told himself. Holbeck Moor had proved to be fertile ground, but it was time to find a new patch. Keep moving. Never dwell.

He lifted a hood over his entirely bald head and started to walk. Fortress Leeds sprang up north of the river, high-end urban village complexes turning up their noses at the seedy squalor further south; the shells of printing factories, dried-up breweries, wool mills spinning a forgotten yarn of yesteryear. Temple Works and Round Foundry. The Malthouse and Marshall Mills. All testaments to a manufacturing age long since gone to rust. Nothing was made nowadays. Only the smokeless Italianate chimneys stood stoutly, like Edwardian gents, gallantly deflecting the winds of change.

Decay was rife below the river line, but up the hill rose aspiration in glass and concrete edifices. Skyscrapers punctured the skyline, their shaded windows blinking coquettishly at a steady stream of accountants, management consultants, corporate lawyers and investment bankers crisscrossing the financial capital of the north.

The Romanian spat as he passed The Old Red Lion and The New Penny – gay pubs full of gays as usual – before riding the rhythmic wave of commuters over Leeds Bridge. The world's first movie was filmed here in 1888. He didn't know the fact and very few did. Entering damp darkness under the arches of the viaduct, he soon found light and rainbow flag-stones in the Freedom Quarter off Lower Briggate. Though the vibes weren't to his taste, he was strangely drawn to the fluores-cent nail salons and carnivalesque show bars.

At the top of Lower Briggate he turned back on himself and wandered around the cobbled streets close to the docks before tracing a curve onto Vicar Lane and returning to the shops. He slipped into Kirkgate Market and sampled the aroma of raw cow and pig, roast chestnuts, flowers, spices; bought a kilo of satsumas with a five-pound note before heading to the outdoor stalls piled high with broken watches, chipped porcelain and vinyl LPs. He picked up an old pen knife and two paper-weights. Another dealer offered him a silver-plated tea set. Dents in the milk jug were too deep to hammer out. He left it.

After checking out the other stalls he removed his hood, spat into a piece of cloth, buffed his boots and tried to blend in with the Gucci handbags parading through Victoria Gate. He admired the gleaming boutiques with their curved glass frontages before exiting on Eastgate, rejoining Vicar Lane, turning left up Merrion Street and right along Wade Lane to the arena, suspended like a bloated spaceship in cemented space.

From there he took the underpass and inhaled deeply as greenery unfastened around him. This was Lovell Park. He glanced around at the loneliness and the emptiness, the signs of liaisons in the night: fag ends, discarded beer cans, tubs of Vase-line. The stench of urine forced him to pinch his nose.

Lovell Park would do, he decided. That lass with the nose ring in the betting shop had spoken of its potential. A recent punter had proposed a meeting too. The Romanian was happy to oblige but the guy had stood him up and gone quiet. Very quiet. Unless he's a bleeding masochist, the Romanian concluded, a continuing arrangement is out of the question.

He balanced on the end of a rotten wooden bench, peeled the skin off a satsuma, swallowed it whole. The sugar rush felt good; as good as his surroundings. My new hunting ground, he thought to himself. A jogger went by, a skateboarder, a German tourist, a child on a scooter. Not one of them interested him, but he was weighing up his territory all the same.

* * *

'I'm on call for another six hours and haven't had a break since morning. But don't mind me. I'm a tin solider. Wind me up and I'll keep on drumming.'

The nurse waved rigid arms to prove her point. Her hazel eyes were set deep in her skull and her hair was ruffled as if she combed fingers through it constantly. Her face was thin, like her figure, and ashen before its time. She wore a long grey cardigan knitted from wool and tiny plimsolls on her flat feet.

Sant did his best to look sympathetic while getting straight to the point. 'We've had a sighting of someone resembling your husband, Mrs Popescu.'

'A tip-off, you mean. You choose your words very carefully, Inspector Sant. You're a shrewd one.' She called out to one of the canteen ladies. 'I've changed my mind, Ethel. Coffee. Two sugars.' She turned to her hosts. 'Anything for you?'

'I'll have a–'

'We're fine, thanks,' Detective Sergeant Holdsworth said, offering Sant a sharp kick under the table. 'We appreciate how busy you are and don't wish to take liberties.'

'You've taken your fair share already,' said Mrs Popescu.

Holdsworth ignored the jibe. 'We're here to inform you of developments. We feel it is important to keep communication open on all sides.'

'Nothing to report, love. I married Nicolae three years ago.

He's been missing half that time. For all I know, he might've fallen off the planet and left me a widow. Except I never got to know him so calling him my long-lost husband is hardly warranted.' She thanked Ethel for the coffee, blew away the steam. 'Every day I pray he's alive. He's a lovely human being. But you know all this. I've told you before. I'm sounding like a broken record.'

'Did Nicolae fear being deported?' Sant asked.

'Why would he? He was innocent. He *is* innocent. Only the guilty are afraid.'

'He may be innocent,' said Holdsworth, 'but a woman he knew from childhood is maintaining that he imprisoned and assaulted her in a flat he was renting at the time, and when officers arrived on the scene, she was crying hysterically and trying to climb out of an upstairs window.'

The nurse pouted. 'It's Ava Yock's word against his. That's all.'

'Two of her teeth were found on the floor,' Sant put in.

'I'm not denying she was attacked. What I'm telling you is Nicolae didn't do it. He's a gentle giant. There isn't a violent bone in his body.'

'How do you explain her being in his flat?' Sant probed.

Mrs Popescu flushed. 'Don't imagine I haven't spent hours wondering. My guess is other people were there that night. Friends of his. She was attacked but Nicolae didn't do it. He was framed. That explains why he fled in the first place, and why he jumped bail after you lot arrested him.'

Sant and Holdsworth stole a glance at each other as the nurse sipped her coffee. They were silently saying the same thing. Love is blind.

'To be one hundred percent clear,' said Holdsworth, 'you haven't seen anything of your husband since you reported him missing.'

The nurse laughed. 'Look who's sounding like a broken record now. Read my lips. I have no clue where he is. Tell me about this latest tip-off – sorry, sighting – if you're allowed to.'

Holdsworth tugged at her ponytail – a signal to begin what they had rehearsed beforehand. Sant liked her theatrical confidence during interviews. He had no argument, either, with the single mother's high cheek bones, dark permed hair, and sculpted Mediterranean complexion.

'What we *can* tell you,' she said, 'is that a member of the public reported seeing a man resembling Nicolae coming out of a pharmacy a few days ago.'

'Was this member of the public high on painkillers by any chance?'

'Actually, we spoke to the chemist who served the man,' Holdsworth continued. 'It turns out he bought a pregnancy kit.'

Mrs Popescu laughed again. 'Case solved! My husband is disguising himself as a woman expecting twins.'

'Something else the chemist told us was interesting,' Sant added. 'She said the same man had come into the shop a month earlier with a younger woman.'

'Really? What were they buying? Don't tell me. The morning-after pill.'

Holdsworth stared at the nurse without flinching. 'You know?'

'I can spot a tall story from a mile off, madam.'

'It's true,' Holdsworth said. 'The chemist remembers consulting the couple on their options.'

'There are two types of pill,' Sant went on, 'and one's more effective than the other. I learn something every day.'

'Because you're a man,' Holdsworth countered, grinning at the nurse. 'Women don't need to learn things they already know.'

Mrs Popescu stayed stony-faced. 'Shall I wrap up this yarn of yours?'

'I don't see–'

'So this woman pays extra for the pill the chemist recommends because it's been a while since my husband shagged her. But even the branded stuff can't work miracles and so Nicolae returns in need of Clearblue. And the moral of the story is that you think I'm lying when I say I don't know where he is. And you also think that after I've heard your carefully crafted tale of betrayal, I'll take a leaf out of Judas's book and lead you to Nicolae's hideout in the enchanted forest.'

Holdsworth softened her stare. 'We can't help if you don't trust us.'

The nurse took a gulp of hot steam, then clapped her hands together. 'A round of applause to you. West Yorkshire's finest detectives weave their magic again.' She stood up sharply. 'You can stick your phony act where the sun don't shine and have a go at stalking real criminals instead. Meantime, I'm off to help trauma victims while trying to recover from the traumatic experience I've had talking to the pair of you.'

Mrs Popescu marched out of the canteen, casting a blaze of fury on anyone who dared to look at her.

* * *

'That went to plan,' said Sant as they headed out of the hospital.

Holdsworth rattled her car keys. 'We ought to recruit her. She might be willing to read criminal minds as well as ours.'

'I'll tell Capstick not to expect an imminent shadowing job on the wily-eyed nurse.'

'But she can't be wily-eyed, Carl. Marrying a brute is hardly an endorsement of her intelligence.'

Sant nodded. 'More bewildering is her stubborn insistence he's innocent of any wrongdoing.'

They got into Holdsworth's XJS, Sant sinking into the passenger seat. He was looking forward to the ride. His colleague's Jaguar was a joy to behold.

'Isn't she a devout Catholic?' Holdsworth asked as she started up the engine.

'I'm led to believe it.'

'Then if she's so religious, why doesn't she tap into her conscience? If there's a hint of a suspicion, she should be coop-erating.'

'That's love for you.' Sant began chewing on a toothpick, his way of quelling the sort of stress he'd treated with nicotine in days gone by. 'Speaking of which, how are you and Capstick getting on?'

She smirked. 'Neither of us are blind, Carl, but we're very much in love.'

'Long may it continue. He's a fine man. Getting good at his job, gradually.'

'I'm teaching him a trick or two,' the detective sergeant said as she steered out of the infirmary's multi-storey car park into the pinkish glow of a February sunset. 'How about your love life?'

Sant snapped his toothpick in half. 'When I think of my ex, Holdsworth, I realise I was hopelessly blind.'

'You and me both, Carl. The father of my child is a loser.'

'We all make mistakes.'

'How about the woman you met during that last case?'

'Haven't seen her for months. Too young for me.'

'What's the right age for you?'

Sant paused for a moment, then said: 'Forty-four is perfect.'

She laughed. 'What a coincidence.'

They exchanged smiles as she gently pressed the accelerator, the growl of the engine rising gloriously to his ears.

'You think Nicolae Popescu is our serial sadist on the loose?' she asked.

'It's possible,' said Sant. 'Bail offenders often re-offend. They lie low for a while till the urge returns. What I can't work out is whether we're dealing with a mugger or a sex offender.' He wound down the window and breathed in the brisk air. 'Popescu's certainly guilty of taking money from Ava Yock by force, whether she owed it or not. What we're less sure about is whether he assaulted her.'

'She was drugged too, like the others.' Holdsworth placed foot on brake pedal as her car veered off a slip road onto the traffic-jammed inner ring road. She was silent for a while, then spoke with urgency: 'I've got a challenge for you.'

'Go ahead.'

'Well, since your latest trick fell flat on its face–'

'*Our* latest trick, Holdsworth.'

She slapped him on the thigh. 'Okay, I'll share culpability.'

'The very least–'

'Are you going to hear me out?'

'Fire away.'

'Since we know Wendy Popescu is religious, our next move should be to pretend we have solid evidence her hubby is guilty of these ongoing assaults on innocent people. She can't be unaware of them. They're all over the news.'

Sant shook his head. 'I can't see it. She's convinced he didn't attack Miss Yock, so why have a different opinion on the other attacks?'

'I read something in one of Brad's textbooks the other day.'

'A treasured volume from his library.'

'Tell me about it. That library's encroaching on our living space. Anyway, some psychologist has written on the subject and reckons that relatives are more likely to come clean if their loved ones will likely commit further serious crimes unless apprehended.'

'Sounds like mind games to me, Holdsworth.'

They waited at the red light causing the hold up. It was the usual emergency road works with no work to be seen.

Holdsworth went on: 'The theory is that potential future offences matter more than past ones because relatives know they can't do anything about the past, but they believe they can intervene in events to come.'

'The theory sounds fantastic,' Sant said. 'The reality's not so sweet.'

'It's worth a try, Carl. We need to empower Mrs Popescu, albeit under false pretences, which might make her open up.'

'Green, Holdsworth.'

'What?'

'The light.'

'Shit.' She waved an apology to the driver behind. 'Well, do you accept my challenge?'

'Let me think.' He flicked the remains of his toothpick out of the window. 'I've thought.'

'And?'

'Challenge accepted.'

'Great. We'll request the pleasure of her company tomorrow. She's on a late afternoon shift. I'll drop you home.'

'And I'll have forty winks before you get there.'

Sant drifted out of consciousness, the blank canvas of his mind superimposing Holdsworth's olive skin and fine cheek bones over the nurse's endless grimace.

3

ANOTHER DAY GOT OFF TO ANOTHER JOLLY KICK-START:
the dreaded public consultation with the SAVE OUR EYES
brigade. Sant gazed over the crowd and noted faces from the
protest the day before. None of them looked attractive except
the boyish one worn by the ever-popular Councillor Dobson.
He was shaking hands with anyone and everyone, his blond
curly hair positively bouncing with exuberance, his eyes
dancing from soulmate to soulmate.

Sant was no politician and didn't enjoy being the centre
of attention. He left that responsibility to Hardaker. The
superintendent was a natural showman, the microphone
attached to this shirt collar purring approvingly at his
polished northern parlance. His kempt red beard and
matching locks had earned Hardaker the nickname 'Chiefman'. He didn't mind the name because becoming a chief
officer was an ambition he harboured intensely, the sooner
the better. Rumour had it that he was about to be made an
assistant chief constable, replacing the role left by Bill
Gilligan after Gilligan's promotion to Chief Constable

following the untimely death of the previous leader of the force, Edward Lister.

Sitting between Sant and Hardaker was another newly promoted. Detective Chief Inspector Stephanie Appleyard was prepared to stick her long neck out and coordinate the highest-profile investigation West Yorkshire Police was involved in. Vicious attacks on men and women involving sexual violence and theft were being meted out weekly, and the growing feeling among detectives was that one or two head-cases were at the epicentre of the thuggery.

Appleyard had secured the promotion because she was brave enough to take on that thuggery. Oh, and she was pretty and female too. Every constabulary in the country was offering its career-minded girls a helping hand up the career ladder until, that is, they hit a glass ceiling above which only the men who appointed them could rise.

'Before my colleague summarises the main action points,' announced Hardaker to the captive audience of sixty sceptics, 'please can I encourage you to come and speak to us on a one-to-one footing if you have any questions. Over to you, DCI Appleyard.'

She was younger than Sant expected of any officer in a senior role likes hers. Her dark brown eyes and the black lash extensions that sheltered them were large and widely spaced, which together with the low nasal bridge and round visage defined her as mixed heritage. She was, in fact, half British and half Thai, had spent her entire life in England and knew little of her mother's side of the family. In contrast to her striking facial features her hands were slander and devoid of rings. She brushed a long black lock from her forehead and looked down at her super-slick iPad.

Sant felt the vibrations of her chair on the plywood floor. She spoke quickly without volume. Hardaker had largely run the show from the start. A reluctant Appleyard now found herself thrown into focus. Sant had at least one thing in common with her – stage fright.

'To sum up action point one,' she murmured, 'it is agreed that mobile and foot patrols will increase their presence three-fold in the Holbeck area, especially Springwell Road, as soon as possible and no later than the start of March. Regarding action point two, the dedicated street cleansing service will continue. Regarding action point three, we confirm a toughening of policing – any sex worker found to be operating beyond the designated zone or outside the defined hours (eight pm until six am) will be cautioned. If an individual reoffends, she will be arrested and subject to a fine.'

'Give us a figure!' shouted a grey-haired man in the crowd.

'Defined hours my arse!' screamed a woman with a pram.

Appleyard looked up nervously, a rabbit caught in the headlights, before sliding a shaky index finger across her screen and returning to her notes.

'Action point three.'

'Four,' said Hardaker under his breath.

'Point four: any residential area known to harbour sex work and drug-related crime will be subject to a Public Space Protection Order allowing officers powers to detain individuals suspected of soliciting and serve injunctions on offenders. And point five: we will monitor crime closely for the next eight weeks through extensive public CCTV use, examining evidence of anti-social behaviour. Should the offending rate spiral we will make a recommendation to scale back the Managed Approach as soon as possible.'

'Close it down!' bellowed the grey-haired man.

'It's not working!' screamed the woman with the pram.

'Act now!' someone else shouted.

'Get 'em off the streets!'

'No more prostitutes!'

A few cheers went up. Appleyard stared at the critics. She'd lost her voice.

'Thank you for your time,' interjected Hardaker, 'and again, feel free to ask us anything. I draw this meeting to a close.'

Disgruntlement sounded like a knife through flesh as the conference room emptied.

'Well done, Stephanie,' smiled Hardaker as he turned off his mic. 'You kept things succinct and didn't react to the heckling.'

Sant said nothing. He wasn't impressed with Appleyard one bit.

The Chiefman arched his pointed red beard in Sant's direction. 'Stay here a little longer, Carl. DCI Appleyard and I have an appointment with Chief Constable Gilligan about the muggings. Okay?'

Sant nodded. 'Send the Old Man my regards.'

'I will,' Hardaker said, 'but I won't call him Old Man. It might piss him off and rule me out of the ACC job. Besides, now Gilligan is top dog, his PA suits him up in official chief officer garb. He's nearly as dapper as me these days.'

Hardaker pulled at the lapels of his pinstriped jacket and grinned. Appleyard returned the gesture before giving Sant a cool once-over. His baggy get-up didn't live up to her expectations.

Sant's superiors withdrew subtly and left him to field the vitriol. As luck would have it, no-one came up. He saw a chance of a swift escape. Ahead of him he noticed Hardaker and Appleyard fielding questions from Dobson and company. The critics were wasting energy, the two detectives having nothing on their minds other than the exit door.

Sant was about to leave himself until a skinny man walking

with a limp caught his eye – the grey-haired lout who'd led the chorus of disapproval. He was carrying a banner upside down. The banner read HONK IF YOU'RE NOT HORNY. The man chanced a glance and Sant put an instant name to the wrinkled face.

Jeremy Donohue. Former caretaker at a down-and-out school under special measures. Sant had arrested him a decade ago after a teenager was reported missing. She'd left home suddenly and without explanation. Donohue, it turned out, was operating a side-line luring pupils he befriended into jobs as working girls. Thanks to Sant the teen was traced to the trafficking racket. Donohue was handed an eight-year prison sentence, a place on the sex offenders' register and a future without meaningful employment.

What possible interest could the man have in joining SAVE OUR EYES: a group that was against prostitution? Sant went after him in search of answers, but before he could renew old acquaintances a woman tapped him on the shoulder and offered her hand. He took it hesitantly.

'Have you a few spare minutes, Inspector Sant? Time for a cuppa perhaps?'

She spoke with a gravelly voice but didn't appear to be suffering from a cold. She was in her early seventies, Sant guessed, and wore an impossible array of layers topped off by a loose-fitting purple cardigan. A pair of half-moon spectacles dangled from a chain around her thick neck. Also hanging from her neck was a lanyard but the badge was hidden underneath her cardigan. She noticed Sant's curiosity and subtly pulled it out. It read DR JULIA PRINGLE, DIRECTOR, CENTRE FOR SEX WORK AND ABUSE.

'Have we met before?'

'Excuse my directness,' she said as she slid the badge out of view. 'I'm keeping a low profile in case anyone asks me what I do.'

'What do you do?' asked Sant, failing to make sense of her job title.

'I'd rather tell you in private. My office is a hop and a skip away. Let me lead the way.'

Sant obeyed. He didn't mind a spot of mystery. It was certainly an improvement on a public consultation meeting.

* * *

Five minutes later Sant took a sip of Yorkshire tea as the mystery unravelled. He sat back on a velvet corner sofa and surveyed the immaculate floral wallpaper of Dr Pringle's office, crammed between a recruitment agency and a pawnbroker's shop on the third floor of a slate-roofed premises originally housing a dance hall and upstairs fish restaurant.

'To put it plainly, Inspector, I'm the architect of it all.'

'What?'

'The Managed Approach. Me and my colleagues set up the scheme from scratch.'

'And that's why you were being discreet back there.'

She rested a teaspoon on her chintz saucer. 'Despite my age, they'd lynch me if I told them who I was.'

'Where did you get the idea?'

She swivelled on an ergonomic chair. 'London, actually. Me and my research assistants conducted a survey many years ago. We found that two out of three on-street sex workers suffered violence from punters. Something needed to be done but London was too big, so we dug further to discern where to focus our limited energies. Second on the list of UK cities with issues is Leeds. The data decided it. We set up base here.'

'Which means London was – for want of a better word – your inspiration for this place?'

'The States, actually. Especially San Francisco. We visited the "John School" as they call it over there. It signalled a revolution in thinking about street sex. You see, historically the blame was always directed at the prostitutes, demonised for doing a job that kept them above the bread line.'

Sant looked shamefaced. 'I've locked up a few over the years.'

'I don't doubt it. The missing part of the equation is the men. The John School changed the goal posts. In San Francisco the policymakers had a Eureka moment. They realised the best way to solve the myriad of crimes linked to prostitution was to criminalise those who use the trade.'

'As opposed to the traders,' the inspector put in.

Dr Pringle swallowed a mouthful of tea before coming up for breath. 'Men had to be taught that kerb crawling was a serious offence, that most of the women they abused were no older than teenagers when they started out, that they were funding drug peddling and money laundering by returning again and again for their five-second orgasm.'

'This John School sounds more like education than punishment.'

'Correct, but the threat of punishment is always there. We established a similar school in this city, called it the KCRP – the Kerb Crawlers Re-education Programme – and recruited our students with help from your colleagues working on sex offences. The men were told they could join the KCRP or face a criminal record and their name splashed over the newspapers. You can imagine how successful our uptake was.'

Sant swirled the tea in the bottom of his cup as if it was going to tell him something. 'You must've had a lot of unhappy punters.'

'Students, Inspector. They came to be educated, not enter-
tained. And it wasn't only experts like me teaching them. We
brought in sex workers to describe what it's like being on the
receiving end. We had sexual health workers. The Coalition for
the Removal of Pimping got involved. We even had parents of
daughters murdered on the game. Tell me, have you ever been
with a prostitute?'

The question threw Sant. He felt a mixture of anger and
humiliation.

'No,' he replied bluntly.

'That's good to hear,' she said, peering at him through her
spectacles. 'I'm being intrusive, I know, but I work on probabilities. You may be interested to know that four out of ten male
officers have had sexual intercourse whilst on duty – and I don't
mean consensual sex with partners on their lunch breaks.'

Sant scratched his ear in irritation at being lectured to. 'So
the John School spurned the Managed Approach?'

Dr Pringle laughed through her nose. 'You could put it that
way. As well as educating the kerb crawlers, we garnered their
views on the MA. They thought the whole thing was a legal
brothel, of course, but it's nothing like it in the true sense.'

'Isn't it?'

'Certainly not. I've seen brothels in Cambodia, Vietnam,
Egypt, Kenya. Those places are vile. Holbeck is completely
different. It's regulated. There are no Class A drugs. The
women feel safe. The Johns have what they want – anonymity.
And the MA makes what they do acceptable. The goal is to
stop paid-for sex altogether, but that's easier said than done.'

'You must've had a lot of resistance in the beginning,' Sant
said.

'From the police?'

'We're not all screwing at work, for your information.'

'I've touched a nerve.'

'Or four,' he said, counting on his fingers.

Dr Pringle beamed widely. 'Point acknowledged. I accept that we had a mixed response when we pitched it. Some of your officers thought we'd end up with more murders. The opposite has proven true. Regulating sex work is much safer than keeping it underground. Four prostitutes a year were killed in West Yorkshire before the MA came in. The haters accuse us of giving pimps a licence to make money. What they don't understand is the pimps are eliminated with our approach. It's just the girls and the Johns. Cash goes direct from pocket to hand and the pimp gets nothing. He's history.'

Sant stroked the tip of his nose. 'What about the movers and shakers above the pimps who pretend to play no part? It must've given them a shock to the system.'

'They kicked up a fuss at first. I even received a death threat.'

'What sort?'

'A letter. It was addressed to the Centre. We have a website. Our address is public knowledge.'

'Do you still have the letter?'

'Of course,' she said. 'I view it as a compliment; as proof we won the battle. Despite the haters and doubters, we fought the corner of the sex workers and defeated the criminals exploiting them. Prostitution was under our control.'

Tell that to the residents of Holbeck, Sant said to himself.

'I'd like to read it if you don't mind.'

'Be my guest.' Dr Pringle pointed upwards. 'I've framed it. It's a prize asset.'

The short note hanging on the office wall was printed in large capital letters:

THOSE WHO STICK THEIR NOSE IN PEOPLES AFFAIRS GET WHATS COMING TO THEM. KEEP

LOOKING OVER YOUR SHOULDER. ONE DAY YOU
WILL HAVE NO SHOULDER TO LOOK OVER. NO
EYES TO LOOK WITH. NOTHING LEFT OF YOUR
TINY BRIAN. SLEEP TIGHT.

Sant read the note twice, then said: 'You must've been
scared.'

'It takes more than words to ruffle me. And besides, nobody
personally known to me is tiny and called Brian,' she laughed.

'I assume you reported it.'

'Far and wide. I wanted the local press to publish it. Word
for word. I showed it to a journalist. She ran it by her editor.
Nothing came of it.'

'What did my colleagues say?'

'I was given armed protection for a few days. Felt like a
queen. Having a bodyguard was quite a privilege.'

'Who looked after you?'

'Quite a few were passed the buck, but one officer whose
name escapes me took charge... that poor man who was killed at
the remembrance service last year.'

'Chief Constable Lister,' Sant replied.

She stared at him and paused. 'Hang on, weren't you the
one–?'

'Who tried to save him. I was too late.'

'How tragic. I had a great deal of respect for him.'

You wouldn't have if you knew what I knew, Sant thought.

'Lister wasn't top rank back in those days,' he said.

'No, but he was quite senior. A superintendent, or so I
recall. He came to see me practically every day for a month or
more. Like an overprotective father, he made sure I had an
alarm fitted to the office. An expensive contraption that alerted
the police immediately it went off. He ordered CCTV too. Oh,
and a daily escort back to my apartment. Someone stood guard

outside the door. A bit OTT, but I wasn't complaining. Better safe than sorry. That's what Superintendent Lister said, and he didn't mind repeating it.'

'He must've wanted you to succeed.'

'Maybe he did,' she said as she drained the rest of her tea. 'He kept a low profile though. I asked him to join me and my colleagues when we presented our ideas to the council. He backed away. Maybe he was concerned about a backlash. He saw the front pages: "Chief Gives Green Light to Brothel".'

'Who stepped into his shoes?'

Dr Pringle raised her eyebrows above the half-moons. 'I thought you would know.'

The inspector shook his head. 'No-one tells me a thing anymore.'

'Well, I suppose a woman is more fitting than a man to spearhead our plans. I refer to your colleague, Ms Appleyard.'

It was Sant's turn to raise his bushy brows. 'Our resident high-flier.'

'And long may she fly high. She was a tad nervous in front of that hostile audience, but she's a clever young woman. She should become the chief constable one day.'

Sant chose silence over protest and moved on. 'That was hardly music to your ears – what the residents of Holbeck were saying.'

She shook her head. 'They're hardly a cross-section of the community, those SAVE OUR EYES freaks. I'd rather listen to the LISTENING WELL campaign. They're more moderate and accept that there's no perfect solution. Sadly, even the moderates embrace ill-informed politicians like that curly-haired buffoon.'

'Rory Dobson is the man of the moment.'

'Not on my watch, Inspector. I've had more than the odd

spat with him. He blames the MA for every crime he can make political capital out of.'

'It's true that crime is rising in this city,' Sant remarked. 'Violent crime especially.'

'See what you're doing. Scapegoating. Like Councillor Dobson does. Rapists are on the loose and you blame regulated sex work. Hardly makes sense, does it?'

He thanked her for the tea and stood to leave, then said: 'I'm no expert. The only thing I know is things aren't improving.'

'Give it time. Time is all we've got.' She offered her wizened hand and he shook it gingerly. 'You mustn't give up on us. Promise you'll keep faith in the MA.'

Sant couldn't recall having faith to begin with. He gave Julia Pringle a parting nod but no ringing endorsement.

* * *

Early evening visiting hours were underway. The doors of Ward 29 buzzed obligingly as Sant and Holdsworth let themselves in. Sant didn't mind hospitals. He knew too well, though, how their veneer of clinical orderliness obscured the bloody horrors of organ transplants, body bags, surgical stirrups and scalpel blades.

The nurse saw them come in from the other end of the corridor. Her dark blue uniform bore the marks of an experienced sister a grade above those in lighter attire. She placed a pair of medical scissors in her breast pocket and stepped swiftly towards the two detectives.

'What's happened now?' She seemed oblivious to patients and visitors peopling the ward. 'Don't tell me. The chemist saw my husband buying milk formula and Calpol.'

'Is there somewhere we can talk in peace?' Holdsworth asked uneasily.

'I'm working in case you hadn't noticed. If you want to talk, do it here.'

'How about there?' Holdsworth pointed to a staff room tucked behind the reception desk.

Mrs Popescu followed the detective sergeant's thumb and sighed as she considered her options. Reluctantly, she approached the sole person in the room – a phlebotomist inspecting a blood pressure cuff. 'Can you bear some company for a moment?' she asked him. He fired off a few remarks before hastily excusing himself.

'Sadly, we've had no more sightings of Nicolae,' said Sant as he found a pew.

'So why've you come here?'

'You may've seen the news about the sex attacks lately.'

Mrs Popescu glared coldly at Sant. 'Surely you don't suspect Nicolae.'

Holdsworth remained standing. 'We've had no reason to, but new evidence has come to light from one of the victims. We can't divulge; however, we think there's a pattern.'

The nurse shook her head. 'Why are you telling me this?'

Sant waited for eye contact. 'Mrs Popescu, if there's anything you know that might help us to trace Nicolae, it would do a huge service to us, and him too. If he's not guilty of these recent offences, it would be best to turn himself in.'

The nurse was silent for a moment, staring at a monitor above her head. Then she made a wailing noise and smacked the palm of her hand on the desk in front of her.

'You've got one hell of a nerve! First you arrest my husband for something he didn't do. And now you're stitching him up for other crimes because he's run out on you. No wonder he skipped bail. You drove him nutty and think you can find him again by pulling the wool over my eyes. Me, who hasn't seen him for two years or more.'

'Let's not make a scene,' said Holdsworth, offering a comforting hand. 'All we ask is you keep us informed. We'll always lend a willing ear.'

'I know what's driving you,' the nurse continued. 'You're no better than those Little Englanders. Nicolae could've been a fine citizen if given a chance, but when the country is over-flowing with bigots like you two, what chance does he have?'

'Now look,' Sant said, his temperature rising a notch. 'Where your husband comes from has nothing to do–'

'I'm through with you,' Mrs Popescu snarled, removing the scissors from her pocket and pointing them ominously. 'Good riddance to bad rubbish!'

She knocked over a plastic chair before storming out. Sant followed discreetly but Holdsworth held back. Sant noticed her delayed move and gave an impression of manning the reception desk while he waited for her. A brittle man with a walking frame directed a quizzing look as he passed slowly by. At last, Holdsworth scurried out of the staff room and gripped Sant's arm.

'Your challenge didn't come off,' he said.

'Maybe not, or maybe yes.'

'What do you mean?'

'A breakthrough.' They pushed through the buzzing doors. 'I stole a glance at one of the computers.'

'Naughty, naughty.'

'It's called detective work, Carl.'

'Never heard of it.'

Holdsworth held out her phone. 'I took a photo of the staffing rota for the rest of the week. Look. Wendy Popescu's name is struck through for consecutive shifts on Friday night,

Saturday and Sunday. She's actually working on Friday till ten, but originally she was on call till midnight.'

'She's scooting off early,' mused Sant, 'to take a long weekend.'

She let go of his arm and slapped it gently. 'My point is she must've booked this leave in the last couple of days or else her name wouldn't appear at all.'

'Good point, Holdsworth. She's got something to do she hadn't planned.'

The detectives looked at each other, their thoughts on one train.

'Your boyfriend has a job lined up,' Sant remarked

'Brad loves a spot of tailing,' she smiled.

* * *

A promising sun had long since set and stubborn cloud was dumping heavy sleet. The Romanian kept to the bushes. He wore a grey hoodie, black nylon jacket, black tracksuit bottoms and steel toe-capped boots. His unshaven face was shielded by the hood and a woolly hat protected his bald crown. On his shoulder he carried a sling bag.

He took out a pouch of Amber Leaf, dipped down to extract a pinch, lifted it delicately and lightly padded it into the boat-shaped rizla he caressed in his other hand. Then he rubbed the ends of the paper between thumb and forefinger, rolling it in the same motion, licking at the corner to seal the joint. He lifted the finished article above his eyeline and slotted it upright into the fold of his hat.

He'd circled Lovell Park for an hour and was wondering whether to stick around or catch a bus to somewhere else. There wasn't much happening. He needed a fix. Someone like his first prize. That man in his sixties. Once the business trans-

CHLOE: PRIME VICTIM 33

action was over, he'd presented the sitting duck with four sharp kicks to the head before robbing his holiday cottage of a gold chain, two oil paintings, a Chinese vase and three hundred pounds in legal tender.

The sleet began to ease. He lifted his hood and unzipped his coat. And then the place livened up all of a sudden. Two roadmen came towards him from the park gates, holding hands and reciting the latest grime hit. The Romanian crouched low behind a thick shrub and watched the teens pass. A minute later another gay couple danced by, sipping froth off cans of Strongbow Dark Fruit as they held each other tightly.

The Romanian left the shrub but dived back in as more footsteps approached. A man and a woman this time, chunky fingers clutching their hefty belts. He sensed a pair of pigs, their black-and-white chequered caps confirming his suspicions.

'My shift ends at eleven,' the male officer grumbled.

The female officer checked her phone. 'Not long now. All quiet here. Fancy Burley Park?'

'Yeah. Might be less gays there. Hang on, aren't Paddy and Trace covering Burley?'

The female officer nodded. 'We agreed to swap with them.'

'Why?'

'Paddy's idea, the shady bastard. Getting paid off I expect. That Aussie junkie owes him.'

'We should be in on the act,' grumbled the male officer. 'I'm fed up getting peanuts for doing lates.'

'Paddy'll get caught one of these days. It's not worth risking your job over.'

'Suppose. I'll stick to taking bribes from benefit cheats.'

The female officer's guffaws evaporated into the night. The Romanian stepped back onto the path and cursed. Corrupt police everywhere. Scumbags. I even hate the ones I'm working for, he grumbled under his breath.

Perching on a wet bench to relieve his shoulder of the weight of the sling bag, he looked down at his pot belly. He felt sleepy, but the cool air forced him to do some stretches to stay warm.

A while later he caught a glimpse of someone he knew. She was called Maria Balgin. Fellow Romanian and slut, she was engaged in business with a drunk youth trying his best to unclothe her. They made split-second eye contact as she walked on. The Romanian felt like beating the shit out of the youth and giving Maria a piece of his mind. I can't afford to get into trouble, he told himself repeatedly, but I'm craving action – if only to save my muscles from freezing up.

Standing up from the bench, he whistled a high note and called her name.

The youth turned around first. 'Who the fuck are you?' he slurred. 'Mr Birdie?'

Instead of answering, the Romanian sprang forward and launched a long-range left hook that poleaxed the boy.

'You son of a bitch, Nicolae.'

'He deserved it.'

'You've knocked him cold.'

'No colder than the weather. You should thank me, Maria. I've made it simple for you.'

She directed her eyes down at the inert figure and lifted them back towards her compatriot.

'Go on,' he said, rubbing his fist against his thigh.

She bent down and came up with a bulging wallet. 'Want a split?'

'It's yours, Maria. Who's your pimp?'

She pocketed the wallet. 'I'm doing things my way now. Nobody takes from me.'

The Romanian put an arm around her shoulder. 'Keep away from the competition. Understood?'

She freed herself from his clutches. 'You heard from Ava?'

'I was about to ask you the same.'

'I'm worried. I didn't think she'd fly without telling anyone.'

'She went to the pigs, didn't she? That was out of order.'

'She got fucked over good and proper. She had to report what happened.'

'And blame it on me?'

'She wouldn't do that, Nicolae.'

The Romanian shook his head. 'As long as she stays away from me and my affairs, I couldn't care less where she is.'

'What about–?'

'Leave him to me.'

She nodded and was swallowed in darkness. The Romanian dragged the youth under a tree, felt a pulse, heard him breathing. He contemplated having a bit of fun but chose to conserve energy. Good things come to those who wait.

He left the boy and sauntered up a slope towards a battered structure that had once served as a rundown public toilet, and even further back, a public toilet in a reasonable state of repair. Graffiti as abstract as Beckett's prose decorated every patch of brick wall. If any action was to be found, this was where he'd find it.

He looked across a small football pitch where a man and two girls were kicking a ball to each other. A tiny dog chased the ball periodically. A father and his daughters getting some late-night practice? The Romanian shook his head as he saw the man taking a swig from a plastic bottle before passing it to one of the girls. She was about fifteen, the man at least four times older. He kept glancing at his phone, his watch, back to his phone, clearly more concerned at keeping time than grooming his way to a threesome.

The Romanian reached for the fold of his woolly hat, found the rolled-up joint, put a match to it. Should be go down there and tell the paedo to take a hike? It wouldn't cause him any grief. The man was weedy. A sucker punch to the stomach was a cinch.

He looked back at the three figures and saw only two. One of the girls was running towards the park gates. She turned to signal a one-fingered goodbye to her drinking companions. The man made a start towards her, limping as he walked, the dog following, tail wagging. He hobbled for a few more strides before giving up on the girl and consulting his watch again.

The other girl pointed and roared at her fleeing friend. She put the bottle to her gob before bursting into more laughter, liquid spraying from her gob into icy puddles around the goal mouth, soaking her ankle-socked feet.

The scene bored the Romanian. He stepped away and rounded the corner of the building that interested him. The Gents was locked. He tried the Ladies. The broken door creaked as he pulled it open. No-one inside. Only a few used johnnies; a damp pack of cigs.

He navigated the building one more time before returning to the footballing action. It had started to sleet again, and as the air was a degree cooler than before, the sleet was turning to snow. The man, the girl and the dog had gone, but the ball was nestling in a massive puddle by a goal post, lonely and forgotten. The Romanian lifted his hood and began retracing his steps.

Then a voice piped up: 'Doing business?'

A fat and very ugly man was standing ten yards below him.

'Sure.'

'What's your going rate?'

'Twenty for a hand. Fifty for the works.'

'You know how to charge.'

'You get what you pay for.'

'You've enticed. I'm in my car. Follow.'

The Romanian reached into his sling bag and pulled out a half-full bottle of vodka. 'Show's on the road. What's your name?'

'Ivor. Yours?'

'Call me Don. Got glasses?'

'Paper cups will do,' Ivor said, merrily jangling his BMW keys.

* * *

Harry Hardaker entered the new extension to his working quarters with a distinct swagger. The swagger of a man expecting people to call him Assistant Chief Constable Hardaker imminently. By his side was Appleyard. She blinked unsmilingly at Sant and Holdsworth before opening the folder she was carrying and sliding out the pages marked with fluorescent green index tabs.

'Thanks for joining me in the new boardroom.' Hardaker said it with a sweep of his arm.

'You've landed on your feet here, Chiefman,' said Sant, tapping the oval table and breathing in the fresh lick of paint. 'Makes a nice addition to your pad. You can watch the Whites from up here too.'

Leeds United's Elland Road stadium was visible from this end of police HQ, but Sant was pushing the limits of reality as the pitch itself was completely concealed behind the South Stand.

'It's not for my sole use, Carl. Anyone can book the space – if I'm not using it.'

'You'll have your own wing once you join the chief officers' team,' Holdsworth said.

Hardaker grinned, lowered his lean figure into a pristine high-back chair and stroked his ginger locks. 'I appreciate it's very late in the day, though we can hardly rest given the current situation. Where's Detective Constable Capstick?'

'Busy,' said Holdsworth, tugging at her permed ponytail. 'She's got him tied up.'

Holdsworth slapped Sant on the arm. 'Excuse me,' she said, repressing a laugh.

Hardaker ignored the banter and continued: 'As you both know, DCI Appleyard is heading up enquiries into the park rapes and I'm overseeing things. We're facing the media tomorrow to provide an update. Stephanie will be the lead spokesperson. I will assist alongside her.'

Appleyard and Hardaker exchanged smiles. *It all ended happily ever after*, thought Sant.

'The state of play is we're dealing with eight violent sexual attacks in a month,' Appleyard said as she shuffled her papers. 'Each one includes robbery of some description. In each case the victim was picked up in a public park or open space. Five of the victims are females. The other three males.'

'Makes you wonder why we haven't nabbed anyone yet,' Sant remarked. 'There'll be a fatality sooner or later.'

'Isn't it odd for a rapist to target male and female victims at the same time?' Holdsworth said.

Appleyard held up her reports. 'We may be dealing with more than one attacker. But there's a pattern forming. As well as motive and location profiling, the same concentration of Rohypnol is used to sedate the victim before the assault is carried out. The assaults follow a pattern too. Punches to the stomach, neck, face. We're dealing with a brutally strong assailant every time.'

'Or two people working together,' Hardaker added.

Appleyard turned to Sant and Holdsworth. 'What we need

from you is the low-down on your safeguarding investigation. Still no sign of Nicolae Popescu?'

'We interviewed his wife again,' Sant said. 'If she knows anything, she's not giving it away.'

'Worth a surveillance job?' asked Hardaker.

Holdsworth glanced at Sant and back at Hardaker. 'Actually, we've got Capstick on it.'

'Ah yes, you said he was busy.'

'He's already tailing her?' Appleyard probed.

Sant took in her long eyelashes. 'We're one step ahead of the game,' he said with a wink.

'We should've been consulted,' Appleyard said.

Silence filled the room. Sant ruffled his black hair for a second before folding his arms. 'It was my call. I'll give advance notice next time.'

'In line with protocol,' the chief inspector snapped.

'Three months in writing.'

Appleyard aimed a stern face at Sant. 'Say again?'

'Ignore the dry humour,' Holdsworth said as she kicked Sant from under the table.

Hardaker swiped a finger over his tablet. 'Popescu allegedly attacked a woman and later jumped bail, which suggests he's guilty as sin. Does this woman fit the victim profile?'

'In some ways,' continued Holdsworth. 'Ava Yock is young, small, fragile. She turned twenty-one in January. Popescu had known her since childhood. There was history between them. She had a debt to pay. Five thousand. She denied owing him anything.'

'What's the evidence against her?'

'We've found nothing,' Holdsworth went on, 'though it's significant that she has no bank account. She's lived off cash for yonks. Maybe Popescu was her loan shark.'

'How about the rape itself?' Hardaker said. 'Comparisons with recent attacks?'

'Similarities,' said Sant. 'Miss Yock received blows to the face and stomach. Ribs were badly bruised. She broke her wrist falling hard after one of those punches. The location isn't consistent, though. Yock said she was attacked in the flat Popescu was renting.'

'If Yock was his first victim, the location may not be so telling,' Appleyard pointed out. 'Serial aggressors only settle on a preferred location after trying out several. Popescu didn't exactly triumph with the indoor strategy either, considering he was arrested on the scene.'

Hardaker gave a double thumbs up. 'Quite right, Stephanie. The first attack is often naïve but if he's lucky enough to escape arrest, the sexual predator learns his lesson and subsequent strikes become more sophisticated. He drugged Miss Yock too, which follows the pattern of the outdoor attacks.'

'Not entirely,' said Sant.

'They were all given Rohypnol, weren't they?'

'Right, Chiefman, but the drug had worn off by the time Popescu attacked Yock.'

Hardaker shrugged. 'Maybe he gave her a smaller dose.'

Sant pinched his rugged nose. 'A more likely scenario is she was spiked before Popescu attacked her, meaning someone else may've doped and raped her.'

'She was adamant it was him,' Hardaker said.

'Yes, but the effects of the Rohypnol complicate things; cast doubt on the reliability of Yock's statement. We've no way of proving Popescu's guilt without his DNA.'

'He jumped bail, didn't he?' remarked Appleyard. 'He's clearly culpable.'

Sant sucked in oxygen before clamping a toothpick

between his teeth. 'As I said, he assaulted her. He also robbed her. Two hundred was missing from her coat. What we don't know for sure is if he was sexually violent.'

Appleyard fingered her reports. 'The violence alone is consistent. Three of the females on our list describe how the assailant used his knees to pin their arms to the ground. He then punches them in the stomach before forcing himself on them.'

'What about the other two?' Sant asked.

'Already unconscious,' Hardaker said. 'They don't recall a thing.'

'I thought you said *all* of them were doped,' said Holdsworth.

'That's right,' said Appleyard, 'but three were conscious enough to fathom what was happening to them. They had had more food than the other two – and less alcohol.'

'And the three males?' Sant queried.

Hardaker consulted his tablet. 'Out cold. Their drinks were laced to high heaven.'

'So what's your call, Chiefman?'

The superintendent looked across at Sant. 'I'm erring on the side of caution. Let's coordinate our investigations.'

Sant snapped the toothpick in two. 'You think Popescu is our man?'

Hardaker eyed each colleague in turn. 'We need to keep an open mind. I see no harm in bringing the cases together. DCI Appleyard will take the lead. I will oversee. Amanda, keep us informed of the Popescu angle.'

'Twenty-four seven,' Appleyard added.

'No problem,' Holdsworth said. 'And you do the same for us.'

Appleyard looked up as she slotted the papers inside her

folder. 'That goes without saying, DS Holdsworth.' She dropped the folder into a filing cabinet and slammed it shut.

As the gleaming glass doors of Hardaker's boardroom closed behind them, Sant spoke to Holdsworth in hushed tones: 'Haven't had the pleasure of her company before.'

'What do you mean? We've worked with her before.'

'But it's never been a pleasure.'

Holdsworth nudged him with her slender shoulder. 'You're under her command now, Carl.'

'I'm not under anyone's command, Holdsworth, and no-one's under my command either. You, for instance, can do what you like as far as I'm concerned. I trust you. That's the difference between me and her.'

The detective sergeant turned to face her boss. 'You've never liked hierarchies, have you?'

'I dislike people who have all the answers and think that solving a crime is about meeting a target rather than meting out justice.'

'Psychology lesson finished?'

'For you, partner, yes – but not for our new detective *chief* inspector.'

* * *

The Romanian needed all his strength to lift the fat man out of his car and dump him in a ditch. He took a moment to recover, made to set off, then cursed himself for nearly forgetting. Retracing his steps to the body, he did a quick search and found what he was looking for. A tatty wallet, worthless, but four crisp twenty-pound notes were not. Petrol money. He couldn't run his newly acquired Beemer without a full tank.

He threw away a few worthless coins, thanked the man, got a snore in response. Sleep tight, he whispered. Not that there was any need to whisper. That Liquid E would render him dead to the world for a good while longer. Then he'd wake and wonder why he was lying prostrate on a bed of snowy grass, nursing a hangover from hell.

Maybe a hangover wouldn't be his only complaint. The Romanian smiled to himself. Just for good measure, why not knock out a tooth? He bent down and struck hard. The fat man's nose exploded under brass knuckles. He struck again and blood streamed from that ugly mouth. Job done.

He turned the ignition and slowly guided the BMW along the dirt track. He loved the rumble of the engine in the back, guiding those rear wheels for extra cruise control. The motor was immaculate. Almost. The puff had puked on the leather upholstery. Still, the mess could be cleaned up and he'd still get six thou. Used cars didn't come cheap anymore. Six thousand readies. Not bad for a night's work.

He made a mental note. Five. The number of his victims. He was getting a taste for men. They had more to lose, usually, and less to cry about.

Experimentation was the key to success. Mixing it up kept the pigs scratching heads wondering how many perverts were on the loose. Who knows? I've no idea myself, the Romanian told himself, but the confusion works in my favour. Dealing with widespread public fear will make bail offenders the least of the pigs' worries.

That bright ball of moonlight was a blessing. No need for headlights till he reached the main road. The blessing didn't last for long, though. A snow cloud drifted under the yellow disc and brought blackness to Earth. The Romanian hit the brakes and the Beemer came to a halt.

He could still see ahead of him as white flakes hit the windscreen, but several risks needed weighing. If he kept the lights on, he'd draw attention to himself. Anyone watching from afar would question why a car was snaking its way up a rough track at the dead of night. But if he carried on without headlights, any number of potential pitfalls awaited him. There was the roadside ditch, for one, and for another, sharp boulders he'd somehow managed to dodge on his way down. They might come back to haunt him by bursting a tyre, scrapping the undercarriage, ruining the suspension.

He peered up at the sky and groaned. The movement of the cloud was glacial, the air thick with fresh snow. He took a deep breath and dimmed the lights as low as he could. Slowly, he pressed the accelerator and kept the speedometer steady at ten miles per hour.

Avoid deep potholes, he told himself, and don't veer to the side, and keep straight along here, and thus the running commentary remained largely prosaic until two white beams whizzed over the hill in front of him and his heart stopped beating. Dousing the lights and crunching the gear stick in one motion, he reversed fast and narrowly missed the stone wall to the left of the track while skirting the precipice on the right. The car bumped and shuddered over rocky debris.

The Romanian cranked his neck and stared at a point somewhere beyond the rear window. He'd passed it moments earlier. A narrow stretch of dirt that fanned out beyond a cluster of overgrown trees. It was once the entrance to a geriatric nursing home, but he didn't know the fact and very few did.

He didn't see the turning until reversing passed it. Mouth wide open, he nearly yanked the gear stick out of its socket. The wheels spun as he steered off the track and rammed the Beemer into the wooded pass as far as it would go. He got out and climbed over rotten fencing long since trampled by trespassers. Crawling under a low ceiling of hanging branches, he landed hard on leafy ground and held his breath. It reeked of disinfectant, but so what? He was safe. Probably.

A pair of headlights floated by. The Romanian wasn't religious, yet he was praying for those beams to dance merrily down the hill, not to stop, no Lord. Surely the driver was a farmer doing an early morning errand. Surely not a pig. He'd told none of his associates about the place. Someone had suggested it to him as an ideal spot, secluded yet close to the action. He tried to remember who.

The car or van or whatever it was coasted on. He couldn't work out the model, though it was making such light work of the rocky road that he assumed it was a four-wheel drive. He closed his eyes in relief as it went by. The coast looks clear, he told himself. Get out of here now. He pulled himself up and began to crawl out of the woody maze, but the clattering of the motor came back. It trundled up the track and came to rest by an opening in the wall where a gate had been removed.

The Romanian trained his vision through the long grass and twigs on a point about fifteen yards in front of him. It took a while to get accustomed to the shadows, but all at once the moon reappeared and the scene was floodlit. He unscrewed his eyes and widened them. The widest eyes he'd ever worn. What he was seeing, unmistakably, was the driver and his passenger hauling something out of the boot the like of which he'd never seen before. It was a smooth and enormous cube of ice, so slick and cumbersome that the pair of them were struggling to get a grasp of it. Eventually, after much steam had risen from the two mouths, the cube toppled over the brim of the boot and thudded onto the gravel.

Driver and accomplice dragged the weight off the track and between the gap in the wall using a rug placed underneath. Next, the rug was unfurled and the giant ice cube toppled down the slope of a snow-coated field until it disappeared. The rug was then tossed into the boot and the masterminds of this mysterious act went with it. The driver jolted the engine into life and the vehicle sailed back up the hill without a murmur.

The Romanian still had his gob open. He was curious by nature and normally examined the things left behind by others. But this thing wasn't normal, not even by his own standards. If it was the carcass of an animal and these people were quack butchers, why dump it in a random field? That block of ice had no reason for existing, no matter what in God's name was inside it.

As he sat back in the BMW, he recalled who'd tipped him off about this haunt. It was the lass with the nose ring in the betting shop. The one who'd told him about Lovell Park too; about a gay friend of hers who'd picked up a lover boy there and taken him here. Should he join the dots together? Under other circumstances, yes, but just then he had neither the time nor the will. He counted to twenty before reversing out of the wooded pass and bolting into snow-white night.

4

As Sant drove down Woodhall Road, the bakery factory on one side and the disused quarry on the other, he sensed flickering blue bouncing back at him from low mist above. The lights came in fits and starts. Piercing the hazy blue were white and red streams of traffic slithering along the dual carriageway beyond.

He came to a cattle grid and parked his Fiesta behind a crime scene investigation van; said hello to a couple of uniforms on guard duty; squeezed through a stile beside the cattle grid.

Taking long strides over endless holes in the road, Sant then straddled an icy ditch to one side and followed a half-beaten path bordered by barbed wire. He heard the distant sound of bleating but saw no lambs. The pong of cow muck seeped into his nostrils. Most of the people he knew hated the stench, but he found it oddly pleasurable. This was what country life was all about. He'd grown up on concrete streets where views of open fields came via the TV set. Seeing and smelling a real farm was much more satisfying. This world was exotic to his fume-infested senses.

He reached the end of the path and saw a white tent erected in an undulating field two hundred yards below. Technicians in matching white outfits were sealing off the crime scene. Three of them on hands and knees were scouring tufts of grass and molehills for traces of anything that could reveal a lead.

The call had come before dawn, but Sant was glad he was on the early shift. He'd be the first detective to lay eyes on things, and that fact pleased him. But he knew Dr Grant Wisdom would be on the case before him. The good doctor appeared from beneath the tent as Sant trudged down the slope.

'You're up bright and early,' he called, pulling his mask below his chin.

'Not early enough,' Sant said. 'What do we know?'

'Nothing until the post-mortem, my boy.'

Sant didn't need reminding of Wisdom's meticulous approach to his job. Each cadaver he encountered was like a work of art. It needed evaluating. By a cool-headed professional. And only a Home Office pathologist like Wisdom had that authority.

The inspector tried a different tack. 'What does the body tell you?'

'What body?'

Sant stopped breathing for a moment. 'There's no body?'

'On the contrary, my boy, we have a pair.'

'Two?'

'Right, but they're hard to separate.'

'I don't understand,' mumbled Sant.

Wisdom adjusted his hairnet. 'Put it this way, we'll need a cryobiologist.'

'You mean... they're frozen?'

'Entirely covered in ice.'

Sant felt his feet sink into snowy ground. 'The weather's colder than I thought.'

'It's not,' Wisdom replied. 'They're straight out of a freezer.'

'Freezer?'

'A bloody big one.'

Sant threw on protective overalls, followed the pathologist into the tent and watched as he chiselled away at an icicle protruding from a huge ice block, placing it carefully into a sample jar which went into a cool box packed with previously filled jars.

'What's your hunch, Grant?'

'I don't have one,' the doctor said. 'I'm a scientist. I work on evidence, not speculation. Besides, only X-ray eyes can see through that glacier.'

'So what does the evidence say?'

'There's not much of it yet, my boy. We'll wait for it to melt. Which reminds me, I must flag up these samples to the lab team urgently. Something strange has occurred with the freezing process.' Wisdom turned to his assistants. 'Let's remove the structure and start loading up. We've done what we can.'

Sant watched as the tent was raised like the lid of a salver to reveal the ice-entombed bodies underneath. Four techs then supported each corner of the obscene ice coffin, gently guiding it into the back of an ambulance. Ordinarily, the bodies would have been loaded directly into a major incident mobile unit specially equipped for scientific analysis, but no such unit was mobile enough to negotiate a dirt track.

As soon as the forensic machinery was up and running and weaving its way to the morgue, Sant turned and headed in the opposite direction, further down the track. He wanted a better feel for the place. He walked unhurriedly as he surveyed his surroundings with a jeweller's attention to detail. The road only got rougher. It was worn out like the quarry it had once served.

He waved a greeting at an officer supervising a cordoned-off section, ensuring unwitting ramblers and stray dogs couldn't trample over sacred killing ground. The officer didn't ask for ID as he passed her. Sant's face was familiar among rank and file.

He circled the cordon and kept on walking, no exact aim in mind. All he knew was the techs had spent less time exploring this barren stretch. He travelled a hundred yards down the lane. Nothing but mud and rubble.

He retraced his steps, this time zigzagging across the track to inspect pits and verges. After a while something glimmered in his vision. The glow came from an object wedged into soil in a shallow ditch on the quarry side of the road. Sant bent down, took a clean handkerchief from his inside pocket, and lifted the shiny thing out of the soil.

A ten-pence piece. He was about to wrap it up in the hankie when another flash of metal caught his eye. Treading carefully along the ridge of the ditch, he picked at it with a spare corner of handkerchief. Another coin, this time fifty pence. He widened his scope and more coins shone through grassy wilderness.

Sant pocketed his sixty-pence parcel and reached for the phone in his other pocket. He started a call to the crime scene investigation unit, then closed the connection when a faint whiff grabbed him. He followed his nose and the scent grew stronger as he stepped lightly down the ditch. He spotted a clump of turf stained with blood, but it wasn't the blood he could smell. It was acidic vomit, and a generous helping of the stuff was splattered among the blood, just waiting to be trodden on.

* * *

The long dark night had given him time at least. Not much, but maybe enough. What am I going to do now? He thought hard. First, get rid of the Beamer. There's no possibility of selling it anymore. As soon as the pigs get wind of that giant ice cube and whatever the hell is inside it, this newfound BMW of mine will be on every police radar imaginable.

Find some place far away, reasoned the Romanian. But the tank was emptying by degrees and under no circumstances could he risk fuelling up. His options were few and far between. He had sixty miles to play with at most.

He thought of places he'd visited but they were all too dense with cameras and patrol cars. Then he thought of the seaside and a town that nose-ringed lass had mentioned. Not too big but big enough to drift about in. He knew it was in the direction of York but thirty miles further. He also knew of roads away from the beaten track of dual carriageways and their prying electronic eyes. He came off the A1 at a junction by a racecourse and followed the country lane east. A few pretty villages and even fewer lit areas adorned this stretch. Once he reached the York ring road, he took the clockwise route and saw the signpost he was looking for. Scarborough. The lass had done business with the pigs there, or so she'd told him. Could he trust her?

He spent an hour winding through more country roads before pulling into a layby about five miles from the seaside town. He reckoned it would be safer to hang fire and join the first wave of rush-hour traffic. He got out and ripped the plastic poppy from the front of the car; considered flinging the thing into the bushes but decided it was risky. Better to dispose of it elsewhere.

The Romanian got behind the wheel again and ten minutes later, as the sun rose over the horizon, he rounded the corner of the North Bay promenade and saw the waves crashing into the sea wall. The sight and smell of salty water made him feel better – freer. He was almost out of fuel and it felt like he'd made it to the end of the earth.

He wanted to get out and saturate himself in frigid open water. Impossible. Instead, he steered up a hill lined to his right with hotels offering sea views and little else. The fronts of the cream-coloured buildings were peeling with age and disrepair, every window advertising VACANCIES and happy-hour offers on alcoholic drinks. The Romanian didn't pay much attention to his surroundings. He had one thing on his mind. Dump the car. He measured out an on-road parking space and steered the Beamer between a Volvo and a Renault Clio.

Hood flung over bald head, he grabbed the keys and plastic flower from the passenger seat, opened and closed the driver's door as quietly as he could. It was still early and there was little sign of life. The hotel guests, if there were any in the off-season, must have been three sheets to the wind. He spotted a bin by a bench and tried to chuck the flower in there, but the damn thing was too big to fit through the seagull flap.

Aware of looking suspicious if he loitered too long, he carried on walking up the hill and down the other side, subtly getting to work on the poppy with his hands while his ears remained sensitive to the sound of a car starting up, a dog barking, a fishing boat motoring to shore. At last, he managed to transform the flower into four bits of mangled plastic. He found a bin wide enough to jam the pieces into and buried them deep. After that, he lost himself in alleys around the market hall, browsed the antiques stalls in the vaults, ate breakfast at a greasy spoon, bought some trainers and got rid of the toe-capped boots to be on the safe side, then phoned one of his associates to arrange a lift home.

* * *

Detective Constable Capstick – who'd been on the look-out for CCTV – uploaded what he'd retrieved. Huddled around the projector in the Homicide and Major Enquiry briefing room were Sant and Holdsworth to one side, Hardaker and Apple-yard to the other, as well as a posse of detectives working on various unsolved murder cases.

'Spotted anything?' said Hardaker as he took a bite from a cereal bar.

Capstick pressed his NHS glasses against his nose. 'Plenty for a Thursday morning. There's a potential witness as well.'

'The farmer who raised the alarm?' Appleyard asked.

'He didn't see a thing,' Capstick said, 'apart from that huge block of ice in his field of course.'

'How's the image quality?' Hardaker asked.

'Good, sir, though the dark doesn't help and the camera's partly hidden behind a tree.'

'Wind her up,' said Sant, who didn't like technology and refused to take the exams designed to turn him into a desktop geek. 'We haven't got all day.'

Capstick expanded a window on his laptop and adjusted the brightness. 'This footage was filmed from the entrance to the baking factory on Gain Lane – the closest any camera gets to the Woodhall Road turning.' He dragged his cursor along a timeline at the bottom of the screen. 'At 1.23am a white BMW driving west along Gain Lane from the A647 Stanningley Bypass gyratory takes a sharp right into Woodhall Road. Now watch what happens.' Capstick clicked on the timeline. 'Eleven minutes later, at 1.34am, a green Land Rover appears from the same direction and takes the same turning.'

Holdsworth scrutinised the projected images intently. 'Hang on, has the BMW left?'

'No. And there's no other way out.'

'Which means the two vehicles were in the vicinity of each other,' Appleyard said matter-of-factly.

'Any way of identifying the drivers?' asked Sant.

Capstick snorted. 'Sadly not, sir. We've got tree branches and pouring rain and pitch-black night to contend with.'

'How long did they stay?'

The constable played with his cursor again. 'Not long. The Land Rover leaves first. Here it goes, turning left at the end of Woodhall Road and back towards the A647. The time is now 1.39am.'

'Stuck around for just five minutes,' commented one of the other detectives.

'And four minutes later the BMW exits but turns the other way, right towards the bakery entrance where this camera is installed.'

'We should get a decent view,' Hardaker said, swallowing the rest of his snack while pointing a finger at the footage.

'Sadly not.' Capstick paused the video, then pressed play. 'As the BMW circles towards us, along comes a lorry leaving the baking factory and going left into Gain Lane, effectively blocking our view of the driver and the number plate. By the time the lorry is out of the way the BMW has gone past the bakery, heading west towards Fagley.'

'Not the same way it came in,' noted another detective.

'Sod's Law,' sighed Holdsworth.

'Not necessarily,' Appleyard put in. 'I suspect the driver of the BMW strategically waited for the lorry before turning into Gain Lane, knowing he would avoid the CCTV.'

'Let's examine all cameras in and around Gain Lane,' Hardaker said. 'DC Capstick, you're the man for that job.'

Holdsworth slapped her hand on the table. 'The lorry driver must've noticed the car.'

'As I mentioned earlier,' Capstick said, 'we have a possible witness. The HGV should be equipped with a dashcam too.'

Sant turned to face the murder detectives sat behind him. 'I'll visit the factory and track down the lorry driver. If he's seen anyone resembling one of our most wanted, I'll let you know.'

'Excellent,' said Hardaker, 'though more urgent is getting an analysis of that blood and vomit you found, Carl.'

'Wisdom's techs are on it. What's your best guess, Chiefman?'

Hardaker plucked hairs off his red goatee. 'Might be the perp's vomit. I'm not sure about the blood.'

'It's not from the corpses,' Capstick said. 'Their blood is encased in ice.'

'Assuming there's a drop left in them,' Holdsworth remarked.

'Do we know how long the cadavers have been frozen?' asked Appleyard.

'Wisdom's not committing to a timescale,' Sant said.

'Then perhaps we keep an open mind,' Appleyard concluded.

Hardaker nodded. 'We can't be sure these deaths aren't the result of a recent sexually motivated attack.'

'Do we know the sex of the victims?' Holdsworth asked.

'Not for certain,' Hardaker said, 'but a tech I spoke to thinks they're both female.'

'We don't know a thing about them,' Sant added.

'That's true, Carl, which is why I see no harm in a joined-up strategy to cover all the bases.'

'Are you going public with it, Chiefman?'

Hardaker shook his head. 'Our press conference has been rearranged for two-thirty. Stephanie and I will play down any link for now.'

'Were the two victims drugged like the others?' Holdsworth queried.

'Tests are impossible until the ice melts sufficiently,' said Hardaker.

'I'll coordinate the investigation in line with what we're doing elsewhere,' Appleyard confirmed as she made to leave.

Hardaker smiled warmly. 'We'll follow your lead, Stephanie.'

Appleyard hesitated. 'Perhaps you can front up the media this afternoon, Harry.'

The superintendent laid a soft hand on her shoulder. 'For sure, I wouldn't want to rush you in.'

'Why were there two motors?' Sant thought aloud, interrupting the Hardaker-Appleyard love affair.

'One to keep watch?' Holdsworth mused.

'Let's find the vehicles and speculate from there,' said Hardaker as he tracked his partner out of the door. 'Oh, and Carl, don't forget forensics. We need the works on the blood and vomit samples promptly.'

Sant grabbed his jacket and followed close behind. 'First, I feel a bit peckish.'

'Enjoy the bread buns, sir.'

'Don't worry, Capstick. I will.'

* * *

The joyous morning smell of freshly baked dough greeted Sant as he parked his Fiesta in the courtyard. He took his time finding the tradesman's entrance before wandering down a blandly decorated corridor and noticing a door with SECU-RITY marked on it. It was slightly ajar. He pushed it open gently and was met by an elderly man with a cigarette hanging out of his toothless mouth. He was shuffling a pack of cards.

'What tickles your fancy?' the man asked.

'I don't play,' Sant said.

'Pity,' he said. 'I'm the watchman. How can I help ya?'

'My name's Detective Inspector Sant.'

The man stretched his lean frame. 'Ah, be about them bodies wot were found.'

Sant nodded. 'My colleague visited earlier.'

'Aye. Ah, forget his name.'

'Capstick.'

'That's him. Brad. Nice lad. I sorted the recordings for him.'

The watchman attached a monocle to his right eye and waved a small hand at a row of monitors by the side of his desk, wired up to security cameras dotted around the factory.

'That's why I'm here,' Sant said. 'I'd like a word with one of your drivers. He left here last night at a quarter to two.'

The man stubbed out his cigarette in a glass ashtray and glanced at a clock on the wall. 'Aye, they come to work about now. Drivers start in the afternoon and set off with deliveries through the night. I'll show ya where they flock.'

Sant followed the man through the courtyard towards another wing of the factory. At least a dozen lorries were parked along this stretch of the complex, all waiting to distribute loaves to supermarkets across West Yorkshire. The first of them was being stacked with goodies, one man hauling crates filled with iced fingers up a ramp while a young woman fastened the crates to the inside of the trailer with rope. Smoke billowed out of pipes at ground level. Sant guessed the industrial ovens were located deep in the basement, with the finishing touches applied higher up the conveyor belt.

They came to an annexe and two flights of rickety stairs before entering a gymnasium-sized social space equipped with coffee machine and catering trolley containing baked delights.

The pool tables and dartboards had seen better days. One of the workers was playing a Wii game, simulating hurdling on an athletics track. Somewhere a radio blasted out a Bruce Springsteen number.

The watchman lifted a ledger from the top of a bookcase housing worn out paperbacks. He fitted the eyeglass hanging from his neck, licked a thumb and turned some leaves.

'Looks like Stan Grainger's ya lad. Clocked off at 1.35am. Would've taken him ten minutes to check his load and set off.' He let the monocle fall from his eye and called out: 'Is Stan in?'

The question was met with silence by fifteen or so employees within earshot until a woman wearing a chef's hat shouted back: 'He gets in at three!'

The man took a mug from a dishwasher and placed it under the coffee machine. 'You're welcome to stick around. Have a cuppa and a Danish. I'm on decaf. Helps me sleep.'

'What time do you knock off?' asked Sant, grabbing a mug and choosing the latte option.

'About midnight. Just live down the road.'

'So you'd be tucked up in bed before last night's shenanigans.'

'That's right. I visit the land of nod easily these days.' He lifted the mug to his mouth, Sant noticing his arm shaking, making some of the liquid spill. 'Sorry, Mr Sant. Hope I didn't get any on ya.'

'Maybe it's best to sit down,' Sant said.

They found a table with a couple of chairs that looked only slightly less battered than the dartboards. Sant looked across and got a good view of the man for first time. He was struck by the depth of wrinkles on his leathery face.

'Sorry, I didn't get your name.'

'William Payton. Call me Willie.'

'How old are you, Willie, if you don't mind me asking?'

'Sixty-five. Ah, feel a lot older though. That's what comes from keeping ya head down all ya life. I'm retiring next year thank goodness.' He poured boiling hot liquid into his mouth and swallowed without wincing. 'Aye, twenty-two I was, the last time it happened.'

'What?'

'Murder. Down that same track. I was taking a shortcut. Found her there. In that field.'

'Who?'

'Rita. She was in a ditch, naked from the waist up. Bits of her clothing strewn all over. Someone had crept up on her from behind. She'd put up a mighty struggle, but the evil sod had kept on hitting her. I rushed off to tell folk. Knew it'd do no good. She was dead to the world. They tried to save her, gave up a few days after.'

'Must've been traumatic for you.'

Willie extracted a whisky miniature from his jacket and emptied the bottle into his coffee. 'Got over it eventually. Us locals called that road our lovers' lane. Had great times down there. You know, our first kiss and a bit more besides. Used to take my lass for a walk every Friday night before we were allowed in the pubs.' He smiled back at an age long gone. 'Aye, all the love went out of that lane the day Rita got killed.'

Sant sipped casually on his latte. 'What year was this?'

'1977. October. Rita was on her way to work here. It was Almond's Bakery back then. Such a shook. I haven't ventured down Woodhall Road since.'

'Did you know the girl well?'

The watchman knocked back the rest of his decaf. 'She was in my class at school. Chatted her up once. But we left school as soon as we could in those days, and I lost touch with her after that. And a few years later someone bludgeons her with a coping stone. Her face was such a mess. The stepdad could only tell it was her when he saw her hands, and the engagement ring.'

'She worked here, you say?'

'Aye.'

'And you?'

'I wasn't here back then. Worked as a cook at the women's geriatric hospital.' He pointed in a direction Sant couldn't fathom before extracting more steamy coffee from the machine and tipping it into his asbestos mouth. 'Fifty-seven beds and two of us doing the cooking. Rushed off our feet we were, me and Jack Hindle, till the place closed. Then it became an old people's home. That's no more neither.'

'Who killed Rita?'

Willie looked pointedly at Sant. 'Over to you and your lot. Ya predecessors failed badly on that front.'

Sant thought hard and finally his brain kicked into gear. 'Rita Mitchell. The wrong man was convicted of her murder.'

'Aye, Simon Coyle did twenty years inside and was innocent all along. Some folk maintain he was guilty, but I'm not so sure. By all accounts he was forced to confess. Excuse my language, Mr Sant, when I say the policemen in these parts used to be bastards. I had dealings with them myself.'

Sant took another sip. 'Does Coyle still live locally?'

'He's pushing up daisies. Had a heart attack. All those years in prison took a toll on his ticker.'

'Did you know him?'

Willie wiped his mouth with the back of his hand. 'He was a few years older. Went to a different school. Not that it did him much good. Unemployed most of the time. Eventually the council gave him a job as a gardener. He was working the day he was supposed to have killed her.'

Sant glanced at his watch. Interesting though the conversation was, he couldn't afford to engage in idle chatter. He half-finished his latte and pushed the mug to one side.

'Aye, that Bird and Wormald set him up good and proper.' The names were vaguely familiar to Sant. 'They put words into his mouth. Convinced him he did it. The poor lad was mentally handicapped. Not badly so, but enough to leave him at the beck and call of those detectives. Cretins would be a better description. No offence, Mr Sant.'

'None taken. I never knew them so I'll reserve judgement.'

'Any policeman worth his salt would've done a better job.' Willie arched his neck closer. 'Ya know what I heard at the time?'

'Tell me.'

'This might be rumour, but a dicky bird told me the police had a prime suspect with no alibi who was seen by witnesses close to where Rita died on that horrible day.'

'Prime suspects are not always guilty.'

'Aye, Mr Sant, but here's the really puzzling thing. This suspect, and nobody knows who he was, apparently got off scott free.'

'You mean he wasn't charged?'

'No, he was arrested at the same time as Coyle, but he was never questioned. For some bizarre reason the police refused to follow their noses. It was as if Coyle and this other man were playing cards together, and it was do or die and the other came up trumps. How about that for a mystery?'

Sant tried not to laugh at the sincerity in Willie's leathery face. 'Most mysteries turn out to be works of fiction, fortunately.'

'But if this prime suspect did exist and there's a record of his identity somewhere, what's stopping you lot reopening the case? I mean, the chances he's still alive are quite good.'

'Unsolved murder files are never closed,' said the inspector, 'but as time passes the probability of conviction is small. And time means money.'

What the hell do I sound like, Sant thought, cursing himself. I'm taking these words right out of the Chiefman's manual on efficient policing, for heaven's sake.

Willie's chin dropped to his chest. 'In a perfect world there's no price for justice. We don't live in that world, do we?' Sant shook his head. 'I shan't keep you any longer. A truck load of flour is expected. Bakers can't do owt without it.'

He grinned toothlessly and left.

* * *

More workers drifted in. Sant devoured two Danish pastries, picked up one of the tatty paperbacks on display, read the first chapter. It was about a deaf boy and a dog, and the dog knew sign language and could sign the Lord's Prayer backwards. He was contemplating whether to start the second chapter when a cleaning lady tapped him on the shoulder and pointed to a tall man who'd just walked in.

'I take it you're Stan,' Sant said as he approached the man.

'Who's asking?'

Sant showed his ID. 'It's about the bodies we found this morning.'

He put up his hairy hands. 'It wasn't me.'

'Don't worry. You're not a suspect.' The man was about the same height, placing Sant directly in line with his airstream and the pungent booze on his breath. 'Last night your lorry was captured on CCTV at the front gate. As you were exiting, a BMW turned right onto Gain Lane from Woodhall Road. You would've had a good view of it.'

Stan looked up at the ceiling and back down. 'Sorry, my mind's a blank. A BMW?'

Sant nodded. 'A white one. Accelerating fast.'

'Now I think of it, I did see a car.'

He headed for the coffee machine. Sant guessed he was searching for something to mask his taste in whatever he'd been drinking by the gallon.

'Do you recall anything about the car or its driver?'

'Not really.'

'Surely you heard the screech of tyres; the rev of the engine?'

Stan gulped black caffeine, exhibiting an even thicker asbestos gob than Willie.

'Can't say I did.'

'You always hit the bottle before work?'

He licked his lips. 'No, well, sometimes.'

'I presume you've got a dashcam fitted.'

'No, I mean yes, but it doesn't work.'

'Have you reported it?'

'No.'

'Why not?' He shrugged but said nothing. 'How much have you had to drink?'

'Only the one.'

'Wrong answer. You're over the limit.'

The man clutched his thumbs to his forehead and inhaled deeply. After silently sobbing for a moment, he said: 'I'm having a rough time. My frigging girlfriend's having it off with my best mate. Give me a second chance, please.'

Sant took him to one side. An audience of finger pointers had gathered around and it wasn't much fun being centre stage.

'Listen, Stan. I'm drawing a line under this. On certain conditions.'

'Name them, I'll keep to them, I promise.'

'First, take a sickie. Second, walk straight home or catch a taxi – leave your vehicle here. Third, never again get behind the wheel if you can't stay off the booze. Understand?'

Stan closed his eyes and tears fell to the floor. A few onlookers moved in, Sant waving them away.

'This is a private matter, thank you.'

They pulled faces and turned back.

'And fourth,' Sant continued, 'sign up to an AA clinic. I've got the T-shirt. No-one likes to talk in front of strangers, but believe me, it works.'

Stan dried his eyes on his shirt sleeve. 'I'll try. I will.'

Numerous eyes were fixed to them like superglue as they exited stage left.

'I'll drop you at the nearest bus stop if you like,' Sant said as they scrambled down the wobbly stairs.

'I'm fine. It's not in my nature to take a Bridewell taxi.'

Sant caught the man's meaning. Police cars were nick-named Bridewells by the locals because they had once delivered criminals to the old Bridewell police station under Leeds Town Hall. The nick had long since shut, but the name had stuck.

Sant bid farewell but as he got into his Fiesta, he heard a cry from afar. He wound down his window and waited for Stan to come stumbling forward.

'Red poppy!'

'How many pints did you say you'd had?'

The man was out of breath. 'The white BMW. It had a red poppy.'

'You certain?'

'Near as damn it. In fact, I saw the poppy before I saw the car. That's why I didn't pay attention.'

'Nothing to do with the booze?'

Stan blushed. 'It won't happen again.'

'Good to hear it, and thanks for the info.'

'Glad I could be of use. Is there a reward?'

'You get the reg number?'

Stan looked deflated. 'Afraid not.'

'Never mind.' Sant turned his key in the ignition. 'When we've solved the case, I'll bring you a crate of something nice. Pepsi or J2o, whatever suits your taste buds.'

The lorry driver considered his options, then said: 'Pepsi. It's better for chasers.'

Sant laughed but Stan laughed louder, like a hooting owl at the crack of dawn.

* * *

Back at Elland Road HQ Capstick was still preoccupied with laptop and projector, going backwards and forwards over the same shots frantically as if his life depended on it. Sant threw his black suit jacket over a coat-stand and sat down hard, his feet like two lead weights. He was out of shape. Running after a drug peddler and roaming a murder scene at sunrise came with side effects.

'Traced the BMW and Land Rover yet, Capstick?'

'The guys handling the other cameras have sightings aplenty, sir, but headlight glares and the like are proving a nightmare when trying to detect number plates.'

'Show me,' Sant said, placing a fresh toothpick between his jaws.

Capstick expanded an image of the green Land Rover on his laptop. 'This should be the easier vehicle to identify because it took the Leeds-Bradford Road route out of Gain Lane. Sadly, both front and back registration numbers are obscured by grit or muck.'

'Land Rovers do get muddy, but rarely so conveniently.

Hopefully the driver forgot to wash the plates afterwards and some discerning traffic officer strikes gold.'

'A premeditated move, sir?'

'Certainly. How about the BMW?'

Capstick opened another still. 'Fewer sightings of this one because it went the opposite way out of Gain Lane, along quieter roads. What I've seen, though, indicates the plates weren't dirtied in any way. Unfortunately, the images are too blurry to pick out details.'

'Keep searching for film, Capstick. We've got a chance, especially with the Beamer.'

'I'll pass on your instructions, sir. But first, pay close attention.' He brought up the video clip he'd been dissecting. 'This is from the same CCTV I showed you earlier, but this footage was recorded later in the night. You'll miss it if you blink.'

Sant watched keenly. 'Run it again.'

The detective constable dragged the timeline back and pressed play. Grainy black and white frames out of sync with real time were set in motion, only windblown trees betraying the stillness of the scene. The overhead view of the road conveyed no sign of life at all.

Then, to the extreme left of the picture, a moving figure fleetingly photobombed the scene before retreating out of the frame. The figure hunched horribly. Someone in pain.

'Rewind.' Capstick clicked a few times. 'Hold it there.' The fuzzy form was fixed in time. 'When was this?'

'3.48am, sir.'

'Two hours after the Land Rover and Beamer left.'

'Just over. The BMW left at 1.43am, the Land Rover a little before.'

'It's a pity we can't zoom in.'

'We can,' Capstick demonstrated, 'but there's not much to go on.'

'Male or female?'

'Looks like a male.'

'Age?'

'Impossible to judge.'

'A drunk teenager?'

'Maybe,' Capstick said, 'in which case we can't blame him for throwing up his beer and kebab if he set eyes on that ice tomb.'

'I see what you mean, but not many teens accidently lose themselves in the middle of nowhere.'

'You've misremembered your youth, sir.'

Sant smirked. 'Speaking from experience, Capstick?'

'Being brought up in the Dales, sir, it's amazing what holes I've wound up in after too many sherbets.'

Sant chewed on his toothpick. 'The other thing to ponder is why he puked. It's not necessarily because he bumped into a pair of corpses.'

'What do you mean?'

'For a start, he could hardly see the bodies for all the ice around them. But also, the vomit I found was nowhere near the bodies.'

'True, sir. Anyone with a humane stomach would be sick close by.'

'Which suggests this man puked for some other reason. It's also likely he puked before he saw the bodies because the spot where I found the vomit is further from the junction with Gain Lane than is the dumping ground for the cadavers.'

Capstick nodded. 'If the man was heading in one direction up Woodhall Road, he's retched before he gets that unexpected shock.'

Sant cranked his head closer to the crouched figure pixeled on screen. 'It looks like he's bent double, trying to heave, but his stomach's empty and nothing's coming out.'

'Forensics found no vomit in that area, sir. You must be right.'

* * *

At that moment the door of the briefing room sprang open and Holdsworth appeared, her permed brown hair bouncing as she flung down a holdall full of papers and leant her weight on a table, one knee raised above the other, hands clasped to her thigh.

'Any news?' Sant asked.

'I've pulled a muscle,' she said, kicking off a shoe.

'You should ease off on that morning workout,' said Capstick.

'So I can serve you breakfast in bed, Brad?'

'My stay-at-home girlfriend makes wonderful scrambled eggs, you know.'

Sant raised his hand. 'Enough of the banter, you two. If I want to know your domestic routine, I'll befriend you on Facebook.'

'But you're not on Facebook, sir.'

'Exactly my point, Capstick. What's in the bag, Holdsworth?'

'Lots of things I've had no chance to digest,' she said, 'though the initial report on the vomit and blood makes interesting reading.'

'A DNA match?'

'Nothing on the database, but the vomit reveals clear traces of you know what.'

'Liquid E,' Sant said.

'Right.' Holdsworth flicked through the report. 'High concentrations of flunitrazepam on every page. Whoever was sick in that field was doped to the eyeballs.'

Sant snapped his toothpick in half. 'Maybe the Chiefman is right about his joined-up thinking. What transpired last night may well be linked to the violence and muggings we're investigating. We should let Hardaker know. It'll do his self-esteem the world of good.'

'Our priority must be finding the man who puked,' Holdsworth said as she rubbed her thigh.

'He's not guilty of anything, is he?' said Capstick.

'Most likely he's a victim,' Sant remarked.

'So who's the perp?' Holdsworth probed. 'The same shady character who dropped off the bodies?'

'We'll need to ask our victim about that.'

'So why doesn't he come forward?' Holdsworth snapped.

'It's a man thing. He's either too afraid or too embarrassed.'

'Or he may not realise he's been assaulted,' Capstick added.

Holdsworth looked bemused. 'You mean, he might blame his ailments on a bad pint?'

'He knows he's been doped,' Capstick said, 'but it may not be obvious if the sex act – if that's what he's been subject to – was consensual. Also, if he was paying for it, he could be accused of soliciting, hence his silence.'

Sant shook his head. 'I take your point about prostitution, Capstick, but not the consensual act angle. No-one consents to sex with a punch to the mouth thrown in.'

'Which means we're seeking a man with a newly busted lip,' Holdsworth said. 'As well as informing on his sadistic rent boy, maybe he'll give us a lead on the corpses.'

Capstick began thinking aloud. 'Can you imagine a situation where a violent individual dumps a pair of bodies at the same time as he dumps a man he's just doped?'

'Unlikely,' said Sant. 'Murderers don't dispose of victims unless they're categorically dead. Also, Liquid E isn't the executioner's poison of choice. It takes a mixture of other drugs to endanger life.'

'Have we worked out where the vehicles come into the picture?' Holdsworth asked.

The inspector discarded his toothpick. 'My guess is one of them was owned by the doped man, and whoever drugged him stole his wheels.'

'I suppose the BMW's the more attractive motor to steal.'

'Right, Holdsworth. The Land Rover must be ten years old whereas the BMW looks new and has a higher street value. Plus, a Land Rover is better suited for transporting bulky objects like bodies. Whether the drivers worked in tandem is another scenario we can't rule out.'

Holdsworth stood and stretched her slender frame. 'What depressing misdeeds we're deal with,' she said as she picked up her holdall. 'Anyway, a ton of paperwork awaits me. By the way, Brad, stay on red alert for the shadowing of Mrs Popescu.'

'That's tomorrow night, isn't it?'

'I like keeping you on your toes,' she said with a smile and a wave.

Capstick tapped on his keypad. 'Good news – we have a development. An email from Sergeant Roy Galley of Scarborough CID.'

'Never heard of him,' Sant said.

'A white BMW has been found. Parked illegally. No poppy on it, but intriguingly, a refuse collector reported picking up bits of red plastic from a street bin nearby.'

Sant got up from his chair. 'Excellent. I'll call Sergeant Galley now.'

'I wouldn't bother. He's leaving work early today. A private matter, he says. Back on duty in the morning.'

'Jesus Christ! Talk about the quiet life. Before I retire, remind me to migrate to the coast and spend the rest of my working life chasing seagulls.' He grabbed his black Mackin-tosh, which had migrated from the coat-stand to the dusty floor. 'I'm off to the seaside, Capstick.'

'You get all the best beats, sir.'

'It's called taking advantage of the perks while you've got the chance.'

'I'll let DCI Appleyard know where you're heading.'

'Following orders, Capstick?'

'She did tell me to notify her of developments.'

'Twenty-four seven?'

Capstick grinned up from his laptop. 'She might've used that phrase.'

* * *

The sun was still clinging to the western sky as he approached the South Bay promenade and turned uphill towards the town centre. There was no snow anywhere, mild coastal breezes staving off the chill felt inland. Sant found the red-brick police station easily and parked on double yellow lines directly outside it. A youthful woman with short dark hair and long white teeth greeted him at the austere front desk.

'DI Sant?'

'That's me.'

The woman smiled impeccably. 'I'm DC Lawson. I believe you wanted to inspect the BMW.'

'Right.'

'One problem,' she said, laughing nervously in a way that told Sant there really was a problem. 'Sergeant Galley left the key for the compound in his desk drawer, but I've gone through every one of this twenty-six drawers–'

'One for each letter of the alphabet.'

Lawson stared at Sant, then giggled. 'Yes, I've checked every drawer and can't find the key.'

'Have you called him?'

'He doesn't have a phone.'

Sant slapped his forehead. 'What?'

'Well, he does, but he switches it off when he's not at work. He'll be in first thing in the morning. You're welcome to stick around till then.'

'Got a cell free?'

She giggled again. 'We've two actually. Not much action in sunny Scarborough at the mo.'

'You ought to come to Leeds, DC Lawson. We've more criminals than doctors and nurses.'

'The summer season brings its fair share of rough diamonds, but the off season is heavenly.'

'I'll ask for a career move,' Sant said as he peered at his watch. 'After six already.'

'Is that a genuine Rolex?'

'Only in my dreams.' He contemplated the return leg and decided against it. 'Any nice places to stay around here?'

Lawson gritted her long teeth – selling the town wasn't her forte. 'The Palm Court might be your best bet, top of St Nicholas Cliff.'

'Any plans for dinner?'

She offered him another pearly beam. 'My boyfriend's cooking tonight.'

'Lucky man,' Sant said as he turned towards the exit.

'Oh, before you go, there's something I should tell you about Sergeant Galley.'

'He's considering full-time employment?'

Lawson leaned forward over her desk and lowered her voice. 'He's had a stress-related illness. A colleague he knew well in his early days died lately.'

'Anyone I might know?'

'Maybe. I'm too young to have known him. Quite a big cheese he was, once upon a time. To the sarge he was a sort of father figure.'

'His name?'

'Jim something. It was in the papers. Oh, that was it – Jim Lackey.'

Sant shook his head. 'Never heard of him. Must've been well thought of if his death was reported in the press.'

Lawson dropped her tone to a whisper. 'That wasn't why his death became news.'

'Then what was?'

'To put it bluntly, he died in dramatic circumstances.'

'Killed?'

'Topped himself. Leapt off Spa Bridge in the middle of the night.'

* * *

Ten minutes later he checked in at the Palm Court. It was almost deserted, but the room offered looked clean enough. He called Capstick to let him know he wouldn't be back in the office before mid-morning, then stuffed two of the hotel's towels into his rucksack and headed out.

Sant could sense that Scarborough remained a lively place despite the downfall of its economic twin pillars in the last century: tourism and fishing. The golden years would never return but the locals had adapted to the shifting sands of time. Most of the fishing was geared towards lobster and shellfish these days rather than mackerel and cod.

Sant's affection for the town had begun as a child when it had been a regular holiday haunt, and now he felt a sudden urge to relive some of that past. The South Bay with its harbour was directly below him, but he remembered the North Bay more fondly. The sand was whiter there, the sea clearer, the streets less cluttered with souvenir shops and amusement arcades.

Time was against him as he jogged up Castle Hill and he was breathing hard by the time he came to the half-ruined castle. He slowed to walking pace and admired the resilience of the medieval fortress tower sat atop its rocky promontory, still standing after centuries of battles and bombs and blundering invaders hell bent on destroying it.

He passed Anne Bronte's grave and quickened his stride again as he turned onto North Marine Drive and headed down-hill to the beach. No-one seemed to pay much attention to him as he scrambled past the Freddie Gilroy and Bathing Belle stat-ues, the multicoloured beach huts, the sign warning him of high seas breaking over sea walls. He jumped from the promenade onto soft drifts of sand, stripped to his boxer shorts and paddled out to sea in barely enough light for a cold dip before supper.

The water was bitter, but he forgot the chill. Reaching waist height in a flash, he sucked in and plunged down, kicking out as hard as he could, icy sea enveloping every nerve and vein. It took several minutes before his naked self could feel again, bloodstream circulating in tune with the perishing currents ebbing over him. Open water always thrilled. It was also ideal for meditation. Sant meditated frequently. Someone he knew had fled to Thailand to become a devout Buddhist monk, Sant learning lots about mindfulness before his friend left England for good.

He thought about his sons. He'd not seen them for weeks, never bathed with them in this wonderful sea. I must put that right, he told himself. I'll contact the ex and tell her about my plans for Tom and Sam. Elizabeth will try to scupper every-thing by fretting over lifebuoys and black and white flags, but hell, risk assessments are not the alpha and omega of humanity's well-being.

Then he thought of Mia. He craved her company, and yet the age difference was absurd. She must have done the maths by now, which explained the long silence. While he certainly missed her, he didn't miss feeling uncomfortable about their relationship. A thug whose name he'd consigned to oblivion had called him a sugar daddy. The label angered him – but was there a half-truth to it?

Growing bolder as bodily sensations came back, Sant swooped deep into murky green and wrapped bundles of seaweed around arms and shoulders. As he rose to the surface like some infant Godzilla, he extended his skeleton to give purchase against the growing violence of the tide. Blinking to wash saltwater from his eyes, he circled before clasping knees to chest and turning onto his back, the waves carrying him backwards, forwards, up and down, wherever they damn well liked.

He floated for a while, spread-eagled, recalling his sister Linda who'd disappeared forever in her childhood prime, and that's why he'd become a missing persons detective when all was said and done... until a gull's squawk broke his mindful trance and brought him upright. He looked for land and couldn't see the shore, but then the crest of a wave died in the distance and he guessed he must be two hundred yards out to sea.

The white of a half sunken fishing buoy bobbed to his left, handily located for him to rest his weight on. He reached out to grab it and jerked back. It wasn't a buoy. It was a jellyfish. He kicked away from the throbbing blob moving in on him, but when he turned around, a whole line of pink and white jellies greeted him, glands expanding and contracting as they enticed the foolish inspector into their trap.

Hand close to his chest, sea fret spreading, he squinted at the violet sky darkening by the minute. Wading frantically as he conjured up a defence strategy, he finally made up his mind and held his frame stiffly before plummeting down into North Sea chill. He twisted sideways and tilted his face up, eyeing the pink blobs circling above, then closed his eyes, kicked out harder, peered upwards once more. They were still there. He repeated the manoeuvre twice before he was certain of evading the invaders.

Crawling through weedy green fluid, he gasped oxygen as he broke the surface. Enough, he thought, and let these waves throw me headlong to sandy reprieve. Ten minutes later he was beached on razor-edged shingle, and after lying there joyfully for a while, his buttocks sinking into silt, he dug himself out and went about retrieving clothes and towels through the salty mist.

He took a gloriously hot shower in his room, threw on a gown, fell into bed, slept deeper than he'd slept for a long time. The alarm on this phone was set for seven, but it was after eight when he stirred. That aquatic adventure had exhilarated and exhausted him all at once. His heart had been beating like a drum machine on that slow walk back from the sea.

The kippers and two racks of toast he devoured at breakfast didn't do much to improve his physique, but while living it up at the Palm Court, one should get value for West Yorkshire Police's money. That muesli diet could get under way from the moment Sant footed his own bills.

5

He was checking out of Scarborough's finest when his phone rang. It was Hardaker.

'Still at the seaside, Carl?'

'Applying the sun cream as you speak, Chiefman.'

'I need you here. Things are moving fast. We've got another victim on our hands.'

'Killed?'

'No. Drugged and raped. Like the rest.'

'Where?'

'Lovell Park.'

'Lungs of Leeds.'

'It happened the night before last.'

'Who is she?'

'A teenage girl. We only got wind of it this morning.'

'That was the same night as the goings-on at Woodhall Road, wasn't it?'

'Right. There might be a connection, though it's too soon to make a judgement. Keep it brief with Sergeant Galley. I've deployed two techs to assist anyway. Get back by noon or as near as dammit.'

'Sure thing. Would you care for a stick of rock?'

The line went dead. Hardaker was feeling the heat. Perhaps the Chiefman's hopes of a promotion rested on an instant solution to this messy affair.

Sant entered the police compound soon after nine-thirty. Galley was still nowhere to be seen but the ever-smiling, ever-arresting DC Lawson gave directions and the happy news that they'd located the key. He signed in under the watchful eye of a tech who was busy brushing the car doors for fingerprints. Then he pulled on a pair of latex gloves and stepped carefully to the rear of the Beemer. As he lifted the boot, he realised it had been closed lightly to ensure the lock didn't engage.

The smell hit his nose straight away. The same whiff he'd inhaled the day before. Sick. Leave it to the scientists, he said to himself. He leaned further under the lid, taking care not to brush his trousers on the bumper. Nothing apart from an empty carrier bag. He closed the boot gently and moved to the front.

A paper cup was squashed into one corner below the passenger seat. Without touching it, he bent down, stuck out his neck and sniffed. Vodka. Then he checked the side compartment on the driver's side. A magazine was rolled into it. He lifted it with the tips of his gloved fingers and unrolled it gently. A tatty issue of *Gay Times*. Things were fitting into place.

'At your service, sir.'

Sant rose to his feet and turned to face a very short but stocky man with long dark sideburns. He was almost as wide as he was tall, and his head was glued to his shoulders with almost no evidence of a neck in-between. His low centre of gravity would be handy in a race with a tearaway, Sant thought.

'Better late than never, Galley.'

'Sorry for the hold up. I'm moving to a new house and it's stressful.'

'Exchanging contracts?'

Galley nodded. 'Today's the day, though the idiots buying our place want some last-minute bonuses.'

'Tell them it's a crime to ask for the washer as well as the oven,' Sant said.

'I wish I could.'

'You can also tell them about the dead people you're investigating.'

Galley shrugged uneasily. 'Point taken. I believe you wanted to see this.'

He held up a transparent evidence bag and Sant noticed the plastic pieces inside.

'Do they form a poppy by any chance?'

'For certain. I've even discerned the letters marked on the stigma?'

'The what?'

'The stigma is the centre of the flower.'

'Don't get technical, Galley.'

The sergeant smiled up at his superior. 'My biology teacher taught me something useful at least.' He gripped a fragment of the plastic through the bag and lifted it to Sant's eyeline. 'There are two Ps on this piece here and other letters on the other pieces which spell out "Poppy Appeal" – the name of the charity that produces them.'

Sant took a closer look but couldn't see much. 'There comes a time in life, Galley, when reading glasses are worth more than a pair of shades. I'll take your word for it.'

'There can't be many vehicles wearing these things in February.'

'Considerably improving the odds that this is the car we're looking for.'

Galley looked pleased. 'It was a good job I called you.'

'Don't get ahead of yourself. Who's the owner?'

'Name's Ivor Danby. We've nothing on record for him. His address and other details were passed to your team first thing this morning. He's local.'

'Scarborough?'

'Leeds.' Galley scanned the BMW. 'It's a beauty, isn't it? You can see why someone stole it. Why they drove it seventy miles and left it here beats me.'

Sant removed his gloves. 'It's been abandoned in a rushed attempt to hide it. Whoever nicked it ripped off the flower because they knew it would identify the vehicle instantly. Sadly for our thief, he's not much good at disposing evidence.'

'But why not try and sell it on the black market? He'd get at least twelve grand as a worst-case scenario.'

'He wouldn't be in the right frame of mind. Not only has he assaulted someone, but he's also had sight of a pair of corpses at the same spot where he's carried out the assault. Which indicates, by the way, that he had nothing to do with the corpses.'

'I see,' said Galley. 'The only thing on his mind was disappearing. He kept on driving till he reached the coast and couldn't go further without winding up in the sea.'

'No shit, Sherlock.' Sant signed out. 'A couple of techs are on their way as backup.'

'Superintendent Hardaker informed me of the same,' Galley said. 'We might've handled things ourselves, but never mind.'

'You've only one guy.' Sant pointed at the man brushing the doors. 'And he looks overworked.'

'Cuts in public spending have strangled small divisions like ours.'

'Don't get political, Galley. Get your guy to examine the vomit. Oh, and take special care with traces. Blood was found at the scene. It's possible some of it's mixed in with the vomit.'

'Sure thing.'

'And grab all the surveillance you can get your hands on.'

'I've an officer assigned already,' Galley said, wondering if he should be taking notes.

'Good, and anyone else at your disposal can ask around hotels and guest houses for single men without prior bookings.'

'You think he's still in town?'

'It's possible. Check cameras at railway and bus stations. If he's returning to Leeds, he won't be going on foot.'

'Noted,' the sergeant replied, keying Sant's tips into his phone to show willing.

Sant took a moment before saying softly: 'It's never easy when you lose someone important.'

Galley glanced up from his phone. 'You've heard then.'

'Word gets around. Fancy a drink?'

'Got time?'

'Not really,' admitted Sant, 'but an ice cream will do nicely.'

* * *

The Harbour Bar, a mock 1950s milk bar specialising in knickerbocker glories and lemon twists, hadn't changed much in appearance since Sant had indulged in its delights as a child. The business had begun over a hundred years, the Alonzi family waving goodbye to the mountains of Italy and setting up shop on the Yorkshire coast. The semi-oval bar was still a dashing yellow with red trim punctuated by advertising mirrors showcasing American brands with vintage slogans like OUR ICES CAN BE LICKED BUT NEVER BEATEN.

Sant studied the laminated menu and was tempted to lash out on his old favourite – a bananarama topped with chocolate flakes and almond nuts – but instead he selected a modest strawberry fayre sundae. With it he ordered a glass of Horlicks on tap, another old favourite. Galley, who wasn't the ice cream type, settled for a toasted teacake and very milky coffee.

'It came as a total shock,' said the sergeant. 'I used to visit him every Sunday. He was in good health. His wife was Old Bill too. They looked after me when I first became an officer, Jim and Judith did. Put me up for six months before I found my own place. I wanted to pay my way, but they refused and were adamant I could stay as long as I wanted. She was a great cook as well.'

'Sounds like a dream ticket,' Sant said as he licked strawberry syrup off his long dessert spoon.

'For someone like me she was. They were both fantastic. Jim showed me the ropes and taught me about the local gangs; the people to watch out for. He learnt a lot about the underworld as a foot-patrol constable around your neck of the woods.'

'Leeds?'

'Thereabouts. He met Judith when they were both juniors training on the job. That was years ago. She actually became more senior than him, spending most of her time filling out forms. That didn't stop her from being incredibly personable though. She was like a mum to me. I've never known what it's like to have a real one. Judith was as close as I got to the real thing.'

Sant looked perplexed. 'You weren't their foster child, were you?'

Galley laughed. 'I was too old to count as a child by then.'

'Is Judith Lackey still alive?'

'Died of cancer six years back. Jim never got over it.'

'Could that explain the suicide?'

Galley swallowed a piece of teacake, then said: 'It took a long time for Jim to get used to life without his beloved, for sure, but eventually he started to cope and all the talk was about collecting old coins and joining the bowls club and more until... until this happened.'

'Was any note left?'

'Nothing.'

Sant took a spoonful of creamy delight. 'Suicides usually write something down on paper. Was his death investigated?'

'Just the coroner's report. There's a standard script because we have suicides off that bridge every year.'

'Can't the council do something about it?'

'Not Spa Bridge. Valley Bridge has high barriers, but Spa Bridge is a Grade Two listed structure. That reminds me. There was a slight query regarding his glasses.'

'Glasses?'

'As to whether or not Jim was wearing them when he jumped.'

Sant combed his black mane. 'In most cases they take them off.'

'Yes, but his were found close to where he lay. Either he had them on and they were blown off as he fell, or he had them in a hand or pocket and they came loose.'

'Was he short or long sighted?'

'Short. He'd worn specs since I knew him.'

Sant sucked on a mouthful of chopped strawberries, the remainder of his ice cream demolished by his long spoon. 'Did they have children?'

Galley hesitated before answering. 'I'm going to say "no" but don't quote me.'

'Come again?'

'Well, Judith got pregnant when her and Jim were going steady. They baby was born prematurely and died almost immediately. Either that or she required an abortion on medical grounds. It isn't clear what unfolded, and it was no business of mine.'

Sant turned to the Horlicks he hadn't touched yet. 'They must've been sad.'

'Maybe they were, but they never dwelt on things. They were both careerists despite all the caring they did for colleagues like myself.'

'You weren't the only beneficiary of a free lunch?'

'Lodgers came before and after me. All Old Bill, it must be said. Jim and Judith had no intention of letting anyone other than police into their lives.'

'Were they afraid of anything?'

'Afraid?'

'Fearful enough to want extra protection at home.'

Galley finished his coffee and placed the spoon on top of the glass mug. 'Sometimes they appeared agitated. They were always busy and serving the public was their duty. That's why all of us officers still hold a great affection for them. And now they're both gone.'

Sant lapped up the milky sweetness residing at the bottom of his dessert glass before downing his Horlicks in one go. 'Time's a great healer. You'll get over it.'

Galley sighed. 'I hope so. I have low moods. Often.'

Sant hailed an aging waitress in a retro yellow dress and paid for the treats with every intention of claiming expenses. The risk of receiving his marching orders from a petty cash department averse to expenditure on extravagances was high, but he'd chance it anyway.

'I'm always at the end of a phone line if you need a chat,' said the inspector a while later as they departed for their cars, 'and before I forget, good luck with the move.'

Galley clasped his small hands in prayer. 'Hopefully I can pick up the keys by the end of the week.'

'In which case, Galley, be sure to look after them better than you do the keys to your compound.'

The sergeant went as red as Sant's strawberry fayre and shrank by several inches, making him very short indeed.

* * *

He did his best impression of a Formula One driver as he sped back to HQ. When his Fiesta wasn't overtaking farm vehicles, he was thinking about Galley's unswerving adoration for Jim and Judith Lackey – surrogate mother and father no less. He wondered if anyone remembered Lackey from his days as a West Yorkshire detective. Maybe Wisdom had come across the man, way back when.

Sant was almost in sight of Leeds when his phone rang and Hardaker's voice blasted out of the speaker.

'Where are you?'

'Getting warmer, Chiefman. Closing in on Seacroft roundabout.'

'Do an about-turn. The BMW owner has come forward and is at the nearest station, which happens to be Wetherby. I've got a specialist in sex crime heading that way, though you're a lot nearer and we need info a-sap.'

'Drugged and raped, wasn't he?'

'Yes, the same pattern. Find out what you can, then go straight to Dr Wisdom at the morgue. He'll update you on the cadavers. We're seeing him now. Clearly you won't be with us in time.'

'I haven't quite mastered being in two places at once,' Sant replied as he rang off.

He circled the roundabout and thirty minutes later walked

into the sole interview room of the 1970s flat-roofed police station flanking the outskirts of affluent Wetherby. A uniformed officer was pouring tea for a giant of a man sporting a bandage over his nose, two busted lips, and a sling over one arm. Sant took a sip of the tea offered to him before perching on a cheap plastic stacking chair. He glanced at the big man's bruised face and tried to recall the name Sergeant Galley had given him. Damn it. All that sea air had dulled his memory.

'If it's any consolation, we've found your car.'

The man peered up through swollen eyes. 'You can keep it,' he said hoarsely.

'It's still in good nick, except for the poppy on the front.'

The big man looked numb. This was no time for flippant remarks.

Sant let the silence grow a little before fixing eye contact. 'Worry not. We'll find him.'

The big man broke into tears. Sant sipped more tea and felt as weak as the liquid he was supping. There was next to nothing he could do. The man needed a trained officer. Sant wasn't trained for this.

'Excuse me a moment,' he said as he went in search of the uniform manning the station. He returned with the name stamped in his brain. 'You tried describing your assailant to my colleague, Mr Danby.'

'I tried,' Ivor Danby croaked, 'and failed.'

The man rubbed his face into the elbow of his leather jacket.

'Do you remember where you met him? Somewhere near the city centre maybe?'

Danby closed his eyes, then stuttered: 'I – I think so.'

'But you're not sure where?'

'He – he's messed up my head. Could've been a dozen places.'

'Parks?'

'Probably.'

'Has anything stuck in your mind?'

The big man breathed deeply. 'It's a blank. The dope knocked me cold.'

'Maybe that's a blessing.'

'Maybe you're right.'

'Why did he take you to Woodhall Road?'

'Where?'

'The track where he abandoned you.'

'I haven't the foggiest idea.'

'You didn't drive him there?'

'Of course not. He doped me first. Then he must've driven me out that way and left me in that ditch.'

'Where you were sick.'

Danby nodded. 'I was out cold for hours.'

'Did you see anything unusual once you'd regained consciousness?'

'A lot of snow falling from the sky. Not much else.'

'Did you notice a large block of ice as you walked up Woodhall Road?'

'Block of ice?'

'About six feet by four feet.'

'You're joking, aren't you?'

'I wish I was, Mr Danby.'

'What was it doing there?'

'You've not heard the news?'

'What news?'

'A couple of bodies were dumped in a field not far from the ditch you finished up in. They were frozen solid.'

'Really?'

'Really.'

'I don't see – I can't think how they relate to what happened to me.'

'Neither can I, Mr Danby, but I'm not ruling out anything. By the way, did you see a Land Rover or any other vehicle while you were in the vicinity of Woodhall Road?'

The man shook his head and went very pale. Silence. Finally: 'Can I leave now?'

'I'd advise you to stay until a trained–'

'I don't want experts. I just want... to bring the curtain down on this.'

Sant could have told him that any ending was far away; the trauma would last. He said nothing though.

'Am I free to go?' Danby asked again.

The inspector gently shook his head. 'It's a bit more complicated than that,' he said after swallowing a mouthful of tea.

'I want nothing more to do with it. Strike my name off your records.'

'We'll bother you as little as possible, Mr Danby, but we're dealing with a dangerous offender. You're not his only victim. We'll need your DNA.'

'Get the others to help.'

'They are. And we suspect there are more victims who haven't come forward.'

Danby closed his eyes and paused for thought. 'If you hadn't come looking, I'd have stayed away.'

'I admire your honesty.'

'I should curse my luck doubly.'

Sant drained the last of his tea and moved the mug aside. 'We make our own luck. And by the same token, we make our misfortune.'

Danby brushed moisture off his triple chin. 'What's that supposed to mean?'

'You were taking a huge risk, Mr Danby.'

'Not really. I meet my acquaintances on a... fairly regular basis.'

'It's called kerb crawling,' said Sant, 'whether you do it in a street or park or wherever. It's a crime.'

'It's allowed, isn't it?'

'Only in the managed zone.'

Danby stood up impatiently. 'I hardly see a difference. Anyway, those I meet – most of them at least – are good guys. They just need help. They appreciate my charity.'

Sant fixed his eyes on the big man. 'You think you're helping them, don't you?'

'They are poor. I'm not. Making a living is not easy for everyone.'

'What do you imagine they spend your cash on?'

'That's their business. They're not children. They're grown men. I hope they use the money wisely.'

Sant got up from his chair and levelled with his interviewee. 'Do yourself and your acquaintances a favour. Find a steady partner. One you're on equal terms with.'

'I already have one.'

'Your wife by any chance?'

Danby looked down at his beige suede shoes. 'This whole affair must remain confidential.'

'I'll do my best,' Sant said half-heartedly. 'Didn't she ask about your injuries?'

'She's blind. Literally and metaphorically.'

'Good for you.'

The man shifted position to ease the aching arm. 'How long must I wait for this so-called expert?'

The fancy digital clock above the front entrance flashed 13:03 and sported a sulky face indicating poor air quality. Sant wasn't feeling great himself.

'Make yourself comfortable, Mr Danby.'

The big man sat down heavily and muttered: 'Easier said than done.'

Sant left in a hurry as more tears slid down Danby's parched cheeks, a life lived in deceit weighing cruelly on his drooping shoulders.

* * *

A white-cloaked Wisdom showed him into the chilled unit and drew out a mortuary tray from the bottom row, specifically designed for bulk. They were still ice-bound, one on top of the other, the block barely different in size or shape from when it was rolled down a frosty field over thirty-six hours ago.

Sant could only see the corpse on top. She was laid on her front, face down, wrists tied together and resting on top of her head. It was hard to be sure, but Sant reckoned she was an adult, albeit a young one. Spidery frost particles were woven on her clothing and her long blond hair. Tiny droplets of water trickled from her neck and shoulders, as if the block was melting from the inside out.

Another thing struck Sant. The clothes. Purple shell-suit top. Baggy pleated jeans tapered at the ankles. He crouched down and glared through the ice at the high-heeled shoes the woman was wearing. One shoe had come away from the foot. Its style seemed dated, yet it was virtually unsoiled.

'She didn't have much dress sense,' the inspector remarked.

Wisdom, extracting samples of ice with a scalpel, bagged a few and passed them to an assistant. 'Might've been one of those retro parties,' he said with a measured Welsh intonation.

'What parties?'

'Don't you follow the nightlife scene, my boy? It so happens that my daughter, who's reading law at Cambridge, incidentally, is a frequenter of seventies nights. Flares, frilly tops, that sort of thing.'

'I once owned a whole wardrobe of the stuff,' Sant said.

Wisdom replaced blue latex gloves before using a long tool to chisel away at the side of the block nearest the woman's head.

'According to my colleague – junior colleague I should add – this attire was in fashion a decade or so later,' the pathologist said.

Sant wanted to wipe the wall of ice to get a better view, but he knew Wisdom would go spare if he witnessed such profanity. 'She's dressed like the girls from my clubbing days. Quite the eighties throwback.'

'The lass certainly has the get-up down to a tee,' said Wisdom, chiming a note of admiration at odds with the woman's sorry state.

'Sexual interference?'

The doctor removed his gloves. 'Too early to say. I can't get near her yet.'

'How about the other body?'

'Can't make head nor tail of it. As you can see, she's directly underneath.'

Sant decided not to bend down, his back still stiff from rugby tackling Skin Fade. 'Nothing to report then, Grant?'

'Not much, other than the ice has partially melted and refrozen, perhaps at multiple intervals. The freezing hasn't been the kind of smooth process typical of a single stint in a sufficiently chilled container.'

'You mean, they've been out of one freezer and into another?'

'Possibly, or moved from one place to another in the same freezer without a power supply, hence the partial defrosting.'

'So they've not been killed recently?'

'Difficult to say, my boy, but my wildest guess is they've been stored in this state for quite some time?'

'Months?'

'Perhaps.'

'Years?'

'Ditto.'

Sant tried to penetrate the ice block by widening his eyes, then gave up and cursed his own stupidity. 'Wouldn't it thaw quicker above room temperature?'

'Yes, but you might not have a case to work on.'

'How so?'

Wisdom placed pair of pince-nez glasses on his long nose and faced the bodies as if they were precious gold. 'DNA cannot be compromised. I've read several papers on the matter. Regulating the thawing of bodies protects the evidence. They're literally stuck together. We can't start pulling them apart.'

'That's all well and good, Grant, but we've a murder case to solve.'

'And it won't be if you're not patient,' Wisdom countered, his body twitching with annoyance. 'Thawing means time, my boy. The cryobiologist I consulted at the Home Office tells me it took fourteen days before a post-mortem was possible in a similar case involving three bodies: a mother and her twin babies.'

Sant tried to shrug off the unpleasant picture developing in his head.

Wisdom continued: 'We mustn't rush and risk muddying the waters for our friends in the Crown Prosecution Service, should the need arise.'

Sant smiled at the note of irritation in Wisdom's voice. He was right though. No matter how fast you hunted down a killer, preparing a careful prosecution took precedence. One lapse could flush the whole investigation down the pan.

'Right, time to hear the thoughts of the Chiefman and his loyal and devoted second in command,' Sant said as he started to leave.

'They didn't reveal a thing to me. All very strait-laced.'

'A perfect description of what they are,' grinned Sant.

'Even more strait-laced than our chief constable.'

'Gilligan been here?'

Wisdom nodded. 'Before you lot. First time he's set foot in the den for ages.'

'Why was he interested?'

'Don't ask me. I'm a mere technician waiting for the ice to melt.'

'That reminds me,' said Sant. 'Do you recall a detective called Jim Lackey? He was with the force thirty or more years ago.'

Wisdom slotted his pince-nez specs in the chest pocket of his cloak and looked up at the ceiling. 'I'm good with names – and his I've not forgotten. The first of your lot I had dealings with. I was young back then, relatively speaking. He was already quite senior. Then he got promoted. I wonder where he is now.'

'No longer with us. Jumped off a bridge.'

'Where?'

'Scarborough.'

The pathologist let out a sigh. 'Now I remember. He moved to North Yorkshire to become a superintendent or some such.'

'Anything stick in your mind about him?'

'Certainly, but it will take a pint or two of your charity to tell it.'

Sant tapped the point of his rugged nose. 'Give me a nudge when you're free.'

Wisdom didn't reply. He was deep in thought, and the inspector knew better than to probe.

* * *

The note on Sant's desk told him to go to Appleyard's office. She had one of her own – a mark of her distinction as a *chief* inspector. It was the same size as the one Sant shared with Capstick, Holdsworth, and A. N. Other waiting to occupy the desk vacated by their late colleague, Sergeant Liam Dryden.

He grabbed a tuna mayo baguette from the catering kiosk before entering the appointed room and glimpsing the news cuttings adorning the walls. They featured stories of criminals Appleyard had brought to book. She was photographed in one or two, hair and eyelashes immaculate, arms crossed in a show of strength against the outlaws plaguing the land. Only random patches of bare wall remained, supplementaries of the lady's detective prowess to be pasted over them at the earliest opportunity.

'Nice of you to join us,' remarked the chief inspector as she swivelled her leather chair towards him. 'Was it fun at the seaside?'

Sant sat down and caught his breath before replying. 'I was doing a job there.'

'You took your time.'

'What was I supposed–?'

'No squabbling,' said Hardaker, motioning a karate chop with his left hand.

Appleyard patted her bun of black hair before leaning back. 'As you've heard, another victim of a sexual assault has been confirmed, and once more, the victim was picked up in a public place. This time Lovell Park on Wednesday night.'

'The same night the bodies turned up,' Holdsworth pointed out.

'And the same night Ivor Danby was attacked,' said Hardaker, standing up and flicking some fluff off his pin-striped suit. 'Coincidence or not?'

'It's difficult to know for sure,' said Appleyard. 'We're talking about a lot of offending over a short span if the perp or perps carried out this assault and the one on Danby, as well as dumping the two cadavers.'

'Unlikely if not impossible,' Sant remarked.

'Not impossible,' corrected Appleyard.

'What do we know?'

Appleyard swiped her screen. 'Her name is Klaudia Armitage, seventeen, residing in Lincoln Green. Picture here.' She held up her phone. 'It's the same pattern. Drugged, struck in the stomach and face, then penetrated.'

'Do we know where she was raped?' Holdsworth said, jotter in hand.

'Not certain. Upholstery fibres were found on the victim's clothing, which suggests she was taken by car somewhere. But it's not clear if she was assaulted in the car.'

'It's a pity she has no recollection of what happened,' said Hardaker.

'She remembers being in the park. That's all. She was with a friend who left for home before her. Lydia Brown, also seventeen. Guess what?'

'She was drugged too,' Sant answered.

Appleyard stared blankly at him. 'The same concoction of Rohypnol, yes.'

'Was she attacked as well?' Holdsworth probed, scribbling lines and arrows with a short pencil.

'She had the sense not to talk to strangers,' Appleyard said.

'What does Lydia recall?' asked Hardaker.

'She said a man offered them alcohol. A cocktail of some sort. They drank it from a big bottle which they passed to one another.'

Sant chewed on a mouthful of baguette. 'Sounds like White Lightning,' he remarked.

'That's cider and it's no longer produced,' said Appleyard.

'Quite the connoisseur,' Sant retorted.

The chief inspector turned her back on him. 'Lydia thinks the man was old and stubbly, but she's uncertain about the stubble as it was dark in the park.'

'Plus she was under the influence,' Hardaker put in. 'Did she get home safely?'

Appleyard swiped her iPad again. 'Yes, but her mother couldn't wake her in the morning. She thought her daughter was having a convulsion. The doctor came and did a few tests and found that she'd taken a spiked substance. When Lydia finally stirred, she told the doctor everything, he contacted us, and we tracked down Klaudia. Sadly, Klaudia lives with a junkie stepmother who hasn't a care in the world for her.'

'And we've no other witnesses,' added Holdsworth, scratching her chiselled chin.

Appleyard checked her screen. 'None we know about. I'll organise a team to conduct interviews and fix posters around Lovell Park appealing for information. Lydia is helping with a photofit as we speak. Oh, another thing, the man had a dog with him.'

'What breed?' Hardaker asked.

'Lydia's not sure. It was small.'

'Make sure we get a photofit of the mutt,' Sant said.

'Actually, we're excluding the dog from our appeal as things stand.'

'Is that wise?' queried Holdsworth. 'The dog might trigger people's recollections.'

'It might,' said Appleyard, 'but it might not. The animal was small and nondescript according to Lydia. If we were dealing with a big dog, that might be worth making public.'

Hardaker nodded. 'Besides, the reliability of any witness answering the appeal can be verified by asking them whether they saw a dog. If they did not, it's unlikely their testimony will be of any use.' He turned to Appleyard. 'Is there a possibility this incident is isolated, Stephanie?'

The chief inspector shook her head. 'Method of attack, victim profile, location, motive. Lots of parallel lines.'

'You say motive is consistent,' said Sant as he gobbled the rest of his sandwich, 'but this teenager wasn't robbed, only raped.'

Appleyard creased her dark brows. 'For your information, her trainers were stolen.'

'But why steal a pair of trainers?'

'Maybe they're an expensive brand,' Appleyard replied, her face flushing. 'The sexual motive is to the fore, but something was taken nonetheless.'

'It's plain we're dealing with two separate patterns,' Sant persisted.

'Explain further,' Hardaker said.

Sant walked around the office as he relayed his thoughts. 'Take the female victims. Yes, things were stolen from them, but mostly of little value. The males, on the other hand, incurred substantial material losses. They've been assaulted too, but the robbery motive is more significant in their cases.'

Hardaker nodded. 'I see your point, Carl.'

'There's a clear difference depending on the sex of the victim,' Holdsworth agreed.

'I'd avoid assumptions if I were you,' said Appleyard. 'You're assuming a perp knows how much there is to rob from a potential victim before carrying out the attack. The premeditated robbery motive is consistent across the board, but it just so happens the females have been less lucrative to the perp than the males.'

'But probabilities are built into a robber's mindset,' Holdsworth countered. 'A sixteen-year-old girl isn't likely to own a sports car. A middle-aged man might.'

Appleyard directed her dark brown eyes at Holdsworth. 'Not all the female victims have been in their teens, which reinforces my point about not making assumptions.'

'That's what criminals do,' said Sant, pinching his nose. 'They weigh things up. Risks. Opportunities. Threats.'

'Leaping to conclusions is always dangerous,' Appleyard said as she tapped her phone with agitated fingers. 'Any other business?'

Hardaker turned to Holdsworth. 'Developments on Popescu?'

'Not yet,' the detective sergeant replied. 'We're hoping Brad's surveillance pays off. Popescu's estranged wife finishes her shift at the hospital later this evening, two hours earlier than originally scheduled, plus she's booked the weekend off. Seems she's got urgent plans we should know about.'

'Good work, Amanda. Let's see what arises. And as for the mysterious matter of the cadavers,' Hardaker continued, 'Dr Wisdom reckons they've been frozen for quite some time, which means they're probably nothing to do with current matters.'

Sant debated whether to mention Willie Payton's take on the unsolved murder of Rita Mitchell, but they had enough to contend with. No way either would he be granted deployment on a wild card investigation half a lifetime old.

'I'll put a Homicide team on that case,' Hardaker went on. 'Popescu is the priority for now. Let's find him and see what we can hang on the lout.'

Holdsworth followed Hardaker out of the office while Sant held back. He waited for Appleyard to look up from her phone. She seemed preoccupied. He gave up and made for the door, then turned around determined to say something.

'We can clear the air over coffee if you like.'

'I'm busy.' She didn't even try to make eye contact.

He took a moment to organise the words in his mind before saying: 'You can spread the load if it's too much.'

'I don't follow, DI Sant.'

'It's getting tougher. We need delegation. You should have a word with the Chiefman and ask him to put me and Holdsworth in charge.'

Appleyard's eyes finally locked on his. 'Are you referring to Superintendent Hardaker?'

'None other than.'

'Is it not disrespectful to call him by a nickname?' she said, tapping away at her phone.

'Not really. He looks like a Red Indian. We go back a long way.'

Awkward silence followed. Finally, she put down her phone. 'Is that all you have to say?'

'I'm offering my support. You take the official lead, no problem. I'm not interested in the next career move. Let me take one rein and Holdsworth the other.'

Appleyard untied her black mane and shook it loose. 'You must think I'm stupid.'

'I never said–'

'In case you haven't registered the fact, I'm your superior. I value your expertise, but no more than anyone else of your rank.'

'Rank shouldn't come into it,' Sant said, his arms outstretched.

'Actually, it should. A police service can't deliver law and order without a solid hierarchy of responsibility. I'd expect you, with all your years of experience, to understand this basic truth.'

Sant bit his tongue. 'What did I do to get at you, Appleyard?'

'It's DCI Appleyard, actually.'

'What's wrong with letting you know that I'm here to help?'

'I'll call when I need you.'

'You need me now. These vicious attacks are spiralling. I'm an old hand–'

'DI Sant, your attitude is condescending, your approach unwelcome, and as for coffee, I've lost a taste for it. Close the door behind you.'

Sant's nostrils flared. He started to say something, stopped, then left, his condescending attitude shadowing him out.

* * *

At dead on ten, Sant left his car on a side street as near as he could get it to the multi-storey car park and headed for Capstick's Punto. His partner had found a parking spot one tier down from the nurse's Vauxhall Corsa but within eyeshot. He'd arrived early on the off chance she might leave early. Not to be. Friday relaxed rules didn't apply to the NHS frontline.

As Sant opened the passenger door, Capstick gave a thumbs up and waved a phone at him.

'Here's a present from Sergeant Galley, sir.'

Sant squeezed into the Punto and stared at a fuzzy image of a streetlight illuminating a slim figure beneath it. He looked closer and saw a man wearing a hood standing in front of a white BMW. He had something in his hand.

'Is it what I think it is?'

'A plastic poppy. And this occurs next.'

Capstick tapped his device and the man became real as he moved towards the surveillance camera filming him, went out of shot, before reappearing and seeming indecisive. The man dawdled for a while, turned back briefly, changed his mind, walked in the direction of the camera once more. As he came steadily closer, the details of the face were amplified by the white of the streetlight.

'Nailed him!' Sant whooped. 'That's Mr Popescu all right.'

'And further down the same road, sir, this happens.'

Capstick loaded up a new video and set it going. Nicolae Popescu was keeping to the shadows as he wandered down a residential street while glancing left and right, clearly terrified of someone noticing him.

'Around now he changes direction suddenly,' said Capstick providing the commentary. 'He's noticed something to his left.'

'A bin.'

'Right, and it's hardly a spoiler if I tell you what he does next.'

Sant clapped his hairy hands together. 'He's about to rid himself of the poppy.'

'He's torn it into fragments whilst on the move, making it less likely to be seen and identified.'

Sure enough, Popescu advanced towards the bin and peeped inside before feeding it bits of plastic and covering them up in the existing waste, his hand shoved deep through the aperture.

'No gloves either,' Sant observed. 'We should be grateful he's not a professional thief. Those fingerprints will be as plain as day.'

'Perhaps he's better at beating up people than profiting from them,' Capstick mused.

'Though there's no denying the robbery motive is central to

what he does,' said Sant. 'He's an all-rounder, getting a buzz from the stealing as well as the sexual kicks.'

'Amanda told me about your squabble with Appleyard, sir. For what it's worth, I think you're right. The male victims have lost more than the females in a material sense – though not in a physical one.'

Sant said nothing. He wanted to try and rid his head of Appleyard's obstinance and concentrate on her virtues. She was a grafter, for sure, and even if she had the bad habit of devoting herself to causes likely to expedite the latest promotion, at least her dedication could not be questioned.

Half an hour later they were still waiting.

'Is she doing overtime?' Sant wondered.

Capstick, who'd nodded off, recovered his bearings by hitching up his thick-rimmed specs. 'Maybe she's on a walkabout somewhere.'

'It's nearly midnight.'

'She might've made it for last orders.'

'If so, let's hope she's not above the legal limit. We'd be duty-bound to stop her, which would mess up the whole thing entirely.'

Sant decided to burn some waiting time by calling Holdsworth. He activated the speaker so Capstick could listen in. She picked up on the first ring.

'Still at work?'

'Where else?' Holdsworth replied. 'Actually, I've got half an ear directed your way, eagerly anticipating what you and my fella uncover on the tail of Mrs Popescu.'

'You're her fella now, Capstick. How do you plead?'

Capstick chuckled. 'Guilty as sin.'

'You hear that, Holdsworth?'

'Just make sure he comes back in one piece.'

'How caring of you.'

'Oh, and I've got some worrying news.'

'Wouldn't be the first time.'

'The social worker looking after Ava Yock has been in touch. She's missing. There's been no contact for over three weeks and she's no longer staying in the place she gave as her address.'

Sant pulled a fresh toothpick out of his inside pocket and clamped it around his jaws. 'Any idea where she's gone?'

'Nope. She's not answering her phone. The social worker says she could be anywhere. I've been in touch with the Joanna Project.'

'What's that?'

Holdsworth made a tut-tut sound. 'Know your facts, Carl. The Joanna Project is a charity supporting women on the game. They think she might've travelled back to Romania. There was nothing to stop her departing for good.'

'That's true. We can hardly investigate unless something fishy turns up.'

'Anyway, at least we've got her DNA stats, as and when we need them.'

'A good thing, but she might be needed in a future trial.'

'Which gives us grounds to start looking for her,' Holdsworth pointed out.

Sant picked the toothpick out of his mouth and slipped it into his pocket as he saw Capstick pointing at a gangly character with ruffled brown hair hurrying out of a lift.

'Mrs Popescu has made a late appearance, Holdsworth. Ta-ta for now.'

The Corsa abruptly pulled out before looping down a slope and swinging right towards the Punto.

'Heads down, Capstick, and don't move till she's out of sight.'

* * *

The small car's lights blinked and its engine revved with intent as it glided down the concrete incline leading to the exit.

'Don't lose her,' said Sant, tapping on the handbrake.

Capstick pressed his foot flat to the floor and thundered forward with such abandon that Sant was thrown back in the seat. Cutting in and out of traffic, they gained on the Corsa in seconds.

'Pull back! You're right up her backside.'

Capstick applied the brakes and let a couple of cars slip in between. 'She hasn't seen us.'

'Let's hope so,' Sant said as he mopped his brow with a hankie. 'We might as well be driving a marked car for all the subtlety you're showing behind the wheel.'

'Maybe I'll stick my siren on the roof.'

Sant gave his partner the death stare. The traffic ebbed and flowed for the next fifteen minutes, Capstick twice going through red lights to keep apace. Then the car in front slowed down and ground to a halt alongside a row of terraced houses.

'This isn't her home address, is it?'

'No, sir. She lives half a mile from here.'

'Keep going. Take the next left.' As they passed the Corsa, Sant saw the woman racing up crumbling stone steps to the door of one of the properties. 'Second from the end. That's the house she's gone in.'

Capstick turned left into a narrow street and drew up behind a tatty old Astra. 'Should we execute a search warrant first?'

'We'll worry about the paperwork anon.'

'Is that wise, sir?'

'Given the long list of offences we can pin on Popescu, I don't think we'll get a complaint.'

'Assuming this is where he lives.'

'Don't you doubt it, Capstick.' The inspector leaned out of the car. 'Follow ten yards behind. We'll approach from the rear.'

They kept low as they darted along a cobbled alley, passing the end terrace before coming to a rotten wooden gate swinging from a rusty hinge. A dim light shone from a room upstairs and steam was rising out of a half-open window. Sant beckoned Capstick towards him.

'Someone's in the shower,' he whispered.

'Been there long?'

'Long enough for the boiler to fire up.'

To one side of the backyard was an empty coal shed. Sant noticed the door was missing.

'Let's hide in here. If the neighbours see us, they'll think we're burglars and call our lot out.'

Capstick looked around him at the decaying stone exteriors, dog turds, empty cans and gin bottles scattered across the foul-smelling alley. 'Do you suppose the locals would think to do such a thing?'

'Not every member of the riff-raff hates our guts, partner.'

The two detectives stood motionless under the shelter of the shed. The flow of steam from the window steadily subsided and voices rose above it, mere mumblings at first that gradually became words of audible quality, though quality words they were not.

'How can I trust you anymore?'

'Shut your mouth, bitch!'

'How dare you speak to me like that!'

'Get out!'

'You've got some cheek! I put all my faith in you. Stood by you all this time. And now you're hell-bent on getting caught again.'

'Leave now or you'll be sorry!'

'They'll find you. You know that, don't you?'

'You've told them?'

'I haven't said a thing.'

'You're a fucking snitch!'

Sobs blurted through the window, then a loud thump, a squeal.

'You shit! I was crazy to marry a shit like you!'

'Get out! Leave me in peace!'

'To carry on your filthy habits?'

Another thump was followed by a crash. The ceiling had caved in.

Outside, Sant weighed up the scale of violence. He couldn't see a thing, but he could imagine plenty and none of it was pleasant.

'We need reinforcements, Capstick. Tell them it's urgent.'

The detective constable requested two uniforms from HQ and stayed on the phone until a civvy confirmed that backup was imminent.

'It's time to intervene.'

'Front or back, sir?'

'Front. It might be unlocked.'

They hopped over a wall bordering the end terrace, sprinted down a side path and rounded the corner. A marked car pulled up at the same time, the officers inside readying themselves as they fitted protective vests over their torsos.

Sant signalled to hold back before scrambling up the stone steps. He stretched a glove over this right hand and held down the door handle. It opened easily.

'After me,' he said to those behind. 'Fast as you can.'

The four men ran up three dark flights of stairs towards the epicentre of the screaming. It wasn't difficult to find. Sant composed himself as he came to the bathroom door. He prepared a short run-up before ramming in the door with his shoulder.

'Police! Down on the floor. That's an order!'

'You bitch!' the man's voice shrilled.

Sant crouched low behind the door, one of the armed officers flanking his side. Then he dived low and twisted sideways towards the bath curtains.

Popescu tracked the dive as he held his wife over the bath, a toilet brush aimed at her backside. Desperate to get out of the way of Sant's flailing arms, the Romanian dropped the brush and his wife in the bathtub and kicked backwards.

'Get down!' called Capstick as he jumped over Sant and attempted to lock the man's arms.

Popescu squatted low to wriggle free but didn't get far. Capstick reacted quicker, bending his knees together and leaning his weight on the small of the man's back. The fourth officer tried to cuff him. Popescu resisted and reached into his back pocket, tugged and tore out a sharp object which he prodded upwards. The end of it lingered momentarily before swooping on the nearest chunk of flesh.

'Ouch!' Capstick stared in disbelief at the needle vibrating like a dart from his right thigh. 'Christ, sir, he stabbed me!'

'Don't move,' Sant said as he promptly extracted the syringe and hurled it into the toilet basin.

One of the officers pepper-sprayed Popescu and the other clipped handcuffs to his wrists as he pressed his face against broken floor tiles.

'Bitch!' the man hollered, rubbing his inflamed eyes over the bath mat.

Sant read him his rights but cast his eyes on Capstick, not the Romanian. His partner was hunched up against the bathtub clutching his thigh in both hands, his massive bespectacled peepers exploring the ceiling with fascination as it began to gently spin.

* * *

The prisoner passed through the metal detector screening barrier before he was brusquely ushered towards a slightly built officer at the charge desk. The desk was encircled by computers and security monitors. The custody suite at Elland Road possessed all the charm of an airport departure gate with its fixed-to-floor rows of seats and white plastic partitioning.

'Surname?'

'Trump.'

'First name?'

'Donald.'

The custody officer glanced up and tried to conceal his disappointment.

'Let's start again. Surname?'

The prisoner didn't hear. He'd spotted a poster pinned to the wall above the officer's head. A man's stubbly face was pictured above the words: WITNESS APPEAL – DO YOU RECOGNISE THIS MAN? WE WANT TO IDENTIFY HIM FOLLOWING THE RAPE OF A 17-YEAR-OLD GIRL ACCOSTED IN LOVELL PARK ON WEDNESDAY 24th FEBRUARY AROUND 11.30pm. HE IS DESCRIBED AS WHITE, SKINNY BUILD, POSSIBLY WITH FACIAL HAIR, 50s OR EARLY 60s.

The face meant nothing. But the date did. It placed him at the scene. He gave the poster some thought, then realised there was no point in stalling further. Things were looking up.

'I'll repeat. Surname?'

'Popescu.'

'First name?'

'Nicolae.'

'Date of birth?'

'17th of September 1976.'

'Nationality?'

'Romanian.'

The officer showed him a printed statement and read it aloud: 'Your fingerprints and DNA form part of the computerised collection, so as such will be checked for any previous crimes. Is that understood?'

He pretended it wasn't, turned his bald head and saw the darkly clad pig who'd busted him. The same pig who'd snapped that fool of a drug peddler. The crooked nose was sniffing his every move. Popescu felt like spitting in disgust. Instead, he grunted loud enough to let the pig realise he was marked. Redirecting his vision towards the tedious piglet questioning him, he was shown to a height chart where measurements were taken.

'Do you have a drug dependency?' asked the charge officer as he returned to his desk.

Popescu shook his head.

'Answer verbally, please.'

'No.'

'You've been arrested and charged with a bail offence as well as suspected sexual offences. You have the right to a solicitor and to inform someone you know that you've been arrested. Understood?'

'Why do I need a lawyer?'

The officer looked up from his monitor. 'You're advised to have one. Shall I arrange for the duty?'

'Do as you please.'

A request for a duty solicitor was duly processed. It was getting late on a Friday night. It would be the next morning before the duty turned up.

'You will be held in police custody until called for interview. In due course you are required to take a swab test to obtain a DNA record. Any questions?'

'What's his name?' Popescu pointed with his head.

'That's Detective Inspector Sant.'

'First name?'

'Next you'll be wanting his date of birth.' The officer tapped a few more keys, then said: 'Would you like to call anyone? Let them know you're here?'

Popescu shook his head and caught sight of someone else he recognised. An Afro-cop who passed him envelopes in the dark. Envelopes full of cash. They eyed each other discreetly. You scoundrel, he thought as he looked away. Okay, get me out of this mess and I'll keep supplying the goods just how you like them. Maybe we can strike a deal, laced with a little extra for insurance purposes.

'That's everything,' said the charge officer.

Two sturdy guards took an arm each and escorted him through a series of chunky metal doors boasting multiple lock mechanisms. No chance of escape. He arrived at a door built even chunkier than the rest. A sign on the wall opposite read: ALL PRISONER'S SHOES MUST BE REMOVED PRIOR TO PLACING PRISONERS IN CELLS – PLEASE LEAVE SHOES OUTSIDE CELL DOOR.

'Shoes off.'

He did as he was told.

'Watch?'

'No.'

'Jewellery?'

He shook his head again.

'In you go.'

The door closed with an inevitable click. The new inmate stretched before curling up on a low steel bench bolted to wall and floor. Time for a good night's sleep, he told himself, and despite facing a night without pillow or blanket the Romanian slept like a babe, pictures of Inspector Sant and that bent pig in blue wallowing in his problem-free dreams.

* * *

The casualty section of LGI was overheating with customers, most of them unwanted. Sant saw Holdsworth as he swerved around the melee. She ushered him into a room and pulled the curtains across. Capstick was snoring on the portable bed.

Sant looked down at him. 'Sweet dreams, partner.'

Holdsworth held a tissue to her nose. 'What if his blood's infected?'

'He'll be on his feet in no time.'

'You don't know, Carl. Heaven knows what was in that needle.'

'They're checking his bloods,' he said, not knowing what else to say.

Holdsworth dried her eyes with a shirt sleeve. 'He's deep in slumber. Completely out.'

'The effects of being spiked.'

'You sure it was just Rohypnol?'

Sant passed her a fresh handkerchief from his breast pocket. 'All we can do is wait and see. He's made of strong stuff.'

Holdsworth stroked Capstick's inert arm above the tube inserted to keep him hydrated. Sant left to grapple with a vending machine which spat out two cups of mocha in exchange for a small fortune. He returned and offered one to Holdsworth.

She shook her head. 'I can't drink a thing. My stomach's all over the place.'

Sant sat and sipped his mocha for a while, Holdsworth

standing by her lover's side, concern etched above her fine jaw line.

An hour went by and finally Sant said: 'Maybe I should drive you home. Your daughter will wonder where you are.'

'She's staying with a friend.'

'Let me take you home anyway, Holdsworth. There's not a lot we can do here.'

She nodded and the cool air outside the hospital offered some relief. Holdsworth lived in an up-and-coming suburb north of the city. Trees popped up at intervals along the wide pavements. The semi-detached Tudoresque homes boasted enclosed driveways with mailboxes and privacy for the families who had moved there in recent times.

Sant parked outside and kept the engine running. 'Want me to see you in?'

'I'll be fine.'

'It's no trouble.'

Holdsworth smiled slightly. 'I can walk ten yards to my door, but thank you all the same.'

Sant kept an eye on her until she was inside. He'd never visited the house; never had a reason to. He caught a glimpse of textured vinyl wallpaper and pictures in elegant frames. Holdsworth had done well for herself. She was making a life out of tough circumstances, single motherhood for the past fifteen years chief among them. At least she'd found happiness second time round. Her and Capstick were perfect for each other. Sant felt sorry for himself when he realised how perfect they were. Finding that *forever one* was no small accomplishment. Sant was just another statistic on that front; another brick in the wall.

* * *

He could have done with a bout of meditation to alleviate the self-pity. But instead of seeking enlightenment, Sant sought his laptop and logged into the staff directory. He was searching for a face he vaguely recognised. Hundreds of uniforms worked out of Elland Road HQ and he couldn't be expected to know them all.

It took him the best part of twenty minutes to find the face of PC Joshua Benn. One of the few black officers in the force. A thick sculptured beard. White teeth letting off a brilliant smile. Smallish build for a bobby, which suited Sant fine.

Benn had joined the ranks six years ago. An all-rounder working with an antisocial behaviour remit. Something of an irony. Sant added the man's number to his contacts and made his way to the relevant office. All he found were empty desks. The antisocial brigade wasn't in demand at this time of night, clearly.

He opted to call from his office phone. Benn would see the number and raise no suspicions. He dialled the number and got an answer immediately.

'Hello.'

'DI Sant calling. Is that PC Benn?'

'Yeah.'

'On duty I take it?'

'Yeah.'

'I need to speak to you urgently, Benn. A missing person I've found is tied up with a gang operating out of Monkswood. I've got information. Should secure a bunch of charges. Where are you?'

There was a sound of clattering and then the voice returned.

'I'm about to clock off, sir. Can we hook up tomorrow?'

'The gang might split by then. Word gets around. We need to act fast.'

'I'm patrolling Gipton just now.'

Sant mapped the location in his head. 'Meet me outside the McDonald's on Easterly Road at two on the dot.'

By the time the inspector pulled his Fiesta into a parking bay, the place had long since closed. It wasn't like the McDonald's outlets in the city centre that stayed open all night, every night. In fact, it wasn't like any McDonald's anywhere in the world. The locals still called it 'The Oakwood' because the art deco building had once been a huge pub known by that very name.

At least he's punctual, Sant thought, as a police car swung towards him at a minute to two. He got out of his Fiesta at the same time PC Benn opened the driver's door. No-one in the passenger seat. No sign of passers-by. That's the way Sant wanted it.

'I've got evidence in the boot, Benn. Over here.'

The constable approached enthusiastically. 'I know which gang you mean. Been tracking them hoodlums for months.'

'Take a peek at this ugly mug.' Sant shone his torch at a glossy photo of a thug he'd long since captured, waiting for the diminutive Benn to look down. A second later he had him in a headlock and his knee in the PC's gut.

'What the hell!' cried Benn.

Sant tightened his grip and waited for the groan, released his arm from around the man's neck and twisted him upright so he was within an inch of dense beard.

'Nicolae Popescu. Tell me how you two are related.'

'Who?'

'The prisoner in custody tonight. I was watching you and Popescu. You did a little too much eye fucking. What's it all about, Benn?'

'I recognised him from somewhere. That's all.'

'Bullshit. I want the full story.'

'Honestly. I don't know–'

'Not good enough!' Sant bellowed. 'When I want to know something, believe me, I get to know it.'

He clasped the officer's hands and cuffed them in the same motion, hauling him over and into the car before slamming the boot closed.

'Let me out! I'm claustrophobic!'

'That's what the staff directory said.'

'Please! Let me out!'

'You going to level with me, Benn?'

'Okay. Okay.'

Sant lifted the boot. 'If I think you're lying, you're staying where you are. Get me?'

He shone the torch in the constable's face and received a frenzied nod. The man seemed younger in the flesh than in the portrait image. A gold band shone from his wedding finger.

'How do you know Popescu?'

'This'll cost me my career, sir. Can you look after me if I come clean?'

'No promises, Benn. The only sources I keep to myself aren't incriminating.'

Benn blinked into the light beam. 'The way it works is – well, I pay the man. In cash.'

'Why?'

'He supplies girls to some of the boys.'

'Girls?'

'Prossies.'

'The boys?'

'Others from the Old Bill.'

'You included?'

Benn blew out air before answering. 'I don't mess around. I'm a middleman.'

'Who gives you the cash?'

'Another copper. He organises things.'

'I want a name, Benn.'

'You'll keep me out of this?'

'No promises, but I'll do my best.'

Benn hesitated before breathing heavily. 'I don't like to grass, sir, but I suppose I've no choice.'

'None whatsoever.'

'Sergeant Tufail gives me the money. In sealed envelopes.'

'Tufail?'

'Yeah, Fawad Tufail. Works in fraud.'

Sant shook his head. 'Must be a new recruit.'

'Been with us a year, sir. He started over in Manchester.'

'So what you're telling me, Benn, is Tufail gives you cash and you hand it to Popescu.'

The constable screwed up his eyes and nodded. 'I can't lie anymore. This shit has to stop.'

'Why does he give the money to you?'

'Don't ask me.' The officer directed his gaze downwards. 'Maybe he thinks this African man's libido gets the better of him.'

'Does it?'

Benn was silent for a moment, then spoke more seriously: 'I'm loyal to my wife and babies, sir, I swear to God.'

'Who else is involved in this – operation?'

'Quite a few. It's low profile and nobody admits to taking part. I don't know who's in it.'

Sant considered his options, trying to absorb what he'd heard. He wasn't naïve. He realised this sort of thing went on and didn't need Dr Pringle to tell him what percentage of officers screwed a prostitute on an average shift. After several minutes chewing toothpicks and listening to excuses, he uncuffed his prey, offered his arm, heaved the man out of his car.

'I should arrest you here and now, Benn. Alternatively, you could hand yourself in.'

The constable brushed dirt and sand off his uniform. 'It will cost me my job, sir.'

'Too right it will.' He paused for thought before fixing his eyes on the young man. 'I'm going to hang fire for a while.'

'Thanks.'

Sant looked up at the starless sky. 'Don't thank me. You're insulting my integrity.'

Benn leaned forward, hands on hips. 'What should I do?'

'Keep your head down. Do your job professionally. I might ask you to do one or two things for me. I might not. Don't whisper a word to anyone about our conversation. If I hear otherwise, I'll come down on you like a ton of bricks. I need the lowdown from Tufail before I decide what to do next.'

PC Benn bowed his head and hobbled back to his marked car. Sant watched him leave before joining the long-haul trucks and Royal Mail vans tearing out of the dark city.

6

The sign on the door read: UNDER NO CIRCUMSTANCES SHOULD THE INTERVIEW ROOM BE USED FOR SOLICITOR/CLIENT CONSULTATIONS. Sant entered the room the worse for wear. Rather than return to his city centre apartment, he'd spent the night snoozing on the office floor, duffle coat doubling up as blanket and mattress, venomous jellyfish bobbing up and down in his dreams. He shivered as he positioned himself opposite Popescu. The solicitor sat to one side, long legs crossed, a little distant. Her arctic expression signalled that this was the last place she wanted to be.

Hardaker and Appleyard were speaking through an intercom to officers in an adjacent room controlling the recording equipment. Sant noticed how Appleyard couldn't keep still, hands constantly reaching for the satchel slung over the back of her chair. And some of that nervousness was rubbing off on Hardaker. The Chiefman could choreograph a press conference without a script – yet faced with a handcuffed prisoner he looked less assured than a filly in a thoroughbred sprint.

'Recording will be underway shortly,' mumbled Hardaker. 'If you want to talk to your solicitor in private, the interview will be stopped for that purpose.'

Popescu said nothing.

'The time is now' – Hardaker swiped his Surface Pro frantically – 'five minutes past nine in the morning. During the interview you'll notice a red light appearing on that black box. When that light is displayed, it means other officers in the room next door are listening to what's being said. Understood?'

Silence.

Hardaker fidgeted with his Pro, glancing at it periodically. 'Those present before you are myself, Superintendent Hardaker, to my left Detective Chief Inspector Appleyard, and to my right Detective Inspector Sant. We expect you to tell the truth. That is all.' He consulted his tablet. 'I understand English is not your first language. Do you require an interpreter?'

The Romanian shook his head and pointed at Sant. 'Get him to start. He jumped me.'

Hardaker kept his eyes on the suspect. 'You have no say in how this interview is conducted.'

Popescu smirked, his gaze settling on Sant.

Hardaker cleared his throat. 'On the 16th of April 2017, you were arrested and charged with the suspected rape of Ava Yock on the night of the 14th. You were seen by officers running from the flat where Miss Yock claims you assaulted her. After your arrest you were granted bail, but you forfeited the conditions of the bail agreement when you went missing seven months later. Have you anything to say?'

'I want you,' he said to Sant.

'Why me?'

'You do rough work.'

Sant made a crease in his eyebrows. 'Meaning?'

'Your hands are worn. You toil for your living.' He nodded towards Hardaker. 'His palms are like a child's. I respect men, not children.'

The Chiefman flushed red. Sant leant over and whispered something in his ear. Hardaker frowned, switched off his Pro, placed it on his lap.

'Your request is granted,' the superintendent said sullenly, 'though I won't be making a habit of goodwill gestures.'

Sant jammed a toothpick between his jaws. 'What did you do to Ava?' he asked, half an eye on Appleyard as she keyed something into her iPad.

Popescu turned to his solicitor. She pursed her lips.

'Nothing,' he said at last.

'Really?'

'I slapped her. Once. I never forced myself on her.'

'She said you did.'

'I didn't. You police believed her. My word is worth nothing.'

Sant relaxed into his chair. 'You didn't stick around to have your word heard.'

'There was no point. She framed me.'

'So you're denying the sexual offence charge?'

'One hundred per cent.'

'You do know we can check your story?'

'Sure. Swab me. Good luck locating my bodily data on your files.'

Popescu aimed a smile at the duty solicitor. It wasn't returned. Not for this lost cause. Another in a long line.

'Describe your relationship with your wife,' Sant continued.

The Romanian laughed. 'Now you're marriage counsellor as well as detective.'

'Maybe you need both,' Appleyard put in.

'Maybe you keep it zipped,' he hissed.

Appleyard's jaw quivered. She looked ill.

'I'll ask you again,' Sant said calmly. 'How was your relationship with your wife?'

The prisoner stayed silent. Then he stared directly at Sant and spoke assertively: 'My woman is good. She helps the old and infirm. Unlike you, she cares for the needy.'

'Is that why you married her?' Appleyard probed.

He glared at her. 'You got a problem, lady.'

'Come off it,' said Sant, noticing Appleyard flinching. 'It was a marriage of convenience. You hitched up with a nurse because she gave you security. Made you look respectable.'

'You are so right,' Popescu sniggered. 'I married Wendy for her wealth. She is very rich because she works for your cash-strapped NHS. We Romanians are very poor by comparison. We gave our money away to pay for the dinghy ride over here. In this country we are – how you say – a bunch of plebs who've landed on our feet. You natives are so civilised. We serve you gratefully.'

'Sarcasm doesn't suit you,' Hardaker said.

The Romanian's stern face grimaced. 'Guess what the first word we learn is. *Enjoy!* It's McDonald English. Ronald taught us everything.'

'I take it you love your wife?' Sant asked.

'I respect her deeply.'

'Are you attracted to her?'

'You calling me queer?'

Sant counted five movements of the second hand on the cheap clock hanging above Popescu's hairless head before saying: 'You have sex with men, don't you?'

The man looked down at his cuffed hands.

'Don't try and deny it,' Hardaker put in.

Popescu raised his head a fraction. 'There's a difference. I give. I never take. I never get humped.'

'So that makes you straight, does it?'

He held his breath for a moment, then said: 'I'm no faggot.'

Sant glimpsed Appleyard out of the corner of his eye. Her face was as pale as baby powder.

Hardaker shook his head. 'Thing's don't bode well for you, Mr Popescu. You're facing time, and lots of it.'

'For jumping bail?'

'Among other offences,' the Chiefman scowled.

'There's plenty on that plate of yours,' Sant added, leaning back in his chair. 'Be upfront with us. The more you admit, the smoother your journey through the justice system.'

The Romanian tried to find comfort in his solicitor. She made brief eye contact before rubbing her cheek with the sleeve of her blouse.

'What do you want to know?' said the prisoner, forcing a grin.

'Your version of events,' Hardaker said.

'What's the point?'

Sant got up and paced the hard floor. 'You're in serious trouble. We know it. You know it. Others do too.' The duty rubbed her other cheek for effect. 'Tell us everything you did and saw while dumping one of your victims in a lonely ditch and stealing his BMW.'

Popescu's face contorted. I can't worm my way out of this hole, he told himself. Not entirely. But bargaining power is a card I'm yet to play. They don't know what I know.

'Let me speak to her,' he said finally.

The solicitor unfurled her sleeves and blinked into action.

'My client and I will take the statutory break.' She studied the calendar on her phone. 'Returning at one pm sharp.'

'And I want coffee after lunch.'

Hardaker spoke through the intercom. 'Stop the recording.'

'With biscuits.'

The duty glanced despairingly at her latest lost cause before following him out of the room.

* * *

Sant made a beeline for the fraud department where one of Sergeant Fawad Tufail's fellow officers told him that Tufail was only partly deployed to fraud, and furthermore, he'd been on sick leave for weeks. A civvy overheard the conversation and had a different take on the matter – Tufail was taking time off on religious grounds as he was observing Ramadan and needed to conserve energy because of his strict fasting regime. Another civvy in human resources gave Sant the address and luckily it wasn't far away, otherwise he'd have left it until after the follow-up encounter with Popescu.

He called Tufail to let him know he was coming and pulled up outside a tall red-brick terrace in Chapel Allerton shortly after. The owner came to the door and closed it behind him. Sant was sure he'd never seen the man, though he'd joined the force a year ago according to PC Benn.

Tufail possessed sturdy shoulders below an egg-shaped head. Smartly dressed even when at leisure, he donned a tailored brown suit and polished leather shoes. The dark-tinted glasses resembled the trendy oversized ski goggles worn by Generation Z, but Sant saw the sagging eyes behind the specs and guessed the sergeant was not much younger than himself.

'I'd prefer if we speak out here,' he said in a hushed tone. 'I don't like to bring work matters into my home if I can avoid it.'

'And you'd rather have no-one within earshot of trouble.'

The man hitched up his tints. 'That sounds ominous.'

'Ever heard of Nicolae Popescu?'

'Yes. He jumped bail. I saw the appeal for information.'

Sant spat out an old piece of toothpick. 'You know him personally, don't you?'

Tufail crossed his arms. 'What's that supposed to mean?'

'He's a pimp. You send him cash for services rendered.'

The sergeant's eyes dilated behind the tints. 'That's categorically untrue. What do you know? Who told you this?'

'I'm not naming names. I want the truth. Have you ever handed over cash to pay for an escort service?'

Tufail swivelled his egg-shaped head to check no-one was watching from inside his house. Then he lowered his voice and looked straight at Sant. 'Such shady business is against all my values, Inspector. It is shocking that this baseless allegation is being made against me. There must be a mistake.'

'So you're denying any involvement with prostitution, lawful or not?'

'Prostitution is a crime, Inspector, as is conspiracy to control it.'

'I agree, though here in Leeds we do things differently, AKA the Managed Approach.'

'And what a sinful enterprise that is.' Tufail shook his head and uncrossed his arms. 'I feel deeply offended. Who do you think you are? Head of Professional Standards?'

'That's not my job,' Sant said. 'This is strictly off the record for now.'

The man's shoulders drooped. 'These lies about me are completely unacceptable. I want urgent action to be taken against the complainant, whoever she or he is.'

The sound of a baby crying came as a relief to Sant. He was

moved by Tufail's forceful defence and felt uncomfortable all of a sudden.

'When are you back on duty?' Sant asked.

'Next week. I'm taking off days here and there.'

'To save energy?'

Tufail looked puzzled. 'Why do I need to save energy?'

'I thought you were a Muslim.'

'I am, Inspector, but I'm not fasting yet. Ramadan isn't until April.'

Sant held up his hand, cursing the wrong information he'd received and his own folly for not factchecking the dates. 'A colleague of mine is clearly confused. You're not on a sickie either, or at least, you don't look sick from where I'm standing.'

'I was perfectly well until half an hour ago,' Tufail remarked. 'These falsehoods are concerning. I have fought hard to succeed without people labelling me as a charlatan. It is deeply damaging to be embroiled in scandalous misde-meanours I have nothing to do with.'

Sant squeezed his disjointed nose. 'I'll only report the allega-tion if there's evidence. If you're not conspiring with the sex trade, there's nothing to worry about.' He made to leave, then took a few paces back as Tufail started to say something. 'Sorry, I missed that.'

'Something needs clarifying, but you'll find out in time.'

'Find out what?'

Tufail shook his head. 'It's out of my hands. As soon as it's cleared up, I'll be in touch.'

'Cleared up?'

'I can't say more. I wish to, but it's a private concern.'

'Even so, your secret's safe with me.'

'In time, Inspector. In time you'll know.'

Sant tried to penetrate those baggy eyes and the glasses protecting them. Despite the riddles coming out of Tufail's mouth, the countenance spoke of a man at ease. 'You don't appear fearful at all.'

'Only for my reputation,' Tufail said as he re-entered his home and closed the door against the unjust world outside.

* * *

Sant felt guilty. Still, it was never wise to trust first impressions. Tufail looked and sounded innocent, but what was he hiding? And who was he hiding it from? Perhaps his significant others knew much about his darker side, and the biggest threat to him was the protective layer that concealed his deviance peeling away to reveal a hook upon which to hang him.

As Sant steered his Fiesta back to HQ, the phone rang and Holdsworth's pleasant profile popped up on screen.

'How's Capstick holding up?'

A clatter was closely followed by a profanity: 'Shit! I've smashed my screen.'

'Forget about it, Holdsworth. A shop in town will fix it for half a grand.'

'I can get a new phone for less than that. Shit!'

'Never mind. How's the lover boy?'

'I'm still by his side, Carl. He was awake for an hour, didn't touch the breakfast they gave him, now he's slumbering again.'

'When he decides to wake up, have a steaming coffee by his side. Not that NHS belly-wash. Something branded. And give him something edible too. Hospital food is one notch above pig swill.'

'It wasn't too bad. I ate it for him.'

Sant chuckled down the line. 'Right, I'm off to fight the second round versus Popescu.'

'How did the first go?'

'He wanted me to ask all the questions.'

'Wow, Hardaker and Appleyard must've been furious.'

'They passed me the reigns even so. Greatness counts for a lot.'

Holdsworth returned the chuckle. 'Well now, Carl the Great, did you make him confess?'

'I'm working on it. It's a pity you're not on the interview panel, Holdsworth. You must be having a quiet day.'

'Just twiddling my thumbs trying to hunt down Ava Yock and her acquaintances. Come off it, boss. When are we ever quiet?'

'It might take a pandemic.'

'Like in *Contagion*.'

'That's pure make-believe.'

'Don't tempt fate, Carl the Great.'

* * *

'Ivor Danby.'

'Who?'

'Ivor Danby,' repeated Sant, pleased at recalling the name for once.

'What about him?'

'You left him for dead. Stole his wallet containing cash to the tune of approximately eighty pounds. And you stole his BMW, abandoned it in Scarborough, binned the poppy in the hope that the car wouldn't be traced. Why didn't you try and sell it?'

The Romanian pursed his lips and averted his eyes from Sant.

'I know why, Mr Popescu. That car placed you at a murder scene. You needed to get shut of it fast.'

'I had nothing to do with any murder.'

'Mere coincidence, was it?' queried Appleyard. 'Woodhall Road is where all the bodies are dumped, is it?'

Popescu glared at Appleyard, but she returned the glare this time, confidence growing.

'It's suitable,' the prisoner replied.

'Suitable?'

'Quiet. Dark. Easy to find. Easy to get away from.'

'Unless someone else uses it at the same time as you,' Appleyard put in.

Sant moved his chair closer to the suspect. Hardaker almost did the same before realising that such a move would make him look like Sant's understudy.

'What happened?' probed the inspector.

The man stayed silent, legs trembling as if pumping in fresh blood.

'We might change our opinion about you if you tell us,' Hardaker added, the Chiefman adopting a softly-softly approach for this encounter.

Popescu looked at his three adversaries, then at his solicitor, finally at his protruding belly. After a long while he spoke: 'I saw a Land Rover.'

'Was this before or after you dumped your victim?' Appleyard asked.

'After. And he wasn't a victim.'

'You committed a criminal act on him,' Appleyard went on.

'He's a faggot. He got what he wanted. They like it rough, those creatures.'

'Let's leave personal views out of this,' Hardaker said.

'They are not personal. They are the principles of my faith.'

'Tell us about the Land Rover,' Sant said, keen to move on. 'What colour was it?'

'I couldn't tell. It was dark.'

'Did you see the driver?'

'No.'

'How was it being driven?'

'Slowly.'

'Did you see it stop?'

'Yes.'

'Did the driver see you?'

'No.'

'How come?'

'I took action.'

'Explain.'

'I saw the vehicle coming. I parked the Beamer off road and hid in some trees.'

'You were waiting to get out of there?'

The Romanian nodded.

'What happened next?'

'The iceman came.'

Appleyard baulked at the description. 'The driver was a man?'

'I think so. And there was someone else with him.'

'Another man?'

'I'm not sure. I was a long distance away.'

'Hiding in the trees?'

Another nod.

'What did they do?'

'Got out. Slid this ice chunk out of the rear door. It shattered like glass as it hit the road.'

'Did they struggle with it?'

Popescu thought for a moment. 'I think so. It was a minute or two before they pulled it out.'

'And then?'

'They rolled it.'

'Where?'

'Down the hill.'

'Using hands or feet?'

'A rug. Pulled from underneath.'

'And after that?'

'They left.'

'Straight away?'

'They didn't hang around.'

'What did you do next?'

'I got out of there.'

'Surely you went to see what had been left?'

'It didn't interest me.'

'Were you scared?'

Popescu stared at Sant. 'I don't know what you mean.'

'Surely you had suspicions?'

'Maybe.'

'But you got back in the BMW and sped off.'

The prisoner nodded once.

'You sure they didn't see you or the BMW?'

'I'm sure.'

'How about your victim? Could the iceman, as you call him, have seen Danby?'

'No. I left him further down the road.'

'In a ditch.'

'I can't remember.'

Appleyard checked her iPad. 'It was the ditch where we found vomit, the contents of which included Rohypnol.'

'What?' Popescu said.

'Liquid E,' Hardaker translated.

'I don't know anything about that.'

'You laced his vodka with it,' said Appleyard.

He glanced at his solicitor and reverted to restless legs syndrome.

Sant sighed. 'You're in serious trouble, Mr Popescu.'

'Deport me.'

'Not before you go to court to face rape and robbery charges.'

'Good luck trying.'

'The cards aren't stacked in your favour.'

'Aren't they? Without my cooperation, you'll have your work cut out.' He eyed his solicitor again before turning back to Sant. 'Let's strike a deal.'

'What do you mean?'

'A win-win pact.' The Romanian broke into a smile. 'In our mutual interests.'

'You know more about this Land Rover than you've let on, don't you?' Hardaker probed.

'It's not about the Land Rover.'

'Ivor Danby?'

'Not him either.'

The Chiefman frowned, not enjoying failure in the guess-work department.

Sant eyed Popescu intensely. 'Where did you pick up Mr Danby?'

'Wouldn't you like to know?'

'Cut the crap. You're not helping your cause one iota by toying with us.'

'But I can help you.'

'How?' quizzed Sant, getting up from his chair.

'With information.'

'Tell all.'

'Not before I receive assurances.'

Appleyard shook her head. 'Your mind games are heading nowhere, Mr Popescu.'

'I will whet your appetite,' he said, spying the red light as it glowed on the recording device. 'Then we talk about the future.

My future.'

'I'll ask you again,' Sant said. 'Where did you pick up Danby?'

The Romanian beamed again before saying ever so slowly: 'Lovell Park.'

Sant slapped his own arm. 'The night of the 24th.'

It was Hardaker's turn to pipe up. 'Go on,' the Chiefman said eagerly.

Popescu teased them with a minute's silence before brandishing his Romance-speaking tongue and translating word for word: 'The faggot wasn't the only one I saw that night.'

'Who else?'

'An old man.'

'What did he look like?'

'Old. And dirty.'

'Dirty?'

Popescu laughed. '*Un pedofil*. Fucking with two girls. One left. The other stayed and regretted it. And I'm your witness – if the terms and conditions are congenial.'

Appleyard was stunned into silence. Hardaker tugged at his goatee in a vain attempt to stay composed. Sant felt those hairs rising on his black mane. The prisoner leant back in his chair and grinned at the duty. She pouted.

'I want a proper dinner and plenty more coffee,' Popescu demanded.

'Stop the recording,' spoke Hardaker through the intercom.

'And after dinner it will be time to do a deal, don't you think?'

* * *

Sant snacked on a fish butty from the local chippy and washed it down with two cups of tea. Then he took the lift to the second floor and Hardaker's boardroom for a hastily scheduled meeting on strategy in the wake of Popescu's revelations. When he got there, however, only Appleyard had arrived.

'Harry's going to be late,' she said as she keyed a message into her phone.

'I thought we were calling him Superintendent Hardaker.'

'He's got urgent business with Chief Constable Gilligan. I think we'll be waiting some time.'

Sant thought about leaving but saw an opportunity to show some tact. 'You did well in that interview.'

Appleyard remained stony-faced. 'What are your thoughts on Popescu?'

'He's telling the truth, most of the time.'

'You think he knows nothing about those corpses he saw being dumped?'

Sant looked out of the window and saw two men hanging from ropes as they cleaned the outside of the football stadium. 'I think he's being straight with us. The description he gave of the block of ice marries up with what we know. It's unlikely he'd talk in such detail if he was party to the crime.'

'Unless he's trying to absolve himself of involvement,' she speculated.

'If that was the case, it makes no sense to meet up with his gang of body disposers at the same location where he's unloading Danby and stealing his car.'

Appleyard pulled at an earlobe as though not liking counterarguments. 'But what about the claim he saw Klaudia Armitage and Lydia Brown in Lovell Park with the man who abducted Klaudia? Popescu has a remarkable habit of finding himself witness to grave incidents.'

'Coincidences do happen,' Sant said. 'That's why perpetrators of crime are frequently victims of crime.'

Appleyard let go of her ear. 'I know the stats. I've passed the exams.'

'Criminals are prime victims as much as prime suspects, you see. They mix with the wrong people and turn up in the wrong places.'

'That's why they're criminals.'

'It's a bit more complicated than that.'

'Not unless you make it so,' she sighed. 'Umm, I wonder if Popescu knows the dirty old man. Or maybe he's bluffing. Making it up from fragments of news and the information we've released.'

'Well, we'll soon find out if he's playing for time. I'll test him out; verify a few facts. There's the question of the dog, for instance.'

Appleyard nodded. 'The dirty old man had a small dog with him according to Lydia, but we haven't made that detail public.'

'Which means if he genuinely knows anything, he'll tell us – as long as he thinks he'll receive some kind of pardon in return.'

'Completely out of the question,' the chief inspector said with an emphatic shake of her round head.

Sant frowned. 'But it's tactical to make him believe we're negotiating with him. He's desperate and heading for a long prison sentence. Any small mercy hanging by the thinnest thread will be snapped up gratefully.'

She shook her head again. 'These tactics aren't ethical, DI Sant.'

'Popescu couldn't care less about ethics.'

'The solicitor might.'

Sant laughed. 'Did you see her face when he grinned at her?'

'She's not enamoured with her client. I'll give you that.'

'And I'll take it! Before you ask for it back.'

Appleyard wasn't listening. She was too busy checking the messages on her phone. Sant gazed into the distance and saw one of the men cleaning the stadium drop his brush pole and bury his head in his hands.

'Did Holdsworth fill you in on Ava Yock?' he asked as he redirected his attention to his colleague.

'She did. Hopefully Ava will turn up before long.'

'She's high-risk and a victim of crime. We should look for her.'

'Not yet.'

Sant's forehead crinkled in bewilderment. 'Why delay? She's critical to the case against Popescu.'

'We've got priorities. Yes, Ava is a misper and must be found, but we haven't got around to prosecuting Popescu yet.' The phone sprang to life and Appleyard answered promptly. 'Are you free? What? Tomorrow? Right, I'll let him know.' She hung up and plopped the phone on the oval table. 'Harry is unavailable for the rest of the day. I'll inform the custody officers that interview number three will have to wait till the morning.'

Sant leant his hefty weight against a wall. 'Must be high-level talks he's having with Gilligan. We can't detain Popescu for a lot longer.'

'Thirty-six hours considering the seriousness of the offences he'll be charged with. But no longer. Even that solicitor will keep her eye on the clock.'

The inspector recalled something that had been on his mind. 'I had a chat with Dr Julia Pringle after the public consultation. She says you're championing the Managed Approach these days.'

'The previous chief constable gave me the role,' Appleyard said without enthusiasm.

'So you believe in licensed brothels as much as the late Edward Lister?'

'I've been an advocate for years. I'm not sure now. Soliciting, gender violence, drugs linked to street sex, all these crimes show no sign of abating. If the MA is forced to close, I won't shed a tear.'

'Don't let Dr Pringle hear you say that. She'd be mortified. You're her dream ticket.'

Appleyard almost broke into a smile. 'I like her, but as an academic she's detached from the reality. Sex workers are being battered day and night, employees of her darling project among them, and the MA punters are put off by the regs. Holbeck is dead half the time. Meanwhile, the underground scene hasn't gone way. Quite the contrary – it's making a comeback. Legal prostitution is not the answer, I'm afraid.'

'At least we agree on something,' Sant remarked, 'which makes a change.'

He fished for an ounce of warmth beneath that long black hair, but Appleyard's broad visage gave nothing away. She withdrew to her phone and more online rabbit holes. Sant felt it best not to prolong his boardroom stay and was breathing steadier once out of there.

* * *

An evening sprinkled with a smattering of downtime – Sant had forgotten such luxuries existed, though in truth, he was never fully relaxed when off duty. He called his ex-wife on the off chance she might permit him to entertain Sam and Tom outside of the formal custody arrangement, and to his surprise she was *supportive* of the idea. Elizabeth badly needed a haircut in order to impress the new man in her life – Sant hadn't met him and had no interest in doing so – so she wanted the boys out of her hair, literally.

They feasted on pizza in Sant's apartment. He rented the place on a shorthold agreement, but this was now his fourth year and he'd grown to like it and his landlord – an elderly lady who lived in the West End of London and was worth a small fortune – always acted swiftly when a problem cropped up. It was a kind of home, though his mother's house felt more homely somehow. Not that he visited her often. Indeed, he got a piece of her mind about his desertion whenever he called by.

After food, they browsed the shops along the side streets. He bought his sons a football shirt each. Sam was a Leeds fan like his dad, but Tom was mad for Liverpool. They wanted the matching shorts too, but dad was no millionaire like all those overrated Leeds United and Liverpool players.

There was just enough time to play a round of crazy golf in a themed bar, which Sant guessed was an American fad imported from over the pond. Sam emerged as the winner, dad blaming his mediocre performance on a pair of drunken students playing behind who kept shouting 'in the hole!' and 'you're the man!' and the occasional expletive he could have done without hearing. Sadly, no grounds existed to make an arrest for idiocy.

They went back to the flat and tucked into a chocolate cake he'd picked up at the local supermarket. He dropped them back at Elizabeth's shortly after ten and decided he was still hungry. After driving around for a while, he settled on an excellent doner kebab place on New Briggate where he took full advantage of the Turkish specialities, ordering almost everything on the menu with liberal applications of chilli sauce.

When he returned to his car, a parking ticket had attached itself to the windscreen wiper. He'd jammed the Fiesta into a tight space and the back end was encroaching onto double yellows. It was a case of the traffic warden who couldn't care less for hungry coppers. Sant, being a member of the local constabulary, could have avoided paying but he decided to do the right thing and donate fifty pounds of his hard-earned wage to the council. Perhaps the injection of cash would fund a few flowers. Despite the onset of spring, the city looked as colourful as a used teabag.

He considered calling Capstick and coaxing him out of that hospital bed he was growing accustomed to, but it was well beyond visiting hours and the detective constable was probably still sleeping off the effects of that Liquid E. Instead, he left his car and the parking ticket where it was and wandered up to Lovell Park.

A layer of frost an inch thick was keeping the grass honest. He walked quickly to keep himself warm, his black Mackintosh offering little protection against the sub-zero temperatures. He wished he'd worn his duffle coat. Few people were roaming the park. Recent events have put the fear of God into folk, Sant thought to himself.

'Looking for a good time?' a husky voice spoke, breaking the stillness of the night air.

The inspector turned on his heel and spied a tall woman flaunting pink-dyed rattail hair above a blank punk expression. 'Not tonight, love. What's your name?'

The woman hooted. 'Now now, mister. You might be police for all I know.'

'Good guess.' He moved towards her and pulled out his ID card.

'Forgive me,' she winced and hurried off, but Sant caught up in no time.

'I'm not interested in arresting you,' he called out. 'I'm investigating an incident that occurred here a few nights ago.'

The woman slowed her stride. 'I know nothing. This is not my... patch.'

'So you weren't here when the girl got attacked?'

'When was it?'

'The night before last.'

She hesitated, then said: 'Maybe. But I didn't see any girl.'

'Where are you from?'

'Sorry?'

'Which country?'

'Romania,' she answered.

Sant was in luck. 'I'm searching for someone who grew up there – she's called Ava. Young. Only twenty-one. Small build. Less than five foot tall. Suffered a horrible attack a couple of years ago.'

She peered down at her tattered Doc Martens. 'I hope you find her,' she said eventually.

'You know her?'

'We are friends.'

'Where do you think she might be?'

She shrugged. 'I'm worried about her.'

Two young lads smoking cannabis strolled towards them, coughing their guts out and guffawing loudly as they pointed at the woman's hairdo and laddered tights.

'I'd like to talk with you,' said Sant as the pair shouted something and wandered off, 'but this isn't exactly a civilised setting. We can walk towards the university.' He waved an arm. 'There's plenty of lighting up there and we can find somewhere to sit. Okay?'

Another shrug. 'I suppose I have no choice.'

'You do but you want to find Ava as much as me, right?' She nodded. 'Your name?'

'Maria Halep.'

Sant smiled warmly. 'First name will suffice. Follow me, Maria.'

They found a bench beneath a leafless tree and talked for nearly an hour. She sucked on an e-cigarette while Sant learnt about her life, or at least, the twenty-three years she'd lived so far. She'd left her native country aged seventeen to do sex work in Berlin before paying a small fortune to a trafficking racket in return for a train ticket to Paris and a bus ticket northwards bound. A few days later she was picked up by a lorry driver who received a fee for her. He savagely assaulted her and tied her up in his lorry among the fruit and veg destined for major UK supermarkets. After the ferry crossing, he untied her, raped her again, stole her cash and finally let her go.

Soon after, she was a polydrug addict working the streets of concrete dives and losing her earnings to the pimps. One night she was admitted to hospital where she almost died, saved by the stomach pump. Granted asylum after spending months in a detox rehab unit, she found a job as a cleaner but lost it as soon as the chain shut up shop. Without an income and unable to claim welfare for technical reasons, she wasted time being referred to one agency after another where people desperate to help her patronised her at every turn. Defeated by a system designed to cure her, she went back to what she knew best.

'What an horrendous time you've gone through,' Sant said.

Maria laughed. 'When you do what I do you learn to accept certain feelings. I've lost count of the overdoses, the infections, the assaults. It comes with the territory.'

'But it shouldn't. You should be safe. Have you heard of the Managed Approach?'

'The legal brothel, right?'

Sant was taken aback. 'You could call it that.'

'It's a total joke. It's meant to be regulated, and that's meant to solve everything. So the customers start off not minding the idea, but soon they regard the red tape as a nuisance and get frustrated.'

Sant could hear Appleyard's words echoing in the darkness. 'I see where you're coming from. The customers are turned off and go on the look-out for authentic sex workers like... well, like you.'

'Not at all.'

'I'm wrong?'

'Absolutely.'

'You're not authentic?'

She laughed again. 'No comment, but you're wrong about the legal brothel.'

'Tell me more.'

'It's those rules – they're not worth the condom packets they're written on. The MA has two faces, you see. The official one operates from eight till late and is patrolled. Tourists and teenage boys get a taste of what they're meant to see, and the security do the job they're paid to do. The other face operates at all hours and outside the restricted zone. I can think of more than ten girls who've doubled their income taking on Johns without the safety controls, but most of them have quit lately.'

'You mean, they're no longer protected?'

She nodded. 'The customers hand over a cash bonus, backhanders are exchanged, the men get what they demand.'

'Rough sex?'

Maria took a long vape before replying: 'Yes, and the rest. Drugs, weapons, you name it.'

Sant pulled out his phone and found a screenshot he'd taken earlier of PC Joshua Benn's profile. 'Do you recognise this man?' he asked, holding the phone in front of her.

She stared for a long time. 'Is he police?'

He didn't answer. 'You've seen him among the girls?'

'I don't recognise his face. What's his name?'

'Confidential information, sorry.'

'Is he a punter?'

'He's admitted as much.'

'Will he be fired?'

'From where?'

'The police force, of course.'

Sant conceded defeat. 'Probably.'

Maria sucked in another vape. 'I still imagine police as good people. Silly me.'

He swiped across the screen and brought up another image he'd prepared, this one portraying Sergeant Fawad Tufail.

'How about him?'

She gasped and put a silver-ringed hand to her mouth. 'He's police too?'

'You know him?'

'He's in the game.' She stared into the distance. 'Pays out cash on the sly. Wads of it.'

'You sure?' Sant showed the photo again.

'I'm certain.'

'Does he pay you?'

'Not personally. He deals with a pimp. Someone who pays me from time to time. He owes me. That's why I'm staying away from third parties.'

'Has this man been your customer?'

She shook her head. 'He doesn't do sex. I've heard from other girls that he has family and is strictly in it for the money. Which makes what he does all right somehow.'

'It's not,' said Sant, clenching both fists under his coat sleeves.

'It's strange though.'

'What?'

'I've not seen him for months. Since before Christmas.

Maybe he's scared of being found out.' She turned to face Sant. 'Are you keeping a watch on him?'

'You'd better believe it.'

'But you've not arrested him?'

'Not yet. I may need help when the time comes.'

She clasped her knees together. 'It will only spell trouble if I get involved.'

'I'll protect you, Maria. You won't be named or shown.'

She put her long arms around his bulk. 'I mustn't take the risk. I have... let's say, I have a duty to someone.'

'Who?' he asked.

'Would it be rude if I didn't tell you?'

He patted her pink hair for a moment, then said: 'No obligation, okay?'

She smiled up at him. 'You are a good policeman.'

He gently released her. 'You mentioned weapons earlier. What sort?'

She straightened her tall frame and the tension in her calf muscles eased. 'Knives mainly. A friend of mine had her face cut last year.'

Sant wrapped his Mackintosh tightly around his chest. 'That explains the protests. The MA was supposed to reduce crime and make it safer to walk the streets at night.'

'And I was born to be Queen of England,' Maria joked.

'Maybe we should rename it the Doomed Approach.'

She wagged her finger. 'It's the pride and joy of the VIPs, I'll have you know. The show must go on and under no circumstances can anyone peek behind the scenes.'

The conversation didn't end until midnight, Sant feeling enlightened after listening to the girl's impassioned views. Technically, he should have arrested her for soliciting in a public place, but that was the last thing on his mind. Sadly, the first thing on his mind was no nearer being found. Maria hadn't a clue where Ava was. She admitted her friend was a fellow prostitute but gave nothing else away. He could tell she was trying hard not to.

As for Nicolae Popescu, she knew him vaguely and was aware that Ava had accused him of attacking her, but she didn't think Ava was hiding from him or any other Romanian expat. Her parting words stuck in Sant's head for a long time afterwards. 'When girls leave the street, they say where they're going. If they don't, they're in danger, or worse, dead.'

* * *

To his mother he was Sean but everyone else called him Bonehead because his head was as hard as bone. The cranium protruded so starkly through the fast-receding hair on his scalp that he looked for all the world like a living skeleton. The scalp and the face below it had the ruddy tan of a man accustomed to the outdoors.

Bonehead was also called Bonehead because he had an unenviable habit of using his head for purposes other than intellectual endeavour. Over the years he'd built up quite a reputation as a doorman who acted decisively when required, butting countless menaces and rendering them entirely unconscious. Despite this track record of aggression, no-one took him to court – a forlorn task because his victims were hardly paragons of virtue themselves. They also suspected Bonehead was guarded by the people that mattered.

They were right.

Bonehead's history of terror had been brought to the attention of a posse of officers for whom he now worked. The posse was small. Only those who needed to know were in the know. The two uniforms patrolling the Managed Approach that Saturday night were among the privileged few. As Bonehead passed their car on Water Lane, they winked at each other and returned to their word puzzles. They would've given him a thumbs-up and a cup of cocoa from their flask had it not been for the surveillance camera fixed to the lamppost above.

Bonehead always carried a small tool as an insurance policy in case he had to handle an awkward son of a bitch, but on this occasion he wouldn't require it. Head and fists would suffice. The assignment was a break from the usual beating. Someone else must have been assigned it first, he presumed, though for whatever reason Hit Man 1 had gone AWOL.

He took a sharp left and navigated the cobbled roads by the docks before crossing a footbridge and dropping down into a wasteland of auto junk and shattered glass. He kept walking past long-deserted locks and sluice gates, vaulting over a crumbling brick wall before slipping through the narrow doorway of a Muay Thai gym (that's what the signage said). A spindly woman manning the building glanced up from the movie she was viewing on her tablet but kept quiet. She'd received a handsome sum to mind her own business.

Bonehead took three stairs at a time and reached the top floor with a blaze of intent. He scurried down a corridor and reached the locked door at the end, as per instructions from the boys in blue. The lock snapped easily. He kicked hard and the wood splintered. The block of rooms beyond smelled of jasmine incense. He opened the first door and saw the Vietnamese girl. The officers had been right. She was an absolute babe. Five feet tall and shapely in the right places. On another night he'd have spent a ton pleasuring this Feast of the East, but not tonight.

As the girl stood to greet him, Bonehead showed her his yellow teeth before launching his skull against her brittle nose. She shrieked briefly and collapsed onto an ironing board, snapping it in half. He shook his head at the red mess blooming over her face. She didn't deserve that. She'd get over it. In a month or two. And then he'd return to give her the time of her life.

Next, he put his ear to the door of the room opposite, heard the groans of a John desperately seeking an orgasm. Two rooms were vacant beyond this one, but the door to the last one was ajar. He peered inside and saw a woman of a certain age polishing her nails.

'Come in, Lovely.' The woman squinted at Bonehead's bloody brow and shook her red wig at him. 'Deary me, I don't like the look of you,' she croaked.

'Wot?'

'You were here last week. Called me names and hit my friends.'

'That wasn't me, old bird.'

She put a fag to her mouth, lighting it with a match that illuminated the red mandala tapestry hanging from the wall. 'Must've been your twin brother. Shall I smoke naked or clothed?' she asked him, taking a long drag.

'Keep ya clothes on and stand when spoken to.'

She took another drag and struggled to her feet. 'The bossy type, are we?'

Tired of the small talk, he threw a left uppercut that sent her flying. She sprawled on top of a lava lamp, moaning horribly. He grabbed her throat and launched his right fist this time, thud-thud-thud. A minute later she was unrecognisable. He flexed his biceps. The boys would pat him on the back; tell him how grateful they were. Another nail in another competitor's coffin. Top marks, Bonehead!

He began to make headway, then noticed a couple of blond teens parading through the door he'd cracked open. They didn't see him until it was too late. He sprang forward and gripped two tufts of fair hair in each hand before slamming heads against facing walls of the corridor. The smaller girl slithered down and out, but the taller one with the dark tan stayed upright, amazingly, and then had the tenacity to spit at him.

That set Bonehead in a rage. The thing that disgusted him most was another person's saliva. He lifted the whore by the neck and threw a right uppercut that sent her spinning. She stayed on her feet until he pinned her arms and headbutted her twice, sending her to the floor in a stream of blood and broken teeth.

Still disgusted, he went to pick her up, but one way or another, she rolled out of his grasp. He could see her reaching for something from behind. He bent down to fix her but didn't see the fire extinguisher until it blasted icy foam up into his yellow-fanged gob.

Crushed against the broken door and coated in retardant, he gave off a formidable impression of the abominable snowman. Stunned by the thrust of the spray, he got to work brushing the white stuff out of his eyes. At last, he could see again.

The whore was still on the ground, not saying much. He gripped shoulder blades between thumbs and forefingers, tugged and worked his hands under her armpits, hurling her eight feet into the air. She struck the ceiling and went through it, then crumpled amid a shower of plasterboard. Not finished, he scooped up the empty extinguisher and sent it plummeting. The metal cylinder smashed into the back of her neck as she tried to get to her knees. As a departing gesture, he brought down the heal of his right boot, snap-snap-snap.

One look at her jawbone and Bonehead's legs started to shake. He drew in quick breaths and got out at pace. The woman at the front entrance saw the trail of foam, tested her imagination, blew out bubble gum and returned to her movie.

Bonehead put one third of a mile of wasteland behind him before puking over nettles protruding through cracked tarmac.

His eyes were watering. He'd cocked up. The instructions couldn't have been clearer. Do damage but not too much. And now he'd done too much. The girl would be hospitalised. Would she recover? He thought of the worst and puked some more.

He didn't think, however, that someone standing in a high-rise flat two hundred yards away might be watching his every retch.

7

A SECOND NIGHT SPENT ON A HARD OFFICE FLOOR OFFERED no sweet dream, though this time Sant slept soundly owing to the copious volumes of oxygen he'd inhaled the night before. Lovell Park has its perks, he mused. Sprouting out of the Victorian age of civic pride, it was coined the 'Lungs of Leeds' because of the sanctuary it provided from industrial miasma – and the park functioned the same way in modern times despite the toxic waste and hypodermic needles.

Sant and Appleyard started the day as they'd ended yesterday, waiting for the Chiefman in the boardroom. Sant preferred the idea of a morning raid on Sergeant Tufail's home. Maria's claim that Tufail was dealing with pimps was a serious matter, but Sant was reluctant to call him out until he was certain of the facts. The best course of action, he decided, was another visit. Tufail was holding something back, undoubtedly, even if the man seemed sure of his own integrity.

At least the detectives had something to look forward to. They'd been promised some DNA evidence from forensics, with emphasis placed firmly on *some* as the lab technicians knew better than anyone how the science of DNA was not the magic wand lay folks believed it to be. There could be no sharing of DNA data on electronic devices until results had been signed off by a senior tech, so when Hardaker finally rolled in, it was a humble piece of paper he was consulting – to be expunged in a shredder as soon as he'd finished with it.

'Hot off the press,' the Chiefman announced as he plonked himself on a swivel chair at the head of the oval table.

Sant pulled out a fresh toothpick and clamped it to his jaws. 'Feel free to leave us on a precipice.'

Hardaker stared at the paper and sighed. 'No trace of Nicolae Popescu on Ava Yock.'

Appleyard's mouth formed an O. 'Seriously? What about Klaudia Armitage?' She spoke urgently as if her life depended on it.

'Again, no trace of Popescu,' Hardaker said grimly. 'Analysis of the upholstery fibres drew a blank too. The fibres obtained from Klaudia were not from the white BMW or any other vehicle connected with Popescu.'

'Unbelievable,' grumbled Appleyard.

'However,' continued Hardaker, 'there's a clear match with samples taken from Ivor Danby. And not only Danby. Another male came forward the other day.'

Sant pulled the toothpick out of his mouth. 'I was right. Popescu is only interested in blokes.'

'You're jumping to conclusions,' Appleyard said.

'I agree,' said Hardaker, 'though Carl has a point too.'

'Backed up by evidence,' Sant added.

'Which is hardly conclusive,' Appleyard retorted.

'What more do you want? A dossier from MI5?'

Hardaker leant forward in his chair. 'Come on, you two. Let's be good to one another.'

Appleyard tugged her bun of dark hair. 'Where do we go from here?'

Sant snapped his toothpick. 'I'll lead the interview again. I want Popescu to think we're on his side.'

'A dangerous game to play,' Appleyard remarked.

'We can be shrewd with what we record – and what we don't.'

'And land ourselves in deep trouble with the CPS?' Appleyard snapped.

'The crown prosecution won't know a thing,' said Sant. 'Plus, a false sense of security will give Popescu the green flag to tell us what he saw in Lovell Park on Wednesday night.'

Hardaker looked meaningfully at Sant. 'It's good he's talking to you. Go to work on his brain. Stephanie is right about the risks, but let's keep to the same strategy.'

Appleyard glared at her colleagues. 'What do you intend to ask him?'

'Allow me a little head space to meditate,' Sant replied.

'There's no time for any of that malarkey,' protested Appleyard.

Sant gaped at her. 'You don't believe in the powers of mindfulness?'

'I may be half Thai but that doesn't mean I spend half my life listening to monks high on *ya ba*.' The chief inspector rose to her feet. 'We must go. We'll be compelled to release Popescu if we're not quick out of the blocks.'

The ringtones of George Thorogood sprang out of Hardaker's jacket pocket. He unearthed his device and answered, stroked his goatee and listened pensively.

'Message me the postcode,' he said. 'Be there in a jiffy.'

'What is it?' probed Appleyard.

Hardaker replaced the phone in his pocket. 'Bad news. A woman believed to be a sex worker is in St James's ICU. The doctor in charge says she was assaulted overnight and may not survive the injuries.'

Appleyard shook her head. 'She's not an employee of the Managed Approach, is she?'

'Her identity is unknown,' Hardaker went on. 'We need to be at the crime scene a-sap. There may be no link to the other attacks, but I'd like to be certain.'

'At least we can rule out Popescu,' Sant said, 'unless he broke out of his cell at the dead of night and came back before dawn to lock himself in.'

Hardaker was tickled, Appleyard not amused in the slightest.

'What about the interview?' she asked. 'Popescu's solicitor will spot the flaw in our procedure and force us to let him go.'

'Don't worry, Stephanie. If necessary, the custody arrival time can be tweaked on the paperwork.'

Appleyard's mouth made another big O. 'Is that wise?'

'Anything goes if Harry says so,' Sant put in.

'Don't be frivolous, Carl.'

'Better than being shady, Chiefman. Far better.'

* * *

Sant surveyed the shards of plasterboard and lumps of dried emulsion peppering the broken floorboards. Three techs crouched at intervals along the narrow corridor, torches in hand, scanning for footwear prints and fibres of hair among the shattered light bulb glass. An oxygen mask discarded at the centre of the debris was accompanied by a plastic evidence marker displaying a black number four against an orange background. Any crime scene without a casualty in attendance always meant complications, but when push came to shove and life was on the brink, paramedics and oxygen masks were price-less – forensic officers less so.

The inspector spent a while talking to uniforms who knew nothing, the techs in no position to talk either. The situation was hopeless. He went to find Hardaker but the Chiefman was busy on the phone. Sant gathered from the conversation that the victim was critical and any hope of interviewing her soon was fading fast.

He stepped outside and popped the collar of his Mackin-tosh against the harsh morning breeze as he went in search of a bacon roll. As he rounded the corner of the former warehouse that undoubtedly housed this underground brothel, he saw someone he recognised. Councillor Rory Dobson, political opportunist par excellence, was letting the local rag and radio reporters know exactly what this latest atrocity said about the safety net the Managed Approach was supposed to be casting over the neighbourhood.

Sant waited until Dobson had spoken to the journalists before making his move. He advanced from the side and called loudly: 'What's the story, Rory?'

Dobson seemed caught in two minds about whether to engage in banter or seek out the next publicity opening. He almost tripped over his white Puma sneakers wondering what to do, the momentum of indecision thrusting him grudgingly towards whoever was addressing him, wooden arm outstretched.

'I don't think I've had the pleasure,' he said in a slightly camp tone at odds with his navy wool suit jacket underlining muscular contours and self-assured mannerisms.

Sant shook the man's solid hand. 'Detective Inspector Carl Sant, missing persons department.'

The young man's eyebrows lifted a fraction before the wide

smile shone out below the blond curls. 'Ah, you're something of a local hero, I believe. It's a true pleasure to meet you.'

Sant dodged the compliment, though a little massaging of the ego never harmed him. 'Why are you here?' he queried.

'I heard the news. Terrible news. Another mindless act of aggression.'

'And an opportune moment to give the press your two pennies' worth.'

Dobson pressed fingers to biceps. 'They ask me for my thoughts. I give them freely.' He pointed at the derelict warehouse. 'Another den of vice operating under the dark shadow of Holbeck. We have a long way to go, DI Sant, before we sort out the sex-work crisis in Leeds Central.'

'Is this the ward you represent, Councillor?'

He nodded and glowed in unison. 'Spanning a mile or so in any direction you choose. I'm proud to call it my own, though it's in need of some TLC. AKA investment. Imagine the potential of this place, for instance. Install windows and decorate the inside and you've got a perfect base for a community hub. Sadly, there's too much of the wrong sort of business around here. It wouldn't surprise me if there aren't fewer than a dozen dens of vice like this.'

Sant decided to make a head start at rocking the boat. 'Thankfully, crimes against sex workers are rare these days. The Managed Approach has made the trade safer.'

Dobson's smile vanished. 'Don't believe a word of it. The evidence is stark. The MA has its own problems with criminals of one description or another. Meanwhile, underground cess pits like this place thrive as never before.'

'You've won a lot of support for your stance on the MA, haven't you?'

'I'm simply echoing the views of the community,' Dobson went on. 'But I endorse public opinion too. Regulating prostitution is not the solution. Incidents like what happened last night prove my point.'

Sant took a step closer. 'What about the prostitutes you represent? They live as well as work in this ward, right? Have you considered their views?'

The councillor shuffled from one foot to the other. 'My role is to capture the mood of the majority. I can't please everyone. What the workers think is their business, but a regulated brothel is only as good as the infrastructure underpinning it. And the truth is that sex work attracts drugs and knives and STIs, regardless of whether it's decriminalised or not.'

Sant could hear the words of Maria and Appleyard ringing in his ears. Dobson shared their dim view of Holbeck, even if his agenda was politically motivated. 'Are you familiar with the ideas of Dr Julia Pringle?'

'That woman's a fanatic,' Dobson scoffed.

'She's quite persuasive.'

'Don't tell me you've been swayed, Inspector. Her *John School* preaching is the reason we're in such a mess.'

'Maybe you should listen to what she has to say before judging her. I can arrange the conversation if you like.'

The councillor shook his head. 'I'm no stranger to diplomacy, but the nonsense she peddles is beyond my powers of tolerance.'

'I guess it would be a PR disaster,' Sant reflected, 'if word got around you were talking to the architect of the very idea you spend so much time lambasting.'

Dobson's face reddened. 'I have no time for mavericks like her. How can an area like Holbeck aspire to prosperity when everyone calls it the red-light district?'

'The managed zone is a former industrial estate,' countered Sant. 'It's removed from the residential parts entirely.'

'Would you like to live near it?'

The inspector answered honestly. 'Not me personally.'

'Neither do the people I give a voice to, nor me for that matter.'

'You live in Holbeck too?'

Dobson pointed in the right direction. 'About half a mile away from the MA. And before you ask, half a mile isn't far enough. Most nights I see crimes outside my front window. Crimes I wouldn't see if there was no brothel down the road.'

'So what's your answer?'

The councillor backed away. 'It would take too much of the day explaining my position. What's the force's perspective?'

Exhibit number four – the lonely oxygen mask – flashed through Sant's mind.

'Tougher and longer sentences would serve as a deterrent,' he remarked.

'Hear, hear. Pimps and prostitutes deserve nothing less.'

'Actually, I was thinking of the thugs who rape and murder innocent women.'

'Couldn't agree more' – Dobson wasn't really listening now – 'but the violence only stops if the sex rings get smashed. And by the way, the jury's out on how the police have handled things. A whiff of unprofessional standards is in the air. Too many crimes linked to human trafficking are going unpunished, and many locals say the streets need cleaning up.'

Sant eyed the young man inquisitively. 'What are these *unprofessional standards* you've heard about?'

'I'll elaborate in due course, Inspector, and that reminds me – I have suspicions about an individual. Not one of your colleagues, I hasten to add. Someone with form.'

'Fire away.'

Dobson pointed a thumb at the growing assortment of cameras and microphones. 'I might be accused of slander if this lot catch anything. Perhaps we can converse in a more suitable location. Meet me after one outside the Palace.'

'Sure thing.' Sant looked up at the grey sky screaming rain – it was about to pour down and give the streets of Leeds Central that wash they needed. 'One last thing. You're an Independent, aren't you?'

'Correct,' Dobson said.

'Must be hard without a party behind you.'

'Far from it. I enjoy being me, free from the whip, committed to no lost cause. I don't even consider myself a politician. I'm merely a working man like you or anyone else. The only difference is what I do mirrors the mindset of the people I serve.'

'So what's next for your campaign?' Sant probed. 'Staging a rally outside this den of vice maybe?'

The councillor beamed before unfurling a small umbrella tucked under his burly armpit. 'I do have other issues to tackle, believe it or not. You'll be interested to know that in tomorrow's scrutiny meeting I'll be pushing, as I always do, for more bobbies on the beat.'

Sant gave an approving nod. 'Maybe I'll join your recruits.'

Dobson snorted theatrically. 'I meant uniformed police. Diligent CID chaps like your good self are overworked as it is.'

Ever the charmer, the inspector figured, as the young man waved a goodbye and an approaching taxi at the same time. No wonder he's a hit with Joe Public. Dobson must need a lot of toilet paper to wipe the arses of all those voting for him.

* * *

'You took your time,' Popescu said as he trundled into the interview room, wrists cuffed, hands clasped in inverted prayer. 'What's the deal, boys?' He leered at Appleyard. 'And girl.'

Sant brushed raindrops off the shoulders of his black shirt, waited for the prisoner to be seated, then started on the script formulated earlier that morning. 'We can't come to mutual terms unless we know what you're withholding.'

Popescu stared into Sant's eyeballs. 'No games. I want something in writing.'

'What for?' Sant said, arms out wide, palms turned up.

'Assurances. I want a fair settlement.'

'Settlement? You want money?'

'Security. If I tell you what I know, I want a full pardon.'

'Some such thing might be arranged,' said Sant, only saying it because no red light was showing on the recording device – the officers controlling the equipment in the next room were following instructions to a tee.

'I want assurances,' Popescu repeated.

Hardaker pulled at the hem of his trousers. 'We'll do our best for you, Nicolae. Tell the truth and nothing but, and we'll pull some strings where we can.'

'I want to hear him say it.'

'Why me?' Sant complained.

'I trust a grafter.'

The inspector felt like looking down at his rough palms but resisted the urge. 'Fine. We'll look after you.'

The solicitor widened her eyes a fraction and Sant smiled back. She'd be briefed later, to guarantee against misunderstandings.

'Keep me out of prison,' the Romanian pleaded.

'We'll do what we can.'

'I want these assurances in writing.'

That word again, thought Sant. 'We'll type something up forthwith.'

Popescu ruminated, legs vibrating, eyes directed to the

heavens, before making up his mind. He lowered his gaze and gestured with a solitary nod. Sant ruffled his dark hair from back to front, and the red light came on by magic.

'It's one thirty-two pm,' said Hardaker for the benefit of the transcript. 'Let's go back to when you first arrived at Lovell Park on the night of the 24th of February. What time was it?'

'He's asking,' Popescu insisted.

'Me again,' said Sant, getting used to the attention. 'Okay, the time was?'

'Nine. It was sleeting. It stopped about ten and the snow came later.'

'And you stayed there until you met Ivor Danby and went off in his car.' Another sole nod. 'When did you leave?'

The Romanian coughed twice. 'Any chance of a drink?' Hardaker unscrewed a small bottle of water and brought it to the man's mouth. 'Must've been eleven,' he said after licking his lips.

'So you were there for two hours,' Sant said. 'Who else did you see in the park?'

'Pi– police. Two of them.'

'In uniform?'

'Yeah.'

'What time did you see them?'

'Maybe ten-thirty.'

Appleyard tapped on her super-slick iPad, then said: 'Can you describe the officers?'

'Not really. Man and woman.'

'Did they see you?'

'No. But I overheard. One of them likes blackmailing benefit fiddlers.' Appleyard stopped typing and eyed the prisoner for clarification. 'Another corrupt lad of yours,' he continued.

Sant ruffled his hair again, erroneously this time, but fortunately the officers in the room next door carried on recording. 'Who else did you see?'

Popescu stared blankly at his accusers. 'Why do you want to know?'

The inspector scratched his nose. 'I'm asking the questions, remember?'

'The man you saw with the two girls – describe him,' Hardaker said.

'I already told you. He was old and dirty.'

'Very old?'

'Old enough to be their grandad.'

Sant began pacing back and forth. 'There must've been something that made you think he was old. What was he wearing?'

'I couldn't tell. It was dark.'

'How about his posture?'

'He had a limp.' Popescu smiled up at Sant. 'That's how I knew he was old.'

'Which leg?'

'Left.'

'Sure about that?'

'Yeah.'

'A bad limp?'

'Not a good one.'

Sant stood still for a moment. 'Did the limp impede him?'

'He couldn't put full weight on his left side.'

'Was he overweight?'

'The opposite. No fat on him.'

An image was forming in Sant's mind. 'Anything else you recall?'

'He smoked.'

'Left or right hand?'

'Right.'

'What was he smoking?'

Popescu shrugged. 'I couldn't smell. He was too far away.'

'How would you describe his behaviour?' asked Appleyard.

'Immoral.'

'Sorry?'

'How else do you describe a paedo?'

Sant continued pacing up and down. 'How did he act? Nervously?'

'A little. He was restless.'

'How could you tell?'

'He was looking at his watch a lot. And his phone.'

'Waiting for someone?'

'Maybe. Or waiting for the right time to leave. He tried to get the other girl to stay. It felt like he was... unsure.'

'Of what?'

'From where I was standing it looked like he didn't want to take the girls but didn't want to leave without them. That's why he was waiting.'

Sant applied toothpick to gnashers and thought hard. 'Did anyone phone him?'

The Romanian shook his bald head.

'How long did you spy on him?' quizzed Appleyard.

'About five or ten minutes. Then I went for a wander and came back. That was when the other girl got pissed and left.'

'Did he chase after her?'

'He limped after her. His dog gave chase as well.'

Sant had been standing by for mention of the dog. He glanced across at Appleyard and Hardaker; saw the glint in their eyes.

'What did you see next?' Hardaker probed.

'More water.' The Chiefman did the honours, tipping the rest of the bottle down Popescu's open throat. 'I lost interest and then they vanished,' he said as the liquid trickled down his gullet.

'In which direction?' Appleyard enquired.

'I didn't notice.'

'Could Ivor Danby have seen the man?'

'The faggot turned up later.'

Sant scratched his chin with the toothpick, then asked: 'After you doped Mr Danby, why did you choose to dump him on Woodhall Road?'

'I already told you. I had nothing to do with the iceman affair.'

'Where did you dump the others?'

'Sorry?'

Appleyard scrolled down her iPad. 'The man you attacked in Holbeck Moor Park a week ago – and the others.'

Popescu tried to fix eye contact with the solicitor but missed hopelessly.

'We have the DNA proof,' said Hardaker. 'Denying it is fruitless.'

'But we have an agreement, don't we?'

Sant discarded his toothpick in a wastepaper bin. 'That will be all, Mr Popescu.'

'I take it you're happy.'

'Happy?'

'I gave you info to catch your paedo.'

'But you're to be charged with sexual offences,' Appleyard informed him. 'Why would we be happy with you?'

Sant admired the retort and tried to catch the chief inspector's eye, but she was staring straight at the prisoner.

'I told you what I saw. And I only rape faggots.'

'That's great to know,' scoffed Hardaker.

The Romanian stared at Sant. 'You'll keep assurances, won't you?'

Sant ruffled his black mane, the red light blinked and died. 'The criminal justice system is beyond my control,' he replied.

'I want an open prison and a short sentence.' He turned to Hardaker. 'You can pull a few strings, chief.'

'Only these,' the superintendent said, yanking the red hairs attached to his chin. 'I pull them all the time. Ouch!' He feigned pain. 'It makes not the slightest difference.'

For once, client looked gloomier than solicitor. Popescu was helped to his feet and led out by two beefy officers, a long sentence in a high security prison the best deal he could hope for.

* * *

Sant made his excuses and left Hardaker and Appleyard with the CPS lawyer, the latter satisfied that at least one sexual offence charge would result in a conviction seen as Popescu's DNA was all over Danby and his BMW, not factoring in the damning CCTV evidence.

Rory Dobson had messaged to say he was running twenty minutes late – but on entering the Palace at twenty past one, Sant saw no sign of Dobson. Temptation getting the better of him, he ordered a pint of Beamish Irish Stout and poured it down his wide neck. The barmaid reminded him of his first love and suddenly the Beamish tasted acidic and he regretted swallowing the stuff, so he chewed gum and allowed his stomach to settle before heading back to the outdoor market where he'd parked. He passed through the bus station and sensed someone behind him; saw Dobson panning his vision in all directions while negotiating the bus lane Sant had just crossed.

'You almost missed me,' the inspector called out.

The councillor slackened his muscles and breathed heavily. 'Let me explain over noodles. I'll get us some great Malaysian street food.'

They took the side entrance into Kirkgate Market and Dobson ordered two portions of *mee goreng*. Sant's mouth watered as he took in the aroma of garlic and chillies, and he was soon rid of the stout's metallic tang. A native packaged the noodles in polystyrene boxes and Dobson presented him with a crisp twenty-pound note. They found a couple of spare stools beside the shop and ate their lunch heartily before striking up any meaningful conversation. Dobson turned out to be a wizard with chopsticks. A blessed fork stolen from the stall next door came to Sant's rescue.

'So why the late show?' Sant said as he spat out a chilli possessing too much kick.

Dobson paused as if deciding how to reply, then said: 'You probably guessed I was watching from afar.'

'Spying, were you?'

'I wanted to make sure no-one was with you, tracking your movements.'

'Who do you have in mind?' said Sant matter-of-factly.

The councillor fiddled with a chopstick. 'Sorry, I'm nervous. I think someone's closing in on me. That might sound silly, but I'm not paranoid by nature.'

Sant picked at a beansprout with his wooden fork. 'Why would that *someone* be tracking me, too?'

'This might sound even more silly.' Dobson paused again before saying: 'I suspect a copper is keeping tabs on me.'

'What've you done wrong?'

Dobson spoke softly. 'Nothing other than stand up for

decent folk who dislike brothels. Someone isn't keen on the influence I'm having.'

'And you think it's a copper?'

'Well, whoever it is knows a hell of a lot about me. My address, my car reg, the places I hang out, my broadband provider, you name it.'

'Broadband provider?' Sant looked around him to ensure nobody was prying. 'Why would that be of interest?'

Dobson scratched his chin. 'Okay, I might as well come clean. I made a mistake when I was a teenager. Eight years ago. I fell in with the wrong people on the dark web. I avoided jail but not one hundred hours of community service cleaning the windows of council houses. Child porn isn't the wisest thing to subscribe to.'

Sant shook his head. 'You don't want your avid supporters discovering your teen fantasies, Councillor.'

'I'd be out of a job if anything leaked,' he agreed. 'But whoever's got it in for me knows everything. The websites I was using, my credit cards, even the amounts I was paying for those disgusting videos. How ashamed I am of what I once considered a bit of fun.'

'You're telling me you're being blackmailed,' Sant concluded.

'Not for money – not yet – but it's only a matter of time. Unless I stop objecting to the sex factory.'

Sant chewed on the fork for a while, then said: 'Why would a blackmailing copper seek to protect the Managed Approach from critics like you? It doesn't need protecting. It's got a license.'

'That's the same question I've asked myself, Inspector, and I'm no nearer answering it. The one thing I'm certain of, and I've heard locals say this, is that some of your fellow officers are pimping prostitutes.'

Sant raised his bushy black brows, pretending to be surprised. 'Go on.'

Dobson shook his curls. 'The last thing I want to do is make unfounded accusations.'

'I'm all ears. You've nothing to fear. Speak your mind.'

'Forgive me, but I'd rather wait before naming individuals.'

Sant reached for his phone with the intention of showing the screenshots of Benn and Tufail, but he stuffed it back into his pocket – such a move would only worsen Dobson's capiophobia.

'The one person I *am* prepared to call out,' Dobson went on, 'is not a copper though he might be in cahoots, if you know what I mean. Countless folks tell me this man's a predator with his hands deep in serious muck.'

'Give me a name.'

'Donohue.'

Sant sighed anticlimactically. 'A veteran offender.'

'I've heard the same,' Dobson said. 'Once a pervert, always a pervert.'

'Does that saying apply to you?'

The councillor's face reddened, not for the first time. 'I was in a pickle with junkies and crooks, as I've explained, and it'll never happen again.'

'Everyone deserves a second chance,' Sant said. 'Even Donohue deserved one. But his two lives might be up. What've you heard?'

'All sorts. He's been seen in skateboard parks and coming out of shops carrying bottles of cider intended for underage drinkers, mostly girls.'

Sant dug into his short-term memory. 'I saw Donohue campaigning with you and your SAVE OUR EYES friends at the public consultation a few days back.'

Dobson tensed his biceps. 'Heaven knows why he was

there. The MA is perfect for perverts like him. Why he wants it shutting down beats me.'

'Don't you feel uncomfortable having Donohue as an advocate?'

'What's that supposed to mean?'

Sant saw he'd touched a nerve but felt like probing further. 'Whether you like it or not, he's supporting the single-issue crusade you've gambled your political future on.'

'Donohue's nothing to do with me,' the councillor said, striving not to raise his voice. 'You may not believe it, but the truth is I have a very low regard for the SAVE OUR EYES contingent. I prefer the moderates. The LISTENING WELL campaign offers a much better mouthpiece for Holbeck.'

'A better vehicle for your public image too.'

'That's a cheap shot.'

Sant held up his hand in semi-apology before asking: 'Have you reported Donohue?'

'That's what I'm doing now.'

'Great.'

'But I'd prefer you to be there when I testify. I'm anxious, as you can tell, and can't trust anyone at the moment, coppers included.'

'You trust me?'

Dobson closed his eyes and relaxed his arm muscles. 'I feel I can take you into my confidence, yes.'

Sant got up to leave. 'I'll do my best to be with you when you need me, though rest assured, I'll place you in the hands of a totally trustworthy officer with absolutely no connection to your past.'

They shook hands and Sant watched the butch young man exit the market at speed, his head rotating one way and another on the look-out for stomping feet pointing his way.

* * *

'It's clear,' said the inspector as he arrived back in Hardaker's boardroom, late but not very late this time. 'We're dealing with more than one sex attacker. Popescu targets men only.'

'He may've attacked women,' Appleyard persisted.

'We've nothing to prove it,' Sant continued. 'Whoever raped Ava Yock is a different beast who may well have attacked other vulnerable girls.'

Hardaker coughed. 'Well, the DNA evidence gets Popescu off the hook in respect of Yock, so we're back to square one in her case.'

Appleyard shook her head. 'We're not going soft on Popescu, no way.'

'Certainly not, Stephanie. He'll be charged with assaulting Ivor Danby. That offence alone will see him locked up for years. And we might be able to pin him to other attacks, so no, he's not getting off lightly.'

'Needle-spiking an officer won't do him any good either,' Sant added.

'How's DC Capstick anyway?' asked Hardaker.

'Last I heard, he was still among us.'

'Where do we start?' enquired Appleyard, iPad in hand and keen to get down to business.

Sant removed his black tie and loosened the collar of his shirt. 'I have a suspect, actually.'

'Since when?'

'About twenty minutes ago.' Sant sat down and wiped sweat from his forehead with a handkerchief. 'I bumped into Councillor Dobson this morning. He wanted to talk in private. We met for lunch.'

'There's something fishy about him,' Appleyard said.

'I'm not his biggest fan either,' Sant said, 'but anyone who needs votes for their livelihood must struggle to keep their nose clean.'

'So he's turned informer to get your vote, has he?' the chief inspector joked.

Sant eyed Appleyard. 'You'd make a fine criminal profiler.'

'I already have the qualification.'

Hardaker combed his red goatee. 'What did Dobson have to say?'

Sant folded his tie neatly and set it down on the oval table. 'He thinks one of the locals is involved in the recent sex attacks. A certain Jeremy Donohue.'

'Didn't you put that man behind bars a few years ago?' Hardaker said.

'I led the investigation into his relations with kids at the school where he was a caretaker. He did five years for trafficking. Should've been ten.'

'Surely if he's offended before,' Appleyard put in, 'we'll have his DNA.'

Hardaker swiped his Pro. 'We would, and there was no match with Yock's attacker.'

'But he might be acting as an accomplice,' Sant said. 'Aiding and abetting.'

'You think it was Donohue that Popescu saw in Lovell Park with Klaudia and Lydia?' Appleyard probed.

Sant nodded. 'Certain things add up. The man Popescu saw had a limp on his left side. Donohue's left leg has never recovered from a car crash twenty years ago. He limps noticeably.'

'Any other identifiers?' Hardaker queried.

'It's the same modus operandi as before,' Sant went on. 'Ply the girls with sweet alcohol and exploit them when they're drunk.'

'What about the dog?' asked Appleyard.

Sant pinched his nose. 'That's a question I've been medi-
tating over. Donohue didn't have a dog before, but maybe he's
using a four-legged friend as a magnet to get his prey.'

'We should knock on his door and check out the dog angle,'
the chief inspector suggested.

'Especially if it starts woofing,' Sant said.

Hardaker tugged at a ginger lock. 'If Donohue's the accomplice it begs the question: who are the clients paying him for a
ready supply of trafficked girls?'

Sant thought of Tufail and Benn, then said: 'Incidentally,
I've heard rumours about one or two of ours abusing their
authority.'

Appleyard gasped. 'Seriously? Who?'

'Not enough proof to name names yet. You will be the first
to know if I have.'

'But you cannot think twice when faced with serious allegations,' Appleyard said.

'And the officers in question will need to be suspended
immediately,' Hardaker added. 'They will, of course, be exoner-
ated pending an investigation confirming their innocence.'

'Bullshit,' Appleyard remarked.

'I'm simply explaining the process, Stephanie.'

'From a male point of view,' she grumbled as she switched
off her iPad and folded her arms.

Sant cast a worried look at Appleyard. 'Give me a day or
two and I'll report names if everything checks out.'

Hardaker glanced from one colleague to another. 'I'd prefer
you to be upfront now, Carl. Stephanie is right. We must act
fast.'

'I'm no slanderer,' said Sant. 'I can't accuse any Dick or
Harry of a serious offence without solid facts. We wouldn't take
that stance with the public and we shouldn't with ourselves.'

'But you're sure about Donohue,' Appleyard continued, 'so

if officers are abusing their positions, maybe we should squeeze the names out of Donohue.'

'Have you enough on Donohue to make an arrest?' Hardaker asked.

'Not quite,' Sant replied, 'but we should put a tail on him, and his dog if he still has one.'

Hardaker let go of his beard. 'I'll grant permission, and what's more, I'll throw myself in the frontline. I've been talking to Chief Constable Gilligan and I'll let you both into a secret, strictly confidential.' Appleyard and Sant nodded in sequence. 'It so happens that the chief constable himself is aware of unprofessional practice among a pocketful of officers.'

'What sort?' a wide-eyed Appleyard said, reigniting her iPad as if it might tell her the answer.

'Gilligan has received a couple of complaints and he's taking the matter very seriously. These are not wolf-whistle grievances or anything of that sort.'

'Popescu mentioned some corrupt officers he'd overheard in Lovell Park,' Appleyard put in. 'We should pursue that line of enquiry.'

Sant pointed a finger at her iPad. 'Find out who was patrolling the park last Wednesday night, pretend you know something you don't, see what they're prepared to own up to.'

Appleyard turned to Hardaker. 'Have we spare capacity to shadow Donohue?'

'Just,' said the superintendent, 'though we're a man down. The last one Carl took on a tail job is still paying for his troubles.'

'Capstick will be right as rain before you know it,' Sant countered with a hint of irritation.

'I'd help out,' Appleyard said, 'though I guess I should focus my energies on Yock.'

Sant creased his brows. 'I thought you wanted to wait on the missing person angle.'

'I did, but now it feels urgent. No time like the present.'

Sant couldn't believe what he was hearing. Appleyard was listening to his advice and following it – eventually.

'Fine by me,' Hardaker said. 'I'll put together a team, Stephanie. And it's worth talking to Klaudia Armitage again, though no rush. You've a heavy load as it is, plus Klaudia's still in recovery mode.'

The chief inspector reached for her suit jacket. 'She's dealing with the trauma by increments. She'd be hard-pushed to identify Donohue anyway – that dope was extremely potent.'

Hardaker offered a parting smile. 'To action stations, colleagues. We've done half a job bringing Popescu to book. Let's put an end to these assaults for good.'

Sant thought the Chiefman was pushing the boundaries of realism, but he left the meeting feeling upbeat despite the grim work to come. Perhaps his superiors weren't as bad as all that. And perhaps humanity lived in Appleyard yet, even if it reached the surface sporadically like those North Sea jellyfish still bobbing in his nightmares.

* * *

Afternoon was fast becoming evening, these early spring days still brief and unrepentant. It was time to catch up on the iceman affair, as Popescu called it. Sant crossed the threshold of the morgue and observed Dr Wisdom with fascination as he meticulously extracted samples of hair with sharp tweezers before dropping them into plastic evidence bags. Two big holes carved out of the ever-decreasing ice cube were being used by Wisdom to find the least complicated route to each cadaver so that ends of fingers and facial tissues could be removed for analysis.

'What do we know?'

The pathologist carefully slotted the tweezers in the correct section of a sterilised tray before lifting two orange autopsy cards from his breast pocket and scanning the words scribbled on them. 'The first question is a why question.'

'Why were they frozen?'

'Right.' He stretched gloves over his withered fingers before examining the back of an ear. 'As I said to your team earlier, freezing as a method for hiding dead people is unusual. There are only two reasons why someone might choose it.'

'To stop the smell.'

'Yes, and the other?' Sant shook his head. 'To disguise the time of death, though usually the perpetrator removes their victim from the frozen state after a few weeks or months.'

Sant looked intensely at Wisdom. 'You've found something out, haven't you?'

'Yes, my boy. We're dealing with a different timescale vis-à-vis these two.'

'Meaning?'

'Let me show you.' Wisdom poked a telescopic pointer through both holes and aimed it at the neck of each corpse. 'Thin nylon cords of the same type. Visible bruising beneath the cords. Evidence of petechiae around the eyes. These features all add up to ligature strangulation.'

'Were they strangled at the same time?' Sant asked.

'Impossible to say, but I suspect not. I've done some preliminary tests on the tissue cells from the hands. Decomposition is more noticeable in one victim than the other. That could mean a number of things when determining how and when these women were frozen, and certainly, it rules out the possibility they died together.'

'Were they both dead before they were frozen?'

'Let me show you something else.' He aimed the pointer through the ice at the nose of the corpse on top. 'Froth from the nostrils is visible. I'll need to test it before I'm certain, though it's almost definitely mucous.'

Sant waited for an explanation, but Wisdom remained deep in thought. 'Layman's terms?'

Wisdom glared at Sant as if he'd sneaked up from behind. 'The presence of mucous means this victim was frozen soon after death. Froth persists in the airways of a recently deceased body even at sub-zero temperatures. But the victim below shows no sign of nasal froth. It's been a hell of a job getting to her, by the way, and I'm not prepared to tip the ice upside down or I might compromise the evidence.'

'No nasal froth, you said?'

'Correct. Absence of mucous indicates she died at least two or three days before she was frozen.'

'So time of death is unclear, though probably years and not the same for the two deceased.'

Wisdom yanked off his gloves and discarded them in a pedal bin. 'That's my educated guess, Inspector, but nothing more than that.'

Sant chuckled. 'I'll take your word for it on that basis, Grant. All of which means these ancient bodies are nothing to do with the crimes of Nicolae Popescu or other recent assaults carried out by person or persons unknown.'

'You know more than me on that front, my boy.'

'And then there's the great unanswered question: why did two people in a Land Rover plonk an ice coffin in the middle of nowhere?'

The pathologist raised his shoulders indifferently. 'Not my area of expertise.'

'What else do you expect to find?' Sant enquired.

The pathologist snorted. 'Very tactful of you. You're almost as inquisitive as our chief constable.'

'So Old Man Gilligan's been snooping around here again?'

'Hasn't he just,' said Wisdom, pointing his pince-nez specs at Sant. 'Gilligan's taking a personal interest in the case. But as I said to him in my calmest Welsh drawl, our patience will be rewarded once the thawing is over because the advantage of a frozen cadaver compared to the usual type is the extent of preservation.'

Sant looked down at the corpses. 'They've hardly altered.'

'Right, my boy. If you'll allow me to get technical for a tick, when ice crystals form, they fix water in intracellular spaces which cause cell shrinkage but not much else, so even if a frozen cadaver goes through partial thawing and refreezing, it will stay in good condition and only begin to decay from the outside in. Unlike you and me and everyone else in the tropical world who will, sure as the Earth is round, decay from the inside out.'

'Run that by me again,' Sant said, 'in the warmer surroundings of a pub.'

'Ah, you've reminded me. You want my recollections of Jim Lackey.'

'Meet in an hour at The George?'

Wisdom dropped his specs in his breast pocket. 'I should be done with the tweezers by then.'

'And keep those blow torches burning,' Sant grinned.

'Patience, my boy. Science cannot be rushed!'

* * *

The George stood on the corner of Park Street and Great George Street facing the Gothic frontage of the original infirmary. The pub doubled up as a cheap hostel for tourists on a shoestring, but despite the carpet coming away from the floor and the upholstery flaking, this little slice of antiquity was teeming with customers thirsty for booze after a hard day's labour.

This humble dwelling bore the stamp of Scottish architect George Corson, from whom the pub took its name. Sant had read an article about Corson and imagined the great man revelling with his ale-drinking companions over a century ago as they drafted blueprints of the Grand Theatre, Central Library, St Edmund's Church, Lawnswood Cemetery, and other institutions of this Victorian city they had so cannily forged.

Sant order a pint of Stella, a small lager shandy and a packet of prawn cocktail crisps at the four-sided bar complete with four-sided faux grandfather clock. He passed the Stella to Wisdom. The sour stout he'd had at lunchtime was playing on his mind again, which explained the sweet shandy and salty crisps.

'Give me the low-down on Lackey,' Sant said as they found a vacant table jammed in an alcove that had once housed an old fireplace, now sealed over for posterity.

Wisdom slid his pint onto a beer mat and folded his arms in reflection. 'Very quiet but very determined. When I started on the force, he was a senior detective with his fingers in more pies than you'd care to imagine. There were plenty of men above him, Gilligan one of them, but nobody messed with him. He had a confidence about him. Colleagues – even those high in rank – thought of him as untouchable.'

'Why was that?' asked Sant as he ripped open the packet of crisps and swallowed a couple.

'It was to do with his previous job.' The pathologist licked beer froth from his upper lip. 'If I said *C3 Division of the Home Office*, would that mean anything?'

Sant sipped on his shandy. 'A forerunner of the criminal cases review board, wasn't it?'

'A bit of a sham, actually, but at least C3 pioneered an avenue for appeal in the event of subsequent evidence indicating a wrongful conviction.'

'Wasn't C3 made up of the Old Bill?'

'Not quite. The board consisted of civil servants who appointed senior police to investigate other constabularies. That's where Lackey entered the picture.'

Sant tilted his head quizzically. 'I thought he was one of us.'

'But before he joined us, he was one of them,' Wisdom said. 'Jim Lackey reached the rank of chief inspector in South Yorkshire Police and was brought to the attention of someone at the Home Office who decided he should join the C3 team investigating us.'

'South Yorkshire was forever looking into complaints directed our way,' Sant remarked.

'Right, my boy. There were four of them if my memory serves me right. Lackey must have impressed the most, ruffling feathers hardly at all but just enough to appear like the impartial outsider.' Wisdom coughed for effect. 'And lo and behold, a career promotion and transfer to West Yorkshire came hot on the heels of the C3 whitewashing.'

'Which cases did he oversee for C3?'

Wisdom guzzled a mouthful of lager, then said: 'Only one as far as I remember. You see, a C3 review was a last resort and rarely approved by the Home Office unless evidence of a wrongful conviction was exceptionally compelling and genuinely new, that is, not previously considered in the original trial.'

'Go on,' Sant said, a few hairs tingling on the back of his neck.

'In 1977 a teenage lass got murdered. The man charged

with the killing was locked up for life but the evidence that convicted him was mostly circumstantial. The whole investigation was bundled by all accounts.'

'Was the victim called Rita Mitchell by any chance?'

Wisdom raised his pint. 'You've saved me a prolonged headache, Inspector. I've been trying to put a name to the affair ever since you mentioned Lackey the other day. Bravo.'

The hairs on Sant's neck were fully grown by now. 'Did you do the forensic work back then?'

The pathologist took a long, slow swig before shaking his head. 'In 1977 I was studying my trade and living out punk fantasies between lectures.'

'So how come you recall the C3?'

'Because that went on years later. In the mid-eighties I think it was. The case was still a hot topic after all that time. From what I recall, too, Rita's killer wasn't identified straight away. It took a couple of years before the trial began. 1979 from memory. What's your interest?'

Sant emptied his glass and wanted something stronger, but there was too much on his mind to let alcohol dull the senses. 'The spot where Rita Mitchell was killed is a stone's throw from the Woodhall Road crime scene.'

'Where the cadavers were found,' Wisdom added.

'Exactly.'

'And you think there's a connection?'

'I don't know.'

'A connection with Lackey's suicide perhaps?'

'Possibly, though the man topped himself a few months back.'

'Before the ice coffin got dumped on us.'

Sant nodded. 'What do you recall about the C3 review?'

The doctor savoured another mouthful of Stella, then said: 'Confusion was my lasting impression. Some of the evidence got lost over the years. Witnesses for the prosecution were changed at the last moment and statements left out altogether because they contradicted the prosecution's version of events.'

'Sounds like standard practice,' Sant remarked.

'But the problem was the files. They were all over the place when Lackey and company arrived on the scene. Word got around they were tearing their hair out. But one of ours stepped in and brought some order to the chaos. Inspector Judith Skidmore was her name. Her and Jim must've hit it off because a few months later they tied the knot.'

Sant nodded again. 'I heard that she overtook her husband as they climbed up the ranks of North Yorkshire Police.'

'I'm not surprised. She was destined to be a higher-up. Tunnel vision, she had. Complete determination to succeed every time. I hardly encountered her but those who did told me to steer clear. She had a reputation for being ruthless if you put a foot wrong.'

The inspector folded his arms in thought. 'So she must've been livid at having to tidy up the mess in the aftermath of Rita Mitchell's murder.'

'I assume so, my boy, and what didn't help was that the man who'd been found guilty of killing Rita had no shortage of backers hell bent on proving his innocence. There was even a TV crew filming a documentary, which triggered the decision to bring out the C3 team in the first instance.'

'Those TV folks must've known a thing or two,' Sant concluded. 'The man found guilty was called Simon Coyle and he was eventually released after his conviction was quashed on appeal.'

'Another blast from the past. Poor Mr Coyle. A prime victim if ever there was one.'

'And to rub salt in the wounds,' Sant added, 'he died a few years after his release.'

'Not our finest hour,' said Wisdom after draining his glass. 'Not by any stretch, my boy.'

* * *

Rather than return to HQ, Sant pointed his Fiesta in the direction of the Harehills address under Jeremy Donohue's record. The night was strangling the life out of an already dreary Sunday, igniting one streetlight after another. The streets, barely illuminated by their lights, boasted exotic names – Cherry Row, Rosebud Walk – and the back-to-back houses became more densely packed as Sant weaved his car deeper into the Harehills Triangle.

It was called the Triangle because that's what it looked like on a map: two diverging main roads underscored by residential routes crossing from one road to the other. As he headed north to the apex of the Triangle, the street names exhibited London-esque influences: Bayswater Crescent, Edgware Avenue, Bexley Grove. The intention was a good one – here lay a respectable neighbourhood aspiring to splendour. But the aspiration was crumbling like most of the buildings in this part of town.

Sant could see it for himself: abandoned cars with missing tyres and all their windows smashed in, broken glass everywhere. And that was before he'd surveyed the houses. More back-to-back terraces were crammed into this city than anywhere else in the country – hardly something worth celebrating.

They were called back-to-backs because they backed onto each other. If you were unfortunate enough to live in one, you had adjoining neighbours on both sides and directly behind. In other words, you lived in half a terraced house surrounded by fellow tinned sardines.

Sant parked outside the property he was looking for, trapped between other red-brick terraces on a short narrow approach called Rossall Road almost at the tip of the Triangle. Two skinny boys were showing off their moves, flipping skateboards high in the air and timing a standing jump to position them perfectly atop the decks as feet and timber slammed down on broken tarmac.

The door of number 7, like the other front doors, spilled out directly onto the pavement. Sant knocked hard and waited. No sound. He knocked again. Nobody answered. The windows were covered by curtains, but Sant noticed lights on upstairs.

The skaters were out of sight now. He took a handkerchief from his inside pocket, placed it over the tatty handle, pressed down with the palm of his hand. The door was locked.

A voice piped up to his left. 'What ya up ta?'

Sant squinted his eyes and spotted an elderly lady on her doorstep pointing a walking stick at his face. 'Hello, I want to speak to your neighbour.'

'Mr Donohue?'

'Have you seen him?'

'Five minutes back. He's in there somewhere.'

The inspector looked up at the lighted window. 'I reckoned he might be.'

'Throwing out wots in that watering can of his.'

'Watering can? I thought these houses had no gardens.'

'They don't.' The white-haired woman shook her stick at him. 'He's got a winta garden indoors and when he opens them windas, it friggin' reeks.'

'Cannabis?'

'A full functionin' farm. Ya a buyer?'

'I'm police.'

She directed her stick skywards. 'I'm telling ya now, every square inch of that dive is blooming with weed. It's about time he woz called to account. Prices have gone up someut shockin'. Daylight robbery if ya ask me.'

Sant turned to the door of number 7 and had a thought. 'Maybe I should try around the back.'

'Good luck with that, Mr Policeman. These houses don't ave backs.'

'Of course,' Sant said, trying not to kick himself. 'I'll knock louder. Good night.'

The neighbour retreated slowly, walking stick clattering between door and frame as she gestured a reluctant farewell.

Sant decided there was no point in knocking a third time. Instead, he returned to his Fiesta, made a three-point turn in five (the street really *was* narrow), took a right and glided down the next road, counted to fifty before swinging around and back on himself. He hit the accelerator, then the brakes as he turned sharply into Rossall Road and pulled up at the spot he'd parked in before.

The lights had gone out at number 7 and Donohue was out too, hastily locking up his cannabis farm. He glared at Sant's headlights before leaping from his doorstep and legging it into darkness.

'Afta the cretin!' shouted the biddy next door as she flung open her door and jabbed her stick vaguely in the direction of Donohue's travel.

Sant teared down the street and took the next one – named Nice Street believe it or not – before coming to the junction with Harehills Lane. Leaving his headlights on and engine running, he abandoned his car and gave chase. He noticed Donohue dodging traffic as he crossed the main road, a motorcycle coming within a few feet of catapulting him into the air. Sant got lucky. A gap between advancing lorries was just wide enough to gamble on. He took a couple of steps towards the first lorry and, as soon as it went by, sprinted to miss the second by a hare's breath, horn blasting a stark send-off in retrospect.

The opposite lane was less scary but no less busy. Sant let two cars go and held his arms aloft at an oncoming bus. The driver signalled and Sant skipped across in one piece. Donohue was still alive too but limping badly. It was the same limp Popescu had described. His left leg wouldn't last much longer.

The inspector took a gulp of oxygen as he prepared to perform his second rugby tackle in under a week, but he needn't have bothered. Donohue caught the foot attached to his good leg against the edge of a flagstone and hurtled into a pile of vegetable crates stacked outside an Indian grocery store.

* * *

Sant lifted him upright, pressed against his back and pushed him firmly against a drainpipe spitting rainwater into a rusty iron grate. 'Someone tells me you've been up to your dirty tricks again, Donohue. You'd better come clean or I'm going to make life awfully difficult.'

Donohue puffed hard and mustered a croaky response: 'Leave off me. Ya screwed up my life once already. Not this time, sunshine. Ya got nothing on me.'

'Why don't we kick off with drug dealing and take it from there?'

The grey-haired man breathed deeply. 'What ya want from me?'

Sant cuffed his wrists. 'The truth. And nothing but.'

'Bout wot?'

'Klaudia Armitage. Maybe you don't recognise the name, Donohue, but you were seen with her in Lovell Park a few nights ago. We found her the next morning in a terrible state, battered something rotten.'

'I dun know what ya on about.'

'Cut the crap. I've a witness who can identify you from a mile off. What's more, the CCTV officers had a field day following your scruffy mug around the park. You're public enemy number one.'

'I neva touched the girl,' he squealed as Sant gripped grey hair and tugged hard.

'You're facing a long stint in Armley Gaol, Donohue. You might not get out alive.'

'If ya had owt on me, I'd be locked up already,' the man muttered.

'We've got plenty. Evidence of grooming. Know what that means? It means you're serving up girls on a plate for someone else's perverted pleasure.'

'Prove it.'

'Don't worry, I will.' Sant reached for his phone and started to make a call. 'First, though, you'll be charged with production of a controlled drug.'

'Wait! Give me a sec.' Donohue swivelled his neck far enough around so Sant could see the corners of his small pupils. 'How about I grass up – I mean, tell ya who me client is and then ya go easy on me.'

It was the inspector's turn to think. This sort of request felt awkward every time. Doing a deal with the criminal underworld was never a sensible idea, but often it was the better of two options. The other – no deal and no information – was worse. Besides, what was wrong with a spliff or two? Weren't states all over the world legalising it anyway?

'I can't let you off entirely, Donohue, but I'll give you a day's amnesty. Clean up your house and get rid of everything you shouldn't have in there before a uniform gets a tip off and comes knocking.'

Donohue nodded frantically. 'Point taken, and this is all I know, understand?'

'Go on,' Sant said impatiently, wiping sweat from his eyes with his overused hankie.

'The client took the girl off me hands. He woz wearing a hoodie and kept his face outta view. I don't know defo who he is.'

'But you've got an idea.'

'I fink. Not to speak to. I've seen him around though. He's ard to miss.'

'You mean, he's a big man?'

'Not big in that way. He's well known. A bit of a crusader. Ya seen him round too, no doubt. The local council leader.'

Sant let go of his quarry, arranged the vegetable crates scattered beneath him, sat down as best he could. 'I thought you couldn't see his face.'

'No, but I seen his general demeana. Oh, and I seen his credit card too.'

'He paid you by card?'

'No, cash. Not a lot in case ya wondering. Anyway, last time I saw him, he took cash out of his pocket and accidently dropped his card. I'm quick, ya see. I bent down to pick it up and spotted the name on't front. Mr R Dobson. He snatched the card off me in a flash. Knew I'd seen it. Aven't seen him since.'

Sant clamped a toothpick between his jaws. 'How many times have you done business with Dobson?'

'I couldn't say offhand.'

'Roughly?'

'Maybe ten.'

'Ten?'

'Maybe.'

'And you're sure it's him every time?'

Donohue rotated his neck a little further. 'He looks the same, for sure. Wears the same hoodie. Light grey, though it's always dark when I meet him so I can't be exact on't colour. There's a logo on't chest but it's too small to make out. The string around the collar is all frayed up and there's a paint stain on one sleeve.'

Sant worked the toothpick against his gnashers. 'Why does he come to you? There's a perfectly legal brothel in town, even if he wants it closed down.'

'He's scared shitless someone'll notice him in Holbeck.'

'He told you that?'

'No, but that must be it. He's got a rep to look after.'

'Not anymore. His political career is all but over.' Sant chewed on the toothpick, trying to absorb what Donohue was telling him. After a while he said: 'I've worked it out.'

'Wot?' the man said, still facing the drainpipe in a show of obedience.

'Dobson and Donohue. Partners in sex crime.'

'Wot?'

'This campaign of yours to shut the brothel was nothing to do with public service,' Sant went on. 'It was about making sure the girls had nowhere safe to work, and the punters had no alternative but to go underground. You two pimps had a part- nership going that stood to earn a fortune as soon as the Managed Approach was no more.'

Donohue shook his head. 'Ya don't know what ya talking about. Ya fink I'm doing this for kicks. Ya cunt be more wrong. I wanna to get away from the past. But now I'm forced to – what ya call it? – groom and supply. I don't ave much choice in't matta.'

Sant spat out his toothpick. 'If you don't like what you're doing, walk into your nearest police station and tell all.'

The man started to cry, tears gushing from his tiny eyes. 'My world ain't your world.' Water dripped from his cheeks and nose. 'Once ya labelled a paedo, there's no way to shake that label off. Any int of me turning rogue and I'll be six feet under.'

Sant almost felt sorry for his prey. 'But you're still accepting money for your little operation, Donohue. How much does Dobson pay you?'

'Enuff to get by.'

'Rubbish,' the inspector scoffed. 'You don't take risks for pocket money, Donohue. You must be a wealthy gent.'

'Not a bit. I earn enuff to feed meself and me dog.'

'Ah, that faithful mutt of yours. I bet he's as high as a kite right now, and just cute enough to entice gullible kids.'

Donohue's sobs turned to spasms. 'My Scamper's an ickle charmer. I'm one ugly son of a bitch but Scamper's a chick magnet if ever there woz one.'

'As well as the liquorice you add to the cider.'

'There's that too,' the man giggled.

Sant wanted to bust his nose into tiny fragments of bone, split those wet lips and let the blood stream down this chinless coward. He thought of Simon Coyle and other miscarriages of justice – the fact that Donohue wasn't locked up for life was a scandal of the highest order. He resisted the urge to mete out his own justice and instead made a call to a civvy who took down location details.

'Ya woz giving me amnesty time,' Donohue piped up.

'I was, but the more I speak to you, the more I realise your truth. Once a pervert, always a pervert.'

Donohue turned around to face his captor. 'I've fessed up to nowt. The way ya've treated me, I won't forget this.'

Sant stood up sharply and rolled the man's head so he was facing the drainpipe again. 'I can deal with a snitch who does drugs, but a snitch who fucks around with children isn't getting a jelly tot out of me.'

A marked car pulled in at the kerb, blue lights flashing a hollow victory. Two uniforms got out and one of them read Donohue his rights on the charge of cultivating cannabis. The grey-haired lout was guided into the back seat and belted up for good measure.

He bowed his head and called out: 'Watch ya back, Inspector. I'll be free by the end of the year if not before.'

'In which case I'll buy you a Christmas tree. It'll save you growing one in your front room.'

Sant watched the car leave and his adrenalin began to drop, but the hormone had acted as a painkiller because when he gazed down at his right shoe, he saw blood. And then the agony registered. He'd done worse than stub his little toe. The sock inside the shoe was soaked, the red stuff everywhere. A trip to hospital – becoming a habit – beckoned. There's always a bright side though – it was a chance to catch up with Capstick.

* * *

It was after eleven-thirty when Sant finally got seen by a senior practitioner – doctors didn't exist anymore. His little toenail had been severed and there was a deep cut between that toe and the one next to it. The good news: no bone damage. He was bandaged up and given codeine to relieve the aching. Donohue's finest leaf would have worked just as well.

He hobbled out of the casualty department and made his way to the ward where his partner was laid up. Capstick looked no different to before, still three sheets to the wind, his body recovering sluggishly from the shock of that used needle.

'Something's changed with him,' said Holdsworth, who had

been at her boyfriend's side all evening and had hardly spoken to him, such was his cold and drowsy humour.

'What's changed?' Sant asked.

'It's like a poison inside him. He's not the Brad I know.'

'It'll wear off. The tests found nothing other than the dope in his bloodstream.'

'But a mishap like this can do strange things to people,' Holdsworth continued. 'It's a psychological thing. Brad's head is not right. He's been like this for forty-eight hours or more.'

'He's gone mad?'

The detective sergeant flicked a stray hair from her olive-skinned cheek. 'He's as calm as ever, but all the emotional energy has drained away. I don't think he'll be back to work for ages.'

Sant contemplated the sight of her chiselled jaw. 'I'll knock him into shape, Holdsworth. Just you wait and see.'

Holdsworth smiled. 'He'll need you, Carl. You make a great pair.'

'It's about time I was leaving.'

'I'll get out of here too. For a short while. Hungry?'

They ate burgers and fries at a takeaway on Woodhouse Lane. A quick fix but no gourmet fare. Sant enjoyed eating with Holdsworth because there were no awkward moments weighing up table manners. Holdsworth was just as messy and ferocious at munching as he was.

'Shall I drop you back?' Sant said after they'd eaten.

'I'm not ready yet,' she said after a moment's deliberation. 'But I've nowhere else to go. Maybe you can show me your place. I've never had the pleasure.'

Half an hour later they were watching the latest Netflix hit and scoffing cream crackers with microwave-melted Stilton while sipping a white wine he'd unearthed from the bottom of the fridge. The drama was worse than mediocre. Sant was just happy to have company for a change. Very few people had seen the bare walls of his flat. Even his sons seldom had a sleepover with their oddball dad. It was a quaint hole for a hermit like him.

'We should do this more often,' Sant said as the credits rolled. 'Bring Capstick along and let him to do the cooking since he's not doing much else these days.'

Holdsworth's face went a little pale as she glanced at her phone. 'I've stayed too long. I should get back to Brad. Did I bring my coat?' she asked, bending over the back of the sofa.

Sant couldn't help but admire her nimble figure as she reached behind. No wonder Capstick didn't mind the age difference.

'You had your cardigan on, I think.'

'Where's that got to?' She was slightly tipsy as she searched around for it.

'Listen, why don't you stay here for the night,' he said as he retrieved the cardigan from between sofa cushions. 'I've had one glass too many and can't risk driving.'

'I'll grab an Uber.'

'There's a spare mattress under my bed,' Sant insisted. 'I'll bring it out here.'

Holdsworth shook her head. 'I should be by Brad's side. He needs me.'

'Not tonight, Holdsworth. One night without you will do him no harm. Besides, he's sleeping like a baby. He won't notice your absence.' Sant fetched the mattress and placed it on a rug beside the TV. 'Don't set an alarm. You're exhausted. Get up when you want.'

'It might be afternoon,' smiled Holdsworth, her fine angular features accentuated by the beam. 'I'm doing the late shift tomorrow.'

'Stay as long as you like.'

'Thanks for this, Carl. Care for a hug?'

'Of course.'

'There's a first time for everything after all,' Holdsworth said as she squeezed him tight, then released her clasp.

Sant felt a shock wave run through him as her silky hand touched the base of his back, the warmth of an erection taking hold. He stood statuesque for a while, basking in the thrill of embrace, before coming to his senses and realising she'd moved on.

'We should hug more often,' he said as he looked around him.

'Sounds like a plan. Good night.'

She tumbled onto the mattress and was asleep in an instant.

8

HE TOSSED AND TURNED ALL NIGHT, AND WHEN HE finally gave up trying to sleep, Sant fathomed the reason for his restlessness. Rory Dobson was front and centre of his troubles. It was time for a Monday morning wake-up call to check Donohue's version of events. How deep was Dobson up to his neck in hanky-panky?

He put the kettle on and saw Holdsworth huddled on the mattress, her permed brown hair covering her face, arms spreadeagled, one hand supporting the back of her head. He recalled the bodies in the ice and came closer to make certain she was breathing. Then he placed two slices of bread in the toaster and when they sprang up she stirred and said something unintelligible before returning to the metronomic breaths of deep slumber.

Sant had done a bit of digging the day before and discovered that Dobson rented a high-end apartment in the Granary Wharf area. The flat was located on the nineteenth floor of the Candle House, a cylindrical tower on the waterside.

Known locally as 'The Candlestick' because the misaligned

oblong windows staggering up the building in five-floor blocks looked like melting wax trickling down its sides, alternative rumour had it the uneven arrangement was intended to make the building appear as if it was tilting – not unlike the Leaning Tower of Pisa. As it turned out, no such appearance had been manufactured despite some finishing touches – textured brick-work, heavy-duty paint splodges – smacking of desperation in pursuit of an architectural fantasy. Try as the planners might, Candle House was no wonder of the modern world.

Sant took the lift which, mercifully, travelled vertically up the building with no funny gimmicks. The nineteenth floor was at the top of the tower and seemed deserted, the walls and front doors of the apartments gathering a thick coating of dust as if the rooms were too expensive to be lived in.

He knocked three times on the councillor's door – the only one that looked like it was in use. Then he noticed something odd: the edge of the door was not flush to the wood frame surrounding it. For the second time in as many days, the inspector removed a handkerchief from his inside pocket and placed it on someone else's door handle. This time he got a result, the handle giving way under minimal pressure. The place wasn't locked – not even fully closed.

He lightly pushed the door ajar and took a single step over the threshold. The hall boasted beach wood-effect flooring and six spotlights dotted along the ceiling. To the left were floor-to-wall fitted wardrobes and shoe cabinets placed at an angle against the grain of the circular wall.

'Anyone at home!'

No response. But he could hear voices coming through the open door of one of the bedrooms to the right. It was the room nearest the entrance and Dobson had converted it into a tasteful study. A long desk was overlooked by Ikea bookshelves stacked with odds and ends albeit very few books. The desk showed off a shiny new MacBook Pro, a PC gaming set-up, two tablets, and a phone – the same phone Sant had seen Dobson holding at lunch the previous day. Further back, a white DAB radio had its telescopic aerial pointing up to receive a news bulletin. He used his elbow to switch it off, then checked his watch. It was a minute past six.

After a quick scan, he left the study and called out once more. Silence. Not expecting to give anyone a heart attack, he wandered past another bedroom, door wide open. Darkness cloaked the musty smell inside. Sant didn't bother to turn on the light. It was clear that Dobson wasn't in. He made a cursory search of the other rooms before coming to the main living space. It was deceptively big, with fitted kitchen units and hidden pockets of curved and angled territory fashioned out of the round expanse.

Seen from above, Sant mused, it would look like a wedge of cake, expanding outwards. An apartment of this size would fetch two thousand pounds per month, service charges excluded. Dobson had said his only job was with the council. Hardly a handsome salary. Surely other funds were required for a swanky place like this.

The inspector retraced his steps to the hall and was about to leave, the darkened bedroom catching his attention like a misplaced afterthought. He switched on the light with his elbow and was greeted by an ornate metal-frame bed planted in the centre. He was no expert on bed sizes, but this beast was twice as wide as his own humble sack. The other feature that drew him in was tougher to define. It was an effect of the whole get-up rather than any single part. The opulent decoration was akin to a classic Hollywood film scene, three cameras on tripods reinforcing the movie-set feel.

Porn. Sant spoke the word under his breath. He turned off the light as if this might shake off the fusty scent. Then he walked into the room, drew back the blackout curtains, opened a window, looked again at the unmade bed, and noticed a pair of handcuffs attached to one of the posts. A long piece of rope was hanging over the headboard. Two brown teddy bears. A blindfold on a silk pillow. All eye-opening, though in another sense, all very predictable.

Things were falling into place in Sant's brain. Dobson was paying off Donohue for a supply of doped girls who he lured to his bachelor pad. Girls like Klaudia Armitage, experiencing her first dose of unsuspecting porn-star fame. It was a team job: camera operator, chief actors, victim, props and toys, lights, camera, X-rated action. Sant tried to work out how many protagonists needed locking up, plus the role Dobson performed in this dark séance. Was he rapist or accomplice? Who else was involved? And did this blue movie-set have anything to do with police officers who should know better?

Sant phoned for assistance before wandering back into the study. The laptop was still running, screensaver displaying a bird's-eye view of Holbeck Urban Village in all its regenerated splendour. Councillor Dobson was proud of his ward. But beneath that aspirational veneer, Sant wondered how many sick videos were stored on his hard drive.

He bent down to look under the desk and noticed a piece of A4 paper folded in half. He pulled out his shabby handker-chief, reached forward and pinched a corner of the paper, lifted it to eye level and unfolded it carefully.

It was a black and white photocopy of two images of what looked like a laptop, though not the same as the one sitting on Dobson's desk. And alongside the images, two screenshots of BDSM sexual violence in progress. The graphic content didn't surprise Sant, but the visual collage did. Why take photos of a laptop as well as the filth it contained? And who owned it?

Something else was on the floor too. Sant reached out with

his fingertips and plucked up a grey hoodie. The string to tighten the hood was frayed, chewed by human teeth as far as the inspector could make out. And when he checked the sleeves, one of them was tarnished with paint. Donohue was certainly right about the identity of the man he'd done business with.

Sant closed his eyes and tried to meditate because, there and then, he felt like smashing up every exhibit in this seedy cesspit. He knew that wasn't a prudent move, and besides, help was soon at hand. A young detective taking exams on the criminology of sex offences took the helm and knew exactly where to direct the police photographer's lens. The spectacle seemed surreal, Dobson's wedge-of-cake flat like a movie studio within a movie studio that had Sant walking in circles as he retreated to his car, gnawing on the first toothpick of a long day ahead.

* * *

'Good job securing the charge against Mr Donohue,' Chief Constable Bill Gilligan announced as he lifted his greying eyebrows and peaked cap with police badge all at once.

Sant had just stepped into Hardaker's boardroom and Gilligan's presence – he'd not bargained for it – was jarring his train of thought. He knew that Hardaker and the Old Man were examining complaints of unprofessional officer behaviour linked to prostitution, but there were more important players to eliminate from abhorrent games of iniquity, surely.

'Cannabis farming is the least of our concerns,' Sant said after a moment's reflection.

Old Man Gilligan folded his arms over his beer belly and leaned back with two chair legs off the floor. 'Is Donohue caught up in these sex attacks?'

'He fessed up, though not in so many words.'

'It's a pity he's not confessing to anyone else,' Hardaker said.

'There's no point in him denying it,' Sant continued. 'It won't take long before there's evidence to charge him with conspiracy to kidnap Klaudia Armitage.'

'He admitted his guilt?' Gilligan enquired.

'Only because he thought there was something in it for him if he grassed up at the same time.'

'Who's he involved with?' Hardaker probed.

Sant settled into the Chiefman's chair at the head of the oval table before saying: 'The man who took Klaudia off his hands is none other than Councillor Dobson.'

Gilligan grunted. 'Nonsense, Inspector. Don't believe a word of it.'

'Why do you say that?'

The chief constable glared at Sant. 'Rory Dobson is an upstanding community leader who's campaigned against the promotion of prostitution, even if he's given West Yorkshire Police a hard time over the Managed Approach. But I don't hold anything against him. And as for accusing him of being a paedophile, that's like accusing Mother Teresa of breaking into the alms box.'

'I'm not the accuser,' Sant said.

'But your taking Donohue's word for it. The word of a convicted sex offender. Why would Rory have anything to do with a known paedophile like Donohue?'

'Maybe he's got a dark side we don't know about,' Hardaker put in.

Gilligan puffed out flushed cheeks and sour odour. 'We'll need more than a crook's testimony if you want to pursue the matter further, Superintendent.'

'We could ask him to volunteer his DNA,' the Chiefman suggested.

'And take a closer look at his luxury apartment,' Sant added. 'One of the rooms is wired for hardcore porn for the benefit of perverts the world over. It wouldn't surprise me if a video featuring poor Klaudia is racking up profits from subscriptions this very minute.'

'Are you serious?' Gilligan pulled on both earlobes as though he couldn't believe what he was hearing.

'A sex offences specialist is combing every inch of the place as we speak,' Sant went on. 'Unless he's subletting and unaware of the perverts he's accommodating, the young man's in big trouble.'

Hardaker tapped his goatee with his lean fingertips. 'I take it he's not been arrested yet.'

'He wasn't at home when I came calling this morning.'

'Are you telling me, Inspector, that you broke in without a warrant?' the Old Man probed, the veins on his cheeks turning deep purple.

'I'm telling you nothing of the sort,' Sant replied. 'The door was open. Maybe he left in a hurry and forgot to lock up.'

Gilligan stood to tuck his white shirt into his freshly pressed trousers. 'Let's hope you left no trace or we've no chance in a future prosecution – if such a measure is necessary, that is.'

Hardaker gave up inputting details on his Surface Pro and turned to Sant. 'Where do you think Dobson is?'

'I don't know, but I suggest we deploy as many officers as we can.'

'And money grows on trees and the fairies actually exist,' the chief constable snapped.

Sant felt like strangling the Old Man. That would see to his bad breath. He exited the boardroom before the homicidal feeling became a reality, glancing back through the polished glass door to offer Hardaker silent sympathy. The Chiefman was a diplomat and deserved a medal for that attribute alone. There were pricks like Gilligan above him and too many below to fill out forms for. The worst of all possible worlds. But that was Hardaker's lot. There weren't enough diplomats among rank and file, and Sant would never be one.

* * *

He decided to grab a quick lunch at home, mainly because he was curious to know if Holdsworth was inside. Perhaps she hadn't woken yet. As he unlocked the door of his flat, he was gripped by an inner urge to see her Mediterranean complexion beneath those brown perms as she helped herself to brunch, not that there was much food about. But immediately he noticed the mattress perched upright against the far wall and the bed linen folded on top – and judging by the room temperature, the heating had long since been turned off.

Being lonely and feeling lonely were two very different psychologies. I'm a private person in more ways than one, Sant reflected, but liking my own company has its limits. I don't love myself. I love the thought of being private when I want to be and passionately involved when the need arises. But Holdsworth? She isn't someone I should feel passion for. She's a fellow officer under my command, her long-term boyfriend the same.

Sant's last and very fleeting old flame, Mia, wasn't any better suited. She was half his age and twice as eligible for nuptial bliss, and what's more, for her it would be first time round. Anyway, Mia had gone quiet on him. By now she'd be in someone else's arms. Someone without half a century of baggage on his aching back. Which reminded Sant of his little toe – it was throbbing again.

He swallowed two more codeine pills, opened his fridge

and realised the wine from the night before was one of the few items still consumable. He chucked away an unopened bag of salad two months past its use-by date, made a stale cheese sandwich and a cup of milkless tea, and committed himself to a supermarket shop as soon as a couple of hours identified themselves as spare. But none were spare just yet. Too many missing people had to be found, whether they were willing to be or not. And since fairies didn't actually exist, Sant would have to take matters into his own hands.

* * *

He enquired at the Civic Hall but none of his fellow councillors or anyone else had seen Rory Dobson since Friday. Then he went to Holbeck and bumped into faces he recognised among the SAVE OUR EYES contingent. They hadn't seen their hero either but assured Sant that they'd vote for Dobson any day of the week as a thank you for all his hard work. Optimism was growing amid rumours that the Managed Approach was going to be shut down for good, but Sant couldn't raise anyone's hopes as he knew nothing about senior police raising fresh concerns over links between legal sex work and illegal shenanigans.

Further lines of enquiry proved fruitless and as the first tinge of violet dusk emerged eastwards, Sant reclined the seat in his Fiesta and settled himself for a mindful nap. The peace and stillness enveloped him, though the first thing that came to mind was the Jake Thackray ringtones crooning out of his phone. It was Appleyard.

'Is that DI Sant?'

'Any luck finding Ava?' he asked croakily.

'I got a tip-off from a barber who styles the hair of sex

workers around Sheepscar. He's seen her in the last hour or two.'

Sant was fully awake on hearing the news. 'Fantastic. Was she getting her hair cut?'

'No, but her friend was. Goes by the name of Maria.'

'I've seen her around. Tall? Pink-dyed rattail?'

There was a pause on the line as Appleyard checked her notes. 'Yes, that may be her. Is there anything you wish to tell me, DI Sant?'

'I don't have sex with prostitutes, DCI Appleyard. I met her during routine enquiries.' Stick that in your pipe and smoke it. 'Where were they heading?'

'The barber's not sure but they were going out together, and not on business.' Appleyard rustled her notepaper. 'The barber said they were wearing different clothes; not working gear, whatever that means. Oh, and Ava seemed nervous. She didn't want to get her hair cut because she said she couldn't let go of her bag in case she mislaid it.'

'I wonder what's inside,' Sant said. 'Stacks of cash maybe.'

'We might get sightings of them as the evening draws on,' Appleyard continued. 'This is the first positive sighting of Ava for some time – maybe she's planning on doing something.'

'Walking into her nearest police station would do nicely.'

'That's unlikely, but she's with a friend, which means they might be travelling somewhere.'

'Or doing something she wouldn't do on her own.'

There was another pause while Appleyard mulled over Sant's words. 'Such as?'

'Wish I knew the answer.'

'I heard you arrested Donohue on a drugs charge. What's the latest on his grooming record?'

'He's in custody so we've got him – and his associates – by the balls,' Sant replied.

'Good news,' Appleyard remarked. 'Right, I'll make sure a descriptor of Ava and friend goes out to local taxi firms.'

He could have done without the formalities, but Sant was growing a tiny bit fonder of the chief inspector. She was learning on the job and at least they were working jointly now, not bickering. Having a focal point on Ava and her whereabouts was exactly what Appleyard needed, though perhaps that focus was dulling her powers of inquisitiveness because she hadn't asked him a thing about the suspected associates of Mr Donohue.

For want of something else to do, Sant headed south following the signs for the M621, coming off at Junction 27 for Gildersome and letting his satnav do the rest. This was the village where PC Benn lived with his family, punctuated by woods and streams, at the very edge of the city perched on a steep hill climbing out of Leeds.

Sant wanted a follow-up with Benn to check whether Donohue or Dobson came into his frame of reference, and he wanted to be open and say to Benn he had no choice but to tell the relevant people what he knew about the PC's involvement in the sex trade. There was no easy way to do it – spelling it out in front of him was the only proper way.

As Sant steered further up the hill and left behind post-industrial mediocrity, patches of fog floated over his windscreen and his headlights bounced off the cat's eyes. Because of these distractions it took him a few minutes to realise something wasn't right. He'd keyed Benn's address into his Maps app – Castle Avenue – but there was no sign of any castle and the app had given up trying to locate anything resembling the street name. Sant searched for Benn's details and then realised his mistake. It was Church Avenue, not Castle Avenue. He'd passed loads of churches but not a single fort or moat.

Before putting down the phone, he saw a notification and

checked the app. A flashing red dot came into view. One of his colleagues was no more than a couple of miles away. He touched the red dot on the map and Appleyard's face popped up. He took three deep breaths and called her.

'Are you following me?' he said.

'No, DI Sant. Where are you?'

'In Gildersome.'

'I'm next door, in Morley. Another tip-off.'

'Go on.'

'Let me pull over.' There was a lengthy break before Appleyard's voice resurfaced. 'Two women matching the descriptions of Ava and this Maria friend were picked up on Belinda Street in Hunslet by a taxi driver. He called the police after he'd dropped them off.'

'In Morley?'

'Yes, an hour ago.'

'Why've they come to this neck of the woods?'

'Not sure. Why are you here?'

Sant answered carefully. 'I want to talk to a constable who lives out this way. He might have some information on Councillor Dobson but he's off duty and not picking up.'

Silence, as if Appleyard was trying to work out Sant's meaning. In other circumstances she might have prodded harder, but he reckoned on her being too occupied just now.

'Right,' she said eventually. 'I heard about the developments regarding Dobson. I suppose it's a convenient coincidence because your help is required locating Ava and Maria. Join me a-sap.'

Sant put hand to mouth and exhaled with relief, then asked: 'Where's the Chiefman? Ah, don't tell me. Having afternoon tea with Gilligan while they discuss his career promotion and protecting the force from public scrutiny.'

'That's a shallow and frivolous remark, DI Sant, and you know it.'

'But it's—'

'I'll await your call imminently,' signed off Appleyard, pointedly extinguishing any hint of dissent that might be hovering in the twilight air.

* * *

Church Avenue was a quiet residential road flanked by sizeable semi-detached houses with canted bay windows and block paved steps to the front door. Long lawns and driveways separated the inhabitants from exhaust fumes and louts on a late-night bender.

Sant followed the road around and noted the even numbers on the inside of the bend. He counted down to Benn's place before crossing to the other side and parking by the wrought iron gates. It was too dark to see clearly, but he could hear a distinct commotion coming from somewhere in the garden. He rushed out of his car and noticed a slim black woman hurrying through the gates, three small children in tow.

'Are you police?' she said, voice cracking.

'Detective Inspector Sant.' He showed his ID.

'Have you found my husband yet?'

'You mean Joshua Benn?'

'Yes, that's what I called about. But I only phoned a few minutes ago. I suppose it's too soon.'

'Is he missing, Mrs Benn?'

'Yes, didn't my call get through to you?'

Sant shuffled his towering frame awkwardly. He could hardly say he was unaware of any call and was visiting her husband because of his connivance in a sex ring. Sometimes concealing the truth harms less than revealing it.

'I was just passing by and heard the noise.'

'Wait a minute.' She gathered up her kids and manoeuvred them into the back of a Range Rover parked on the drive.

'Can I take a look inside?' Sant asked as he shut the gate behind him.

The woman's face was streaked with fear. 'You can, though I'll warn you now – there's blood and plenty of it.'

Sant shifted his gaze towards the open door. 'Has he had an accident?'

'I don't know, but something's horribly wrong. His car's gone. I've had no word from him. If he's injured, I'm the first person he'd contact. I'm his wife, yes, and I'm also a pharmacist with training certificates coming out of my ears.'

'When was the last time you saw him?'

'This morning. Before I went to work. It was his day off today.'

Sant pointed to the house. 'Have you been in yet?'

'Yes. No. I mean, I walked in, like you do. But as soon as I was in' – a pair of tears fell from her smudged eyelids – 'the floor was soaked red. I called his name but there was no answer.'

'Stay where you are.'

Sant approached with care. As he came to the steps leading to the front door, he noticed a trail of red drops. Still fresh. He placed his trusted handkerchief on the centre spot and gently pushed the door fully inwards. The blood was more noticeable in the hallway, one section of carpet having completely changed colour as if some poor soul had been laid out there before being put out of their misery.

The sound of doors slamming gradually reached Sant's senses. He turned around and saw an ambulance and two police cars. He held up his ID and signalled with his other arm. The paramedics came first, followed by a uniformed officer who fished into his jacket pocket and pulled out two shoe covers. Sant pulled them over his black Grenson brogues and entered the house tentatively, treading as close to the skirting board as he could without touching it.

The kitchen was deserted. A mug of coffee, half empty, had gone cold on the black glass dining table. Sant checked the other downstairs rooms. Nothing amiss. The only blood was in the hall. Whoever had been attacked was coming into the property or answering the door. Either way, they had little chance to do much else.

The uniformed officer called from upstairs: 'All correct up here.'

Sant acknowledged the info and tiptoed out of the hallway before it was cordoned off, his breath turning misty as it met the cool air outside. He stood in the middle of the lawn, turning his back on the blue lights illuminating the scene, trying to sort the facts in his head. He was sure PC Benn was in trouble, whether villain or victim, but it wasn't too late to save a life. A lot of blood had been spilt but no more than half an hour ago if Sant's guesswork was good.

He relayed his thoughts in three sentences to a scenes-of-crime officer carrying a large holdall of forensic utensils. Then he walked towards the Range Rover. Mrs Benn saw him coming and cut short her phone conversation before stepping out of the vehicle and tying up her hair. Sant overheard the word 'mother' as she ended the call.

'Any sign of him?' she asked as she dried her eyes on a blouse sleeve.

He shook his head. 'Have you an idea where he might be?'

'Maybe he's gone to a hospital.' She checked her phone for updates but not for long. 'You can find out for me, can't you?'

Sant made sure he secured eye contact before posing the

difficult question. 'Is there anyone, Mrs Benn, who would want to harm your husband?'

'Not that I know of,' she said without delay. 'I mean, he's a policeman. You know the risks.' She brushed away more wetness on her cheeks. 'Oh my, this is not like him at all. A bad thing has happened. I know it. It's definitely his blood.'

'You sure?'

'I've seen it before.' Tears poured and she began to howl with anguish. 'When you've been with someone for so long,' she sobbed convulsively, 'you can smell them, even when they're not there.'

Sant nodded but couldn't empathise; hadn't loved anyone enough to sense their presence everywhere, not least his ex, whose presence he was glad to be rid of – so under no circumstances could he dispute Mrs Benn's account of true intimacy.

'Is there anyone who wants him dead, Inspector?'

Sant asked himself the same question and the only individual remotely springing to mind was Sergeant Tufail, out to revenge a tell-tale conspirator. But Tufail didn't know who the snitch was. Sant had taken great care to protect his source when confronting Tufail with the allegations Benn had made against him.

Nothing swirling around the inspector's mind made much sense. The one thing he did know was the young mother facing him would discover some dark shit about her husband very soon. He dodged a straight reply to her question and guided her in the direction of a female officer keeping the children occupied by showing off her body tech.

* * *

'Where are you?' Appleyard's voice sounded robotic over the radio waves.

'At PC Joshua Benn's house,' Sant responded, 'except Benn and his car are nowhere to be seen and there's enough blood on the carpet to turn it scarlet.'

'What has this PC Benn got to do with anything? I don't understand.'

'Neither do I.'

There was a short delay before Appleyard spoke again: 'Is Benn the one with information on Rory Dobson?'

'Dobson? No.'

'I thought you said you were seeing someone for that reason.'

'Yes. I mean, not–'

'What in God's name are you hiding?' Appleyard snarled down the line. 'Is Benn one of the officers you suspect of going with prostitutes?'

Sant let out a long sigh. 'It's easier to talk off the phone. Where can I find you?'

Appleyard returned the sigh. 'Eating chips. Parked outside Hillycroft Fisheries on Bruntcliffe Lane.'

'What car?' Sant asked, realising he hadn't a clue what the chief inspector drove around in.

'My own. Ford Focus.'

He gripped the steering wheel tightly as he left the chaos of Church Avenue. So much was weighing on his brain, it was hurting almost as badly as his little toe. He needed to offload his theories. Holdsworth or Capstick were ideal sounding boards, but Appleyard?

He pulled up behind her Focus, opened the passenger door and sucked in the rich aroma of fried potato – felt no pang of hunger nonetheless.

'I'll start where I left off.' Appleyard spoke coolly. 'Is Benn involved with prostitutes?'

Sant twirled the knob on the heating controls to reduce the blast of red-hot air blowing from the ventilation grill. 'He denies having sexual relations but admits passing money to a pimp, though not his money and he didn't know what the payment was for.'

'And you're telling me this now,' Appleyard said as she filled her small gob with an extra-long chip.

'I was going to blow the whistle,' Sant explained, 'but first I had to check a few facts about others he'd accused. And besides, I'd no proof of any offence.'

'Isn't the sex trade against the law?' she remarked, lodging some of the chip in her cheek.

Sant felt his temperature rising and wound down the window. 'You know as well as I do – we're taking a different approach in this city.'

'That's beside the point,' Appleyard put in. 'PC Benn has confessed to unprofessional conduct. You should have declared this to me or Superintendent Hardaker as soon as it came to light.'

'Fine, I'll report Benn formally once I've had a chance to breathe. And there's someone else too.'

'You've turned a lot of blind eyes lately, DI Sant.'

He ignored the quip. 'According to Benn and others I've spoken to, Sergeant Fawad Tufail is making a nice living from pimping.'

'Wrong,' she said, avoiding Sant's startled look.

'Wrong?'

'Did nobody tell you? Tufail has been undercover for weeks trying to smoke out the real pimps.'

Sant clenched his fists. 'Great to know I'm not worthy of being in on the spy act.'

'Look who's talking,' Appleyard retorted. 'You're not exactly upfront or transparent yourself.'

'I suppose Tufail is under strict instructions to keep his second life confidential.'

'Did you challenge him?'

'In no uncertain terms.'

'Good to know he's following orders.' Appleyard let the uneasy silence grow for a while before posing a question: 'Do you think Ava and Maria came here to call on Benn?'

Sant cracked his knuckles to release his frustration, then said: 'It's possible but the taxi didn't exactly take them to Benn's front door, did it?'

'Maybe they wanted to throw us off the scent. They got dropped off here and look, it's only half an hour's walk to Church Avenue.' She showed him the route on the app.

'That's a possibility,' Sant said. 'There's nothing to go on though; no proof that Benn and Ava even know each other. When I showed Benn's photo to Maria the other day, she didn't recognise him.'

'But the prostitution link might explain Ava and Maria turning up at Benn's house,' pondered Appleyard.

Sant nodded. 'It might explain the violent altercation in his hallway.'

'And the blood?'

'That too. Someone's in a life-threatening condition at best.'

Appleyard slipped another chip between her lips. 'I'm still not registering Nicolae Popescu's part in all this.'

The inspector pinched his disjointed nose. 'He's one of the pimps Benn has dealt with. Benn confessed to knowing Popescu but claimed to be a mere middleman straightening debts. I reckon he lied to me.'

'Hell almighty!' The chief inspector flung the remains of her snack on the top of the dashboard. 'Withholding this information is seriously bad news, DI Sant.'

Sant opened the door to leave. 'I couldn't care less. I do things my way and get results.'

'Where are you going?'

'To sit in my car. And down some painkillers. I can do without the high volume in here.'

Appleyard pointed an index finger downwards. 'I'm ordering you to stay, DI Sant. We have urgent issues to sort out.'

'Concerning me?' He jabbed a thumb at his grumbling stomach.

'Not directly, no.'

'Who?'

'Ava and Maria of course.'

Sant pulled the door shut. 'Let's get to work, then. Any sign of them?' He jammed two more pills under his tongue before gulping them without a drink.

'What are you eating?'

'Codeine.'

Appleyard exhaled deeply. 'I thought you were making up the bit about painkillers.'

'My toe's killing me.'

She almost saw the funny side but shook her round head instead. 'Right, I've set the ball rolling. Details of Benn's car are being circulated. His phone is being tracked for a signal. Hospitals are on alert. A team of constables is doing the usual rounds – petrol stations, pubs, supermarkets – but no leads yet.' She took a sip of tea from a paper cup. 'Now think – where could the two of them be heading?'

'Depends.'

'On what?'

'On whether Benn is in the driving seat or one of them is.'

'Okay, let's say Benn is the driver. Where is he taking the two women?'

Sant swallowed drily. 'They could be anywhere. If he's the aggressor and suddenly feeling guilty, he might unload them close to a casualty ward.'

'No word from hospitals yet.' Appleyard took another sip of hot liquid. 'Did the scene at his house give anything away?'

Sant twirled a new toothpick in his fingers. 'The blood's from one person only – could be any of the three. Mrs Benn is convinced it's her husband's.'

'Surely that means nothing.'

'Probably, but she's a pharmacist. Maybe she's got a nose for it.' He put the toothpick to his mouth and snapped it in two.

Appleyard thought aloud. 'We're still assuming without eyewitness accounts that Ava and Maria came to call on Benn. Is that a safe assumption?'

Sant scowled at his surroundings. 'This isn't an area you visit in passing.'

'The tea's better than standard.' She smiled briefly. 'Sorry for not offering you anything. I guess those painkillers aren't doing much for your appetite.'

Sensing the pills dissolving down his system, Sant rested his broad hands on his dicky stomach. 'The tea might've helped,' he said.

'You can finish it if you like,' she said, offering him her cup.

Sant grabbed it in double quick time. 'Sometimes, you know, I imagine us in a stress-free working relationship.'

She was about to reply when a call came through. Hardaker's voice piped up instantly.

'A Renault Megane matching Benn's has been spotted by a farmer. Abandoned off Gelderd Road. We're heading there now but you're closer. I'll get a civvy to text the exact location.'

'Have you got back-up?' Appleyard queried.

Muffled conversation finally gave way to a resumption of the Chiefman's precise tones.

'Assembling a team may take longer than normal,' Hardaker replied. 'We're short on scenes-of-crime personnel as many of them are responding to the other incident.'

'At Benn's house?' she asked.

'Correct.'

Sant twisted his head to speak into the phone. 'Is Gilligan with you?'

'Yes.'

'Tell the Old Man to stay indoors. He might get his feet wet.'

Hardaker carried on as if he'd heard nothing. 'This business is urgent enough for Chief Constable Gilligan to choose the frontline. We're weighing up this evolving case against those worrying allegations of police malpractice we keep hearing about.'

'That reminds me,' said Appleyard, directing her lash extensions meaningfully at Sant. 'Benn is one of the officers under suspicion of liaisons with sex workers and their agents.'

'Who told you that, Stephanie?'

'DI Sant found out. He'll reveal more in due course, won't you?'

'Absolutely,' Sant answered emphatically.

'You aren't holding anything back, are you Carl?' muttered Hardaker.

'Nothing that couldn't wait till a host of perverts and victims of sexual abuse were tracked down, Chiefman.'

Appleyard closed the connection before Sant had finished. 'Stop point scoring. This is not the time or place.'

The inspector brushed the back of his hand over the irritating stubble growing on his chin. 'Why is Old Man Gilligan so keen to come out here?' he wondered.

'You heard the superintendent. This is a pressing matter.'

'But what's really in it for him? Since I've known Gilligan, he's been a behind-the-scenes pen-pusher like most of the top rank; never central to what's unfolding on the ground.'

'Unlike you and your worker's hands.'

Sant held out his palms and stared at them intently. 'You're sounding like Popescu. Any relation?'

'Stop asking questions,' Appleyard giggled, scrunching up her food carton to repress the sound of her laughter.

'Have we got a location yet?'

The chief inspector checked her messages and keyed in a postcode. 'Five minutes away. Your car or mine?'

* * *

'It's down there,' she pointed.

Sant traced an imaginary line from Appleyard's finger and jerked his Fiesta sharply to the left, coming to a halt fifty yards along a farm track where the headlights of Benn's discarded Megane were glaring at a bemused cow. The car had been left crossways on a rising grassy verge such that the force of gravity was holding the offside front and rear doors wide open.

It was an eerily remote spot. Apart from farmhouses, a Jewish cemetery and a depot containing skips, the rest was raw nature, nothing greeting the ear except the murmur of motorway traffic and the hoot of an owl far above.

The two detectives kept low as they moved in, peering through the windows of the Megane and seeing no-one inside. Sant shone his LED torch towards the rear and noticed the same strain of scarlet that had decorated Benn's hallway. Whoever had been hurt or killed in his house had been deposited on the back seat.

Appleyard went around to the boot and tried the latch with a gloved hand. It was locked.

'Where do you think they've gone?' she said.

'Follow the red trail.'

Sant guided his torch away from the car and placed a spot-light on five drops of the fresh stuff still dripping off tufts of weedy grass.

They walked at pace through a gap in a hedge and kept to the parameter of the farmer's field. The hedge ended abruptly at a steep bank leading to overgrown shrubs. The sound of running water bubbled below. Between the shrubbery Sant could make out a wide stream, rainfall and melting snow combining to swell the channel. A section of drystone wall running down to the stream sparkled with what appeared to be icing sugar but was, indisputably, glazed frost.

'It's marked Farnley Wood Beck on the app,' said Apple-yard, her phone doubling as a torch and map. 'Where next?'

Sant cast his vision along a makeshift path running parallel to the bank and saw little of interest. The grass was long in places and there was no sign of recent trampling. 'I suppose the only way is hell bound,' he said finally. 'Easier to haul a body downwards than across a horizontal.'

Cautiously but with swift movement, they traversed the slope and squeezed through a narrow clearing in the under-growth which ended in a flat patch of muddy marsh beside the heaving flow.

'I've spotted something,' said Appleyard, aiming the torch on her phone so Sant could see. 'A shoe. And look, another. The same kind.'

'Time for some wading,' the inspector said.

They went with the force of the beck at a depth that reached Sant's knees and Appleyard's thighs. The water was icy cold. Neither detective felt it at first, until an all-embracing chill penetrating air and water seeped through their bones. They were descending into a mossy abyss untouched by life or human endeavour.

Ten minutes later they clambered out of the beck at the other side where the ground had become flatter than the bank they'd come down. Appleyard swung her phone in both directions, but Sant motioned her to douse the light and then all they could sense was the trickling of discharge. They strained their ears to latch onto anything other than the monotonous gush.

It took an eternity – a vibration: the sound of metal striking something hard. A tree root or rock. Someone screeched from behind the fallen trunk of a sapling. A shout of 'Go!' and a ripple of scurrying feet.

Appleyard started to sprint, Sant doing his best to keep up while trying to ignore his throbbing toe. They negotiated the hump of the downed trunk and Appleyard gasped as they hit the ground running.

'I can see them,' she called back. 'Twenty metres away.'

They gained by the second and after clawing their way through a cluster of thick shrubs, Sant called out: 'Police! Get down, that's an order!'

One of the two figures was flagging and the other looked to the heavens before breaking stride. They put their hands up and fell to the soaked earth. As Sant came closer, he recognised one of them. There was no mistaking the hairdo even in the dimness of the wood, though the rattail had been trimmed and was no longer pink.

'Stay down!' Appleyard commanded. 'Hands behind backs!' She cuffed one of them and Sant the other.

'Easy on them,' he said. 'They pose no risk.'

'I'm taking no chances,' Appleyard roared, but there was a note of triumph in her roar. 'Check their pockets for weapons.'

Sant pulled out a pair of gardening gloves from a coat pocket, a silver ring, an e-cigarette recently vaped. 'Hello Maria, I spoke with you a few nights back.'

The tall woman turned her head and looked up but was panting so hard she couldn't speak.

'Which means she's Ava Yock,' Appleyard concluded. 'We've been looking for you, Ava. You're a hard nut to crack.'

Ava met the remark with moans and then tears that flowed as fast as the stream nearby. The petite girl began shaking violently. Appleyard removed her jacket and wrapped it around her with a tenderness Sant found moving. He let go of Maria and perched on a muddy mound.

'Where's Benn?' he asked.

Maria got up on her knees and nodded towards the fallen sapling tree from which they'd fled.

'Show us.'

They retraced a route through tangled bushes and twisted roots jutting up from earth like the arms of a long-buried giant. Eventually they came to a small crater formed by the base of an oak that had toppled in autumn storms. It was this mature tree that had brought down smaller ones with it, the sapling included.

Sant rested his weight on the mighty trunk and stared down. Benn was prone inside the crater, huddled up among drooping branches still clinging to the dead oak. A kitchen cleaver stuck out of his groin. The two women had tried to conceal the body but had left the job unfinished.

Appleyard cast her beam through the heap of death and dislodged the thickest of the branches carefully, allowing it to spring away from whatever was keeping it fixed down. Sant bent down and directed his gaze at the face. The black skin, white teeth and sculptured beard looked no less alive than three days before, when he'd jumped the constable and forced him to confess. But the deep chest gashes still leaking fluid told a different story – this was the man's final comeuppance.

Appleyard hiked up one side of the crater to gain a better view. 'Can you positively identify him?' she asked Sant.

'Joshua Benn,' he answered.

Appleyard stepped back and addressed the two women. 'Why did you kill him?'

Maria glanced at Ava. 'Tell them.'

Ava spoke in Romanian to her friend while wiping dirt from her sunken cheeks. Then she set her bloodshot eyes on the detectives and spoke in word-perfect English: 'That policeman molested me. He almost murdered me. He's done the same to others.'

'But you accused Nicolae Popescu of assaulting you,' the chief inspector remarked.

Ava bowed her head to reveal a butterfly tattooed on the back of her thin neck. 'That was a mistake. I hate Nicolae for what he's turned into. He's a monster just like that policeman. He dopes people too and I suspected him to begin with. Now I'm certain it wasn't him.'

'How so?' Appleyard probed.

'I heard the news about the other girl.'

'Klaudia Armitage?'

She raised up her neck and tilted her gaunt face. 'It happened to me in the same way. A random John plies you with cheap alcohol but instead of using you himself, he forces you into someone else's Benz. You're confused. You don't know where you're going. Next thing you're aware of is the B.O. of the thug on top of you.' She held her breath before releasing more groans and sniffles. 'I did my research, checked the facts with peeps on the street, it added up. That piece of shit deserves nothing better than an open grave. You can spit on the *negru* before pulling him out. I forgot to do it myself.'

* * *

The two friends were ushered into a waiting police car. Officers with dogs and a stretcher passed by before entering bleak undergrowth in search of a dead colleague. The dogs weren't needed anymore but any excuse for a workout was welcome.

Sant and Appleyard brushed off thorns and bits of bark from their clothing as they returned to the abandoned Renault Megane. Two technicians combing for evidence inside were talking to a third tech stood at the rear of the vehicle receiving instructions from someone on the phone. Human resources were so stretched that even forensic investigators had to be outsourced these days. CSI call centres in the public service – press one for robbery, two for a riot.

Sant began speaking to the tech who was on the phone, but she signalled for him to hold off. 'What's up?' he asked after she'd ended the call.

'We've found a body.'

'Another?' quizzed Appleyard. 'Are you sure?'

'Absolutely,' the tech replied.

'Isn't one enough for today?' Sant said, the pain in his toe cranking up a notch.

The tech pointed to the open boot of the Megane. 'You're welcome to take a look, but I'll warn you first, he's not a pretty sight.'

Sant and Appleyard stepped around the tech and caught a glimpse of a pale face hardly brightened by the lamp set up for criminal examination. Again, Sant found himself identifying a corpse. A gagged and cuffed Councillor Dobson was lost to the world. Lumps like golf balls on the young man's forehead told a tale of blunt force trauma.

Appleyard came up close to inspect the handcuffs and saw they were police issue. 'Who the hell arrested him?'

Sant clocked onto a theory forming in his scarcely conscious mind. 'Benn would be my guess. He killed Dobson and stored him in the car while he popped back to the house for something, only to come to grief at the hands of his own nemesis – or nemeses.'

'You mean, Ava and Maria were unaware of Dobson's body in the boot?'

The inspector nodded. 'They had no use for the boot anyway. It was easier for them to haul Benn into the back seat than lift his bulk into the rear.'

Appleyard thought aloud. 'Why would Benn want to do away with Dobson?'

'I'm guessing again,' said Sant, 'but it's odds-on Dobson's penthouse-apartment-cum-pornographic-film-studio has something to do with it.'

'How long has he been lying there?' Appleyard asked the tech.

'Not long. The chest feels slightly warm. He must've died no longer than ten hours ago.'

Sant calculated in his head and decided ten hours was plausible. A lot of nastiness had unfolded between then and now, which was often the way. Crazy people did crazy things all at once and without moderation. Benn met his end just hours after ending Dobson's.

Appleyard poked her head under the rear door. 'Any idea of the murder weapon?'

'A type of hammer most likely,' the tech said, 'but don't quote me. Dr Wisdom will go spare if he discovers I'm giving away information without the proper checks in place.'

'Let me see the wounds,' Appleyard said as she switched on her phone torch.

Sant gripped her coat sleeve as she made to stoop. 'Not a wise move,' he said firmly.

She shrugged him off. 'I'll go about my work free of restraint, DI Sant.'

'He's right to hold you back.' The tech spoke to Appleyard calmly but resolutely. 'You don't want to see the yawning hole where the occipital bone should be. The strands of brain poking out of the back of the skull look like a mixture of raspberry gummies and strawberry laces.'

Appleyard diverted her eyes to shut out the imagined terror and took a step back to ensure there was no risk of glimpsing Rory's gory, gaping, pick 'n' mix crown.

'Did you unpick the boot?' Sant asked the tech.

She shook her head. 'I think it was Dave. Dave, did you unpick the boot?'

Dave called back. 'It was already open when I got here. Ask Tim.'

The tech pointed out Tim and the two detectives made a beeline towards the man. He glanced up from the clipboard he was scribbling on.

'Did you unpick the boot?' Sant asked again.

'Kind of.' Tim tucked the clipboard under his white overalls to keep it dry, flakes of snow starting to fall. 'A fire and rescue officer did the heavy lifting before I arrived.'

'But you oversaw things?'

'I was first on the scene, yes, but the chief had already given the orders to break in.'

Sant scratched his head, now aching in tandem with his toe. 'The chief? Gilligan?'

'That's him. First time I've seen the bloke in the flesh. I was on my best behaviour. Didn't want to piss him off or owt.'

Sant was silent for a moment, then asked: 'Did he say anything?'

'Not a chance. He was well past saving. The medics said as much.'

'I don't mean the man in the boot. I mean Gilligan.'

Tim laughed at his own mistake. 'Ah, he didn't say much. Wanted to know if the victim was dead or alive, that's all.'

'So he raised the boot first?' Appleyard put in.

'No, a fire and rescue officer prised it free. The chief constable was alongside us, watching on.'

'And everything was above board?'

Tim nodded. 'The chief looked anxious but when he saw the chap was dead, it was too much for him. I thought he might faint. He pulled himself together though. Looked much brighter after a minute or two. Good of him to come out and do some dirty work, I suppose.'

Maybe, thought Sant, or maybe not. There was something odd about the Old Man expending so much energy on present matters. Sant was dumbfounded at Gilligan's depth of investment. He caught the expression on Appleyard's face and even she seemed perplexed. All was not well in the police state of West Yorkshire – and the slaying of one rogue officer who had beaten to death a well-respected politician, albeit a troubled sex predator, wouldn't make it a lot better.

9

THE NEXT DAY MISS AVA YOCK CONFESSED TO THE FATAL stabbing of Benn. It was an unambiguous testimony. She'd stolen the cleaver from a chef she knew – hid it in her handbag. Benn answered his front door, the knife was out, the blood began spurting. The backstory was left out for now, but once known, a long queue of criminal barristers would line up to defend Ava, making a case for voluntary manslaughter rather than murder. Sant reckoned the young Romanian would be charged with the lesser offence and receive a ten-year sentence, out in five.

Maria Balgin admitted to deceiving Sant when pretending not to recognise the photo of PC Benn he had shown her. Her reason for denying knowledge was that she wanted to talk to Ava first, tell her what she'd found out from Sant, and let her friend decide the next step. Tragically, that next step was revenge because Ava was no longer in any doubt that the man who had raped her was Benn.

One aspect of the attack on Benn was puzzling enough to

compel Sant to look again at the man's profile. He checked the staff directory and saw that the officer weighed over seventy kilograms despite his diminutive stature. Maria was rangy, but Ava was frail by comparison. Could they have lifted all that body weight without help? Sant didn't think it possible, which meant a third person must have come to their aid.

Initial DNA checks were completed by the afternoon and although the results were stamped as *preliminary*, they were as clear as the icicles drooping from roofs after the overnight frost. Benn was incontrovertibly Yock's assaulter. He'd also had inter-course with Klaudia Armitage and two previous victims of park abductions where no perpetrator had been identified until now. Benn liked them young and naïve and drugged up to the eyeballs.

Sant knew that once the facts were made public, prominent spokespeople would raise hell and call for all officers to be DNA-ed before starting the job. He had to admit that Benn's wickedness would have hit a brick wall had such a policy existed, but he wasn't in favour of surveillance as a general rule. Instead, the jovial words uttered by Benn on the night Sant had accosted the brute rankled him – this black man's libido really had got the better of him.

Dobson's DNA, surprisingly, showed no matches with the national database. Perhaps the councillor was a voyeur rather than a participant. Or perhaps his victims hadn't reported the offences. Perhaps they were like Maria, let down by a system meant to support sufferers of human trafficking. Ironically, the Managed Approach – a progressive model intended to beat the pimps at their own game – appeared as dead as Dobson. A joint report by the council and police authorities was being commis-sioned, which rang a tolling bell for regulated sex work in the only UK city where it was permitted. Poor Dr Julia Pringle, architect of it all.

Uncertainty remained surrounding Benn's motive for killing Dobson. The forensic team scouring Dobson's hard drive discovered no shortage of homemade X-rated videos featuring BDSM and then some. None of them featured Benn. What this suggested to Sant was that Benn had been black-mailing Dobson rather than the other way round. The inspector mulled over the possible scenarios and surmised that the two men had struck an agreement. Benn promised not to interfere in Dobson's money-spinning operation if Dobson supplied him with the kind of girls featuring on the councillor's naughty flicks.

At some stage in the recent past, however, the agreement collapsed. Dobson must have grown sick of feeding victims to his extortionist and threatened to call Benn's bluff.

Benn's curt response came in the form of the photocopied sheet Sant had found in Dobson's study, warning Dobson about the laptop the constable had stolen from him – containing all the evidence needed to bring about a public shaming. Stand-off turned to war of words, no doubt, and Benn decided the only way to make certain Dobson wouldn't renegade on their agree-ment entirely was to detain him under false pretences before erasing him for good.

Sant regretted his delaying tactics, Appleyard quick to remind him of the errors of his ways. If he'd called out Benn sooner, he'd have been arrested on suspicion of unprofessional conduct and denied the opportunity to unleash his wrath on Dobson. But Dobson was no great loss to society, Sant reckoned. The warped young man had played the blame game with the MA, fearing legal prostitution would drive those new-blood teens away from his and Donohue's porn-star grooming racket.

Donohue was the luckiest link in the chain. For one, he was still alive, and for two, conclusive evidence he'd conspired to abduct Klaudia was proving harder to obtain than predicted – all of which meant he'd serve time for his cannabis-farming exploits and be free to carve out another niche in the illicit sex trade. Sant would keep an eye out. There was always one scumbag with a knack for dodging proper justice.

Another lucky individual was the officer Popescu had over-heard in Lovell Park bragging about bribing benefit cheats. Despite internal enquiries, there was nothing hard and fast to discipline the man with, or the female officer he'd patrolled alongside. A verbal warning was the upshot of the affair. At best, it might deter. As for the benefit fiddlers, they wouldn't be so fortunate.

At last, good news reached Sant's ears. The working girl subjected to the warehouse brothel beating was pulling through. Doctors told police the girl was sitting up in her hospital bed, jaw clamped but healing gradually, a grin forcing its way across her bludgeoned face. DNA tests on her clothing showed no trace of Benn or anyone else on the database. Whoever had pounced on her was another sorry excuse for a human but not, Sant supposed, someone connected to the Benn-Dobson-Donohue triangle.

More happy news came by way of Holdsworth. She put her head around the office door and told Sant, with unrestrained joy, that Capstick was back home and brushing up on legal knowledge via his beloved textbooks – in other words, he was much like his old self and totally rid of the Liquid E complex. Sant was delighted and promised to visit as soon as he could.

Holdsworth also shared a slice of workplace gossip. Appar-ently, Hardaker was no longer in the running for the vacant Assistant Chief Constable post. Rumour had it that Old Man Gilligan wanted a woman to fill the role. Poor Harry Hardaker. The ambitious Chiefman wouldn't take the knock-back lightly.

* * *

The last person Sant saw that Tuesday was Grant Wisdom. The case of the frozen cadavers remained disturbingly unexplained. Like the grievous incident in the warehouse brothel, it had appeared integral to the main events but now seemed unrelated.

'Do we know anything more?' the inspector asked as he entered the morgue.

Wisdom placed his pince-nez specs on his long nose. 'The cause of death is not yet established but asphyxiation is probable,' he said in those deep Welsh undertones. 'They were both in their twenties at time of death.'

'Any idea yet when they died?'

Wisdom combed fingers through his silver hair. 'Not anything scientific, my boy. My estimates are not supported by anything salvaged from flesh or bone.'

'But you've got something to tell me,' Sant probed.

The pathologist took off his glasses. 'Cast your mind back to our discussion at the crime scene.'

Sant laughed. 'My memory's gone to rack and ruin after ingesting jellyfish-infested seawater and wading down Farnley Wood Beck.'

'You get around, my boy. Anyhow, when you first saw the cadaver on top, you remarked on her dress sense and we concluded that she'd been to one of those retro club nights.'

'I remember,' Sant said.

'However,' Wisdom went on, 'I've finally managed to get to the clothing labels and it's clear she's dressed in garments actually manufactured in the 1980s. They're not retro outfits churned out in China in the last few years. They're the real thing.'

Sant stared at the corpses. 'They've been frozen for decades.'

'I wouldn't make that claim yet, but I'm most of the way to making it. What's even more compelling is this.' Wisdom replaced his specs, opened a cabinet drawer, pulled out an evidence bag and lifted it towards the ceiling strip light. 'See what I see?'

'A pound note,' Sant confirmed.

'It ceased to be legal tender in 1988. They're something of a collector's item nowadays. I found it and two like it in the pockets of the cadaver below.'

Sant shook his head. 'How the hell have these women gone undetected in a frosty grave for so long? Whoever stored them must've used the same chest freezer connected to the same electricity supply practically all that time.'

Wisdom returned the bag to the cabinet and used his shoulder to slide the drawer shut. 'Moved from one freezer to another is more likely. Some of the decomposition is uneven, suggesting partial defrosting for short but not very short periods under fluctuating temperatures.'

'Faulty appliances?'

'Perhaps, or interruption caused by relocation.'

A sudden idea presented itself to Sant. 'If we're looking at a cold case stretching four decades back, these women might have something to do with the Rita Mitchell murder investigation.'

'And the C3 enquiry that followed years later,' Wisdom put in.

Sant nodded. 'The timeframe fits.'

'And the place,' Wisdom added. 'As you told me in The George, Rita was killed in the same spot where we found these cadavers a week or so ago.'

'And maybe Jim Lackey's suicide is bound up with this messy history too. I told you as much, didn't I?'

Wisdom moved not a muscle except to say: 'Coincidences happen, Inspector, but some coincidences are more astonishing than others.'

10

He sat back in the passenger seat and whistled through his yellow teeth. He'd been with girls of the night before, most of them mingers. This young lass was way above average and even had her own set of wheels. He'd been sexting her online for days on end, but as they say in the prayer books, good things come to those who wait. He met her dark eyes as she glanced away from the road, the cute halo fastened to her upturned nose gleaming in the light of the moon.

'Ya one eck of a babe,' he told her, reaching out and stroking her thigh.

'You're not a bad looker yourself,' she replied.

'Except I don't ave a reet lot of air on me head,' he laughed.

'I prefer the bald look,' she lied.

'Just wait till I get ya in bed,' he said as he tipped the remains of the beer bottle down his throat. 'I've got plenty of air down below, and a huge shaft ready to bring ya pleasure.'

'I can't wait,' she said. 'It's been so long since someone screwed me.'

'But ya a hooker, aren't ya? Ya must ave more holes than Swiss cheese.'

She laughed. 'I'm a very fussy hooker, actually. I choose my clients with care and not really for the money at all.'

'Bollocks,' he said, fists tightening into cricket balls. 'I bet ya loaded. Ya'll ave rich old blokes payin' for ya services till the cows come home.'

'I charge what I like,' she said, getting bored of the small talk.

'I bet ya do,' he replied, thinking back to the slut he'd almost killed and wondering how many jabs it would take to crush that upturned beak. He eyed the nose ring and was reminded of someone the boys in blue had told him to look out for. Could this lass be the one they were after? The disk he'd lifted from her handbag might tell him something, but he was in no rush. Besides, his next hit was that feminist lesbian responsible for the brothel. He'd give her a hiding to begin with.

The girl caught the man's sneer and wondered when the dope would take effect. She'd had it supplied from the Romanian she'd planted in Lovell Park, knowing sooner or later he'd take an interest in the groomers mucking about down there. But the drug was weaker than she'd hoped. Had she dropped enough of it in the bottle? She hoped so, though as the Romanian had taught her, there was an art to spiking. Not too little to wear off, not too much to turn your prey into a gormless zombie.

'Where the eck do ya live? We're way out in the sticks.'

'Not far,' she said. 'It's a bit of a mansion to be honest.'

'Mansion?'

'Massive. One of my wealthier clients gave me the key; spends his life in the Bahamas. You know, tax avoidance and all that.'

'Fuck me!' he bellowed. 'I'm gettin' excited.'

'How awful of me – I've forgotten your name.'

Another lie.

She knew everything there was to know about him, his track record of brutality included, plus the fact he couldn't swim. That university degree she'd never finish hadn't been a complete waste of time.

'Me mam named me Sean. Ya can call me Bonehead, even though me biggest bone ain't in me head if ya get wot I mean.'

She laughed again. 'What's your preferred position, Bonehead?'

He placed a thick hand over his genitals and started to rub himself. 'Listen babe, I'll shag ya which way ya like. This fella's desperate to make ya day.'

She saw his jaw drooping out of the corner of her eye. The Liquid E was kicking in at last. Thirty seconds and he'll be a pushover, she said to herself.

'We're nearly there,' she informed him as they came to a bridge over a narrow river. 'I'll pull up here so we can take a breath. Wow, what timing!'

Bonehead jerked his head and rubbed his eyes. 'Bleedin' eck, this beer's sharp. Might be a good fing to get... oxygen... in me... lungs.' He glimpsed the label on the bottle, then tipped it upside down, dregs splashing over his cargo pants.

'Oh dear, you've had an accident.' She stopped abruptly, got out and raced around to the passenger door. As she yanked it open, he nearly toppled. She grabbed him to break his fall before dragging him out, her athletic arms taking the weight under his shoulders.

'You're a hefty lump of pig-loving shit,' she panted. 'Luckily, I'm in practice at lifting fuckwits. Who do you think you are anyway? Ah, I've cottoned on. You're Hit Man Bonehead. A hard man who wets the bed with his tiny penis. A hard man who tramples on girls and leaves them for dead.'

He mumbled a response and wobbled on his feet. She steered him to the steel railing of the bridge and stared down at the swollen channel. The rapids were visible, the current racing hard. Perfect for a staged suicide.

'It's a good job the girl survived,' she continued, 'or your final minutes would've been more painful than this. You got off lightly, Hit Man Bonehead. Oh, and never steal what doesn't belong to you.' She plucked the disk out of his leather jacket pocket and brandished it in front of his heavy eyes. 'It won't mean much to you, pig-lover face, but the video recorded on this piece of plastic contains ample evidence to destroy that fascist, murderous, misogynistic chief constable who hires you.'

Chloe Lee had had enough. She retreated a few paces before lunging and tossing the lout over the rail. He flipped like a dismal Olympic diver, splashing horribly and receiving *nil point* from a realm of kingfishers judging the execution. She rubbed her hands together and whispered into the darkness: 'That's for all the women you've violated, pig lover. Enjoy your watery grave, and if such a place exists, I'll see you in Hell.'

ABOUT THE AUTHOR

Dan Laughey is a crime writer. First and foremost. In between times, he's a lecturer at Leeds Beckett University where he teaches a course called 'Youth, Crime and Culture' among other things. He has written several books on the subject including *Music and Youth Culture*, based on his PhD in Sociology at Salford University.

Before academia he enjoyed a brief career in public relations, became a high school teacher, barman, waiter, trader, door-to-door salesman, car park attendant, film extra and convenience-store manager – not necessarily in that order.

Dan was born in Otley and bred in Ilkley, West Yorkshire, a hop and a skip away from the Leeds setting of his *Chloe* mystery novels featuring DI Carl Sant. He now lives in the Leeds suburb of Guiseley and shares his time between England and Thailand, where his in-laws live. His wife and two sons keep him occupied when he's not writing, and all three are technologically savvier than him.

Dan's books have been translated into four languages (French, Hebrew, Korean and Turkish) and published in India as well as Europe and North America. He's presented guest lectures in Amsterdam, London, Dublin, Montreal and Bangkok, and has appeared on BBC Radio and ITV News in addition to providing expert commentary for *The Guardian, The Daily Telegraph, Yorkshire Post* and *Yorkshire Evening Post*.

Dan's hobbies include hunting for treasure at car boot sales, watching football and playing the occasional round of golf. He also enjoys running and gambling on the horses – no connection between the two – and can't get enough of his wife's Thai cuisine.

Follow him on Twitter @danlaughey and Facebook fb.com/laughey

* * *

To learn more about Dan Laughey and discover more Next Chapter authors, visit our website at www.nextchapter.pub.

Chloe - Prime Victim
ISBN: 978-4-82417-499-4

Published by
Next Chapter
2-5-6 SANNO
SANNO BRIDGE
143-0023 Ota-Ku, Tokyo
+818035793528

8th October 2024

.

Milton Keynes UK
Ingram Content Group UK Ltd.
UKHW040711031224
452051UK00006B/123